Eve of

By
Mark Cascarino

3

Dedication

To my wife Kim and two children, Penny and Elliot, who share a lot of characteristics to their namesakes but prey not their experiences.

4

Acknowledgements

A special mention to my English Teacher and a great help at the start of this book Jeff, who sadly passed before publication. I don't think he realised how much his encouragement meant.

My great friend and beta reader, Claire, and of course, the wonderful Wendy, who kept me right with my blurb.

Table of Contents

6

Prologue (Harbinger)

I don't do beginnings and I don't do endings. All I can tell you right now is that I'm standing on a hill. This is the place and time, the where and when I've been told to be. I'm here to witness; I'm the Harbinger. I come before times' significant events to bear witness.

On one side, a cold valley stands before me, washed out by the forces of water and ice. I stand and watch a hidden concentration camp in the Highlands of Scotland. The lingering inevitably of death and decisiveness of history-changing moments make my very view worthwhile. On the other side reside in caves an ancient group of humans, trying to free prisoners from those who have succumbed to darkness.

I'm not a too unsympathetic character to either of the sides. I just won't lean either way. My job is to study, not to interfere; I'm the Harbinger, a balance of sorts. I am a sign of affairs parallel to that of the history, pressed for a service reserved in a manner for my Master. My Master picked me to be his Harbinger. I gather around him more devoted and loyal, imbued

with power and sagacity. I refuse to name my Master; it's forbidden.,However, I can talk of my travels through time, and all that has brought us here to this battle in front of us. It has existed since the dawn of time and will exist beyond the rest of us.

Unable to disclose my Master's identity, I will discuss its beginnings, however – its brethren and children. How the world formed and how the world works. Should I give you the genuine history of the planet you refer to as Earth? For the truths to surface, it's important to forge the context of every story, making it comprehensible. The Earth is an unfamiliar name to you, a name given to it by your ancestors and their Gods, 'Pandora.'

I'll tell you the truth, the balanced truth not tipped in favour of one God over another, unlike what humans are in favour of doing. I'll tell you of the Light Bearer, tales of her adventures through Pandora, her dreams, and her battles.

To watch this scene unfold, you need to understand the events that followed it. As I say events, I talk about the ones that happened centuries, millennia, and aeons ago. It all concluded to set the battle in motion from the beginning of time.

My Master has given me the memory of events before my time, and I'll share these with you with my very own memories. All I know is hardwired as my memory; I learn or remember anything out of the sheer experience. You'll find my tone changing when telling stories of the past, the tales of the Eternals and Pandora, reflecting my disinterest in what has already happened and my interest in observing what is to come – watching things unfold, guarding the prophecy.

I'm very interested in the emergence of this new light bearer. She is one of many, in a long line of bearers, but also the last. She has tasted pain and has fought her own demons to survive.

Now, to decide the fate of this world and the creation itself, she must fight actual demons. She will have to decide who lives and who dies. She will have to kill people she holds dear to her heart, only to save you all.

She is Penny White, the bearer of Light.

I, the Harbinger, am here to observe the ultimate battle. I'm here to witness her death as the creature made of shadow stalks her, ready to pounce.

10

Chapter 1:
The Whispering Book

Mark's green eyes were stinging from the smoke, filling his nose and mouth. As he walked towards the window, whispers bounced around his head, "You aren't going anywhere."

The shadow emerged with petrifying hands to grab him tightly. The trembling boy now had the terrifying realization that he wasn't leaving. As he fell on his knees, his hands burned from the heat igniting from the flooring. His stomach twisted, leaving him to die. Whispering became unbearable now, echoing in his head, "You will be with the Shaitan, embrace this Holy moment of the cleansing fires."

His left eye hurt; the memory of his dad hitting him to the ground was still fresh. As anger built, fear was replaced by rage. His dad deserved to die. His mother didn't protect him.

"You bring it on yourself," she would say nothing else. They both deserved to die.

He was reflecting on the deal that he made with the whispers. They told him how to do it and how they would take care of him later, as they promised. In a twisted way, they actually kept their promise, as they have freed him from his trauma.

He has caught his parents off guard, knocking them out with a cricket bat, making it easy to cable tie their hands and feet. Firstly, his father, and then his mother, as she crouched over his dad's body. The exhilaration made him laugh maniacally before a burst of deep, uncontrollable laughter followed.

The whispers cheered him onwards, giving him the confidence for the next thing to come. He grinned, pouring whiskey and vodka over his parents' bodies. As he reached for the lighter, the air became electric. He realized his dad could never hurt him again. The smoke was choking. His eyes stung. He couldn't cry anymore. The floor just then fell with a bang. Mark was dead when he hit the ground, landing on his head, breaking his neck.

Earlier that day, Mark was in class. There was nothing abnormal about the day, just another school day. He enjoyed his time at school.

His teacher, Penny Whyte, was patient and kind, also very beautiful. She was tall with grey eyes, her thick long black hair, almost always tied, and brushed the curves of her slim body. "Right, guys, we all had so much fun yesterday. Wasn't it strange being in a Victorian classroom? I'm looking forward to hearing your reports. Remember what we talked about, focus on what advantages we have now compared to then?" Penny remembered the day she decided to teach and also the day she told her brother.

12

"Why would you want to look after other people's brats?" Elliot didn't much like children. She had just told him about being accepted by a university.

Elliot would sit on his usual barstool, where Penny more often than not found him. She had given up on trying to convince him not to drink, but more and more, he sounded like their dad, "You don't want me sober!" He was full of pain and agony. It was as if everything around him sucked the life out of him. Penny had not seen him laughing in a very long time. Ignoring him in her excitement, "I want to shape them, even inspire them. Nana taught us so much! She told us stories, taught us lessons that we didn't even know we were learning! If it wasn't for her words, I wouldn't have seen Gary for what he was. That is what I need to pass on."

Elliot sunk the last of his pint, looked Penny up and down. He had the same grey eyes, but that was where similarities ended. "Fine, but don't expect me to be your assistant. I love you, but I don't do kids." Penny smiled at the memory, feeling pained once more. A year had already passed, but it still hurt her.

Elliot had his demons to deal with, and Penny had faced down her own challenges. She walked a dark path and made a mess out of her life. Anger and rebelliousness sabotaged her late teens. She found herself at the crossroads in her twenties.

Penny had a boyfriend, Gary, a tall skinny man with an unsympathetic temper. He was nice enough to start with, and she liked him very much.

On a rare night, right after work, Penny was off to a pub. "Can I buy you a drink?" She looked over her shoulder; his aftershave hit her like a wall, and she choked on the smell. He looked embarrassed, and that made her giggle. She was going to polity decline, but felt she should hear him out, given it was rude choking on his smell. It started exactly that night.

Penny stopped talking to people and drifted away from her old life. It began slowly; one by one, comments about her friends became frequent, however. Gary attached a string to her; he could now control each of her steps and pull her away from people. He was holding tight the string to keep her from looking elsewhere, at anyone at all. Soon, he pulled it too close to have her move in with him. Gary assumed, against all else, that she needn't work. He decided to cover things on his own. On the first day of moving, he drove her to work so she could quit her job. She was now reliant on handouts, only getting them when she behaved and did housework to his standards. She lived in a tight suite, decorated with the rage of the man she loved. He reminded her of her dad with his controlling behaviour, albeit he didn't drink. It was a given why she fell so in love with him. She didn't like being controlled, but there was safety in it. She knew it wasn't rational.

When he first hit her, he reasoned finding text messages from a concerned male friend, who was apparently only looking after her. Afterwards, he was full of apologies and promises. He always bought her with empty apologies and makeup; it was never changed behaviour. It soon became a part of their relationship. He would buy her makeup, not to be nice, however, only to help her hide bruises.

He was far from realizing the price Penny had paid for this short-lived love. Fitting, she could also rid her life of him. She had her life sorted from the moment he hit her. Saving the bits of money he gave her, skimming some from grocery misses, her escape was in her hands. When she finally stood her ground to leave, it was only natural he came after her. A thin layer of fear ringed on her skin as she paced her movements, frantically calling the police. He followed her to his very end, in a jail cell, with Penny being sent to a women's refuge in Dundee. He was charged and arrested for his ploy to keep his girlfriend trapped.

It was as if the chase hadn't stopped, first a father who never came home sober, and then a maniac boyfriend who held her in his palms. She had spent most of her childhood being raised by a single dad and unbefitting word for a man who was the worst kind of drunk. Now with Gary, she was left empty-handed. Penny took her time to open up; it took her years of counselling before she told someone about her life. She was able to get the help she desired. She took charge of her life, went back to school, and got her qualifications. Eventually finding happiness, now living by herself. She would visit her book club and support others in a women's refuge. She had finally made a good life for herself, putting her past behind her.

15

Penny was watching them all squirming in their seats, elbowing each other, not wanting to go first. It was always the same. They would get so nervous. "Christopher Fisher and Mark Abbott, you're up first." Penny thought a lot of Mark. He was as shy as her, and she had doubts about his father. His unusual behaviour reeked of signs, making her feel more protective of him. She kept herself from accusing his dad as yet, at least not until there was evidence. He brought back memories of her dad, but she shook them off.

They were studying her favourite part of the curriculum, Victorian Britain, right now. Christopher and Mark were coming to the front to give their presentation on the school trip. Miss Whyte got ready to take notes on their presentation, to grade later – more than likely, with a huge glass of wine.

"Well, we got onto the bus here at school, we weren't sure what to expect, but we had done some research in class beforehand," Chris started. He was a confident kid, popular and athletic with boyish hair and a charm that got him in and out of trouble. Mark couldn't be more different. He was small and shy, much like Penny, lacking confidence and hesitating. Something about him made her uneasy, and it made her think about her own behaviour as a kid.

"When we got off the bus, I thought we were at the wrong place; the school was just an ordinary school, it was a normal grey building with a normal playground with normal children playing, but Miss Whyte told me

16

to be patient," Chris continued. Penny remembered Chris's displeasure when the bus stopped.

Walking down the metal bus steps, the structure of an ordinary school presented itself. It was break time, and the kids were out playing. The noise was what you would expect during break times, with lots of shouts and screams. Some girls were playing hopscotch, and some boys played football on the grass. It didn't feel very Victorian, but she had been there the year before and knew they wouldn't be disappointed. "We then walked inside, up some creepy stairs that smelled like mould. That's when I got paired with this one," Chris nodded his head in Mark's direction, to the delight of the class. Noticing Miss Whyte's look, the class went quiet, and he carried on. "We then got dressed in Victorian clothes and went inside. Mrs. Hyde was mean, and the whole place smelt of cat's piss!"

Miss Whyte sprang up, "Okay, Chris, you can go sit down, and Mark can carry on." Chris slunk back off to his seat as Mark continued giving the presentation.

Chris was right though, the place did smell of cat piss, of old books also. There was a damp smell wafting from the bare stone walls, cold to touch, deprived of any ray of sunlight. Upstairs in the loft, there were a series of rooms. One had a sign that said 1901 on its heavy black door; it was the classroom. There was a separate room full of Victorian clothes for
the kids to wear. "I want you to pair up in twos," Miss Whyte had demanded. There was usual fuss and arguing. She then

told everyone to go and stand against the wall, and she paired each of them. It was how Chris and Mark became partners, and if that hadn't happened, the two might have never become friends. Mark would have never met a friend like Chris.

The Victorian classroom felt cold and grey walled up with the same bare walls as outside. Tables were arranged side by side, alongside an aisle running down the middle for Mrs. Hyde to walk up and down studying the pupils. There was a blackboard at the front, and a sentence was inscribed on it, "Horrible boys and girls shall be punished, and we shall reward good boys and girls with knowledge." It seemed odd to Mark, but it was Victorian. She had Lucy hand out slate and chalk for them to copy the sentence 20 times.

With slate and chalks distributed, Mrs. Hyde started walking around the class, peeking over each student's shoulder. She stopped at Mark's desk and looked over Mark's shoulder, "That, my boy is terrible, my dog has better writing relieving itself in the snow." Chris let out a giggle; she glowered at him, "Get that mischief out of your eye, boy!" she said in a booming voice. Mark let out a nervous giggle as Mrs Hyde stormed over to the front of the class and picked up a massive leather strap. Marching back to their desk with loud footsteps, she slammed down the big heavy leather belt. The bang echoed against the bare concrete walls. The thing looked thick and forked, like a snake's tongue. "If you two think that's funny, you can laugh outside," she bellowed and frog-marched them into the hallway.

Chris and Mark just looked at each other in shock. The two of them stood outside in punishment. After a few minutes, Chris started fidgeting uneasily, "I'm bored, going to see what else is around here."

"You will get us in more trouble," Mark whispered, a little late; however, Chris was already in the next room.

Mark followed him into the room, wanting to persuade him to come back, but Chris just teased in a callous tone, "Not like anyone would notice you missing!" then he ran off.

Mark stopped in his tracks. He knew Chris was right; even his own parents didn't like him much, always fighting and drinking, uninterested and indifferent towards him… If ever his dad noticed him, it was to give him a kick or a punch. He thought about all the times it happened, the anger burning inside of him, and the rage that had bottled up for years. Looking around, he saw newspapers, yellow with age. He picked one up, smelling its musty scent. "A RACE TO RUIN," read the front page. It was the story of William Palmer, The Rugeley Poisoner, Sheffield Independent, 17th of September, 1888. *Wow, these newspapers must be over a hundred years old*, he thought to himself. He walked around the room, glancing at the front pages, laughing at how people spoke so funny. A distressful tremor of pain across his chest made him wince. It was his ribs; they felt bruised; it happened the night before.

Mark started thinking of the previous night running his hand over the bandages he had wrapped around himself the very morning. He had embarrassed his Dad by crying, got thrown to the ground, and kicked in the chest. "Men don't cry," his anger was enervating the memory – the memories, and too many of them. Memories of all the other times it happened. How his mum would pretend not to see, tell him that it was his fault. His anger was turning into a rage at the thought of her memories, a rage that he hadn't felt before. Something in the room was helping it, and he liked it.

He didn't notice the room getting colder at first until he heard the voice. He shouted at it, his anger spilling over from his memories, "Give it a rest. I know it's you, Chris; I'm going back without...." He briefly stopped as he realised the voice was a whisper, and it was inside his head. Chris had already wandered away. Mark could see his breath in the air, watching it vibrate with energy.

It wasn't normal cold; it felt almost electric, similar to an old TV that had just turned off. A coldness that sucked joy and energy from just anyone. Mark then understood the whispers, "Your rage is delicious," it had said. "Go to the wall, move the loose stone; there is a gift," it added. When he moved the stone out of the way, there he found it, wrapped in cloth. It was a book bound with leather that felt cold and unusual. He couldn't put his finger on it. "OPEN IT!" the voice bounced around his skull this time; he heard it and felt it. Mark dropped the book and ran out of the room screaming, running straight into Miss Whyte and Mrs. Hyde. He could see Chris standing in the same place they stood before, looking baffled. They just looked at each other.

Mark knew no one would believe him, so he made up something, "I was looking for a toilet and got lost and scared." He snapped out of his memories, "Mark, that book in your bag, where did it come from?" At first, Mark wondered if he was talking out loud while he was daydreaming. When he looked over, the leather-bound book was half out of his bag, on the floor. Miss Whyte walked over and picked it up, "I don't know how that got into my bag, miss, and it's not mine! Chris must have put it there." The lie had left his lips before he had realised it. Miss Whyte might have believed him, but she was watching Chris the entire time, "I lost you for 10 minutes while you looked for the toilet, but Chris was with me the whole trip."

A series of luckless events followed Mark later that day. Chris beat Mark up on the way home for trying to get him into trouble. His drunk dad gave him a slap. He had a call from the school informing him his son had stolen what was considered a rare book.

The most serious of events happened before any of this. At the Victorian classrooms, Mark sneaked back and took the book before the bus had left; the whispering was back. He must have lost his mind. Sitting, he could hear the whispering again. This time, he listened to them and what they were telling him to do, and an icy grin filled his face.

Chapter 2: The Eternal War (Pandora)

Ifra regretfully watched over Angel; she thought about how its creation was a mistake. The Seraph created Angel for a greater cause; Ifra saw him as a child, but for the rest of them, he was a weapon.

Ifra was first to be created by the sparks to fight for them against the evil force that gave him the birthright to lead the others. Ifra saw how miraculously her brothers and sisters were brought to life by the sparks. Now she feels pain at the thought of what some of them have become, but she also can't hate them as they are one of her own. Ifra closed her eyes and summoned her kins that were still loyal to a council. It was a special connection between them. She connected with them through her mind. It was time for them to decide on what to do with Angel.

Angel watches over Pandora, fixating on its beauty. From his vantage point, he can see every colour of the rainbow. How life flows in and out, tides rise and fall back, and the moon replaces the sun. Up north, he can see the White Mountains, and to its South, there are the towering glaciers. Switching his gaze to the centre of Pandora, he takes a good look at the brown volcanoes, firing out deadly lava and destroying everything it touches. Angel smiles, unmoved at the destruction; "this is the great cycle of Pandora," he whispers to himself.

From the ashes, there will be buds of trees sprouting sky-high to form thick canopies of the forest. Life will spring from death, and death will come to all. This is the natural order of things-- only ever watching. But, Angel was never permitted to go to Pandora. His creators unintentionally made him an eternal being.

"Pandora, in my long existence, you are my only companion, and even though you don't reply, I feel the need to speak. I know that you can somehow hear me as I know you are still alive. I see it in your seasons as they change; I see it as you try to find your balance. You bring life to your surface only to have it stripped away by disaster. You are embellished by the glory of the Sun and grandeur of the moon; you are enlivened by the populace, yet the gust of ashes flurrying around tells a different story. The ash becomes life. But, now I fear they have forgotten about me; they meant for me to die. Did I not have the right to live?" Angel thinks back to when he was made self-aware of his purpose in Pandora – to end the eternal war, to destroy the Shaitan. He knew this because The Seraph made sure to walk Angel through the history of the war on his creation.

This tranquil world wasn't always at peace with itself; it was repeatedly destroyed by the inevitability of war. And every time it was destroyed, it would revive again, there would be life springing from its ashes; Pandora wanted to live, and it knew how to survive. The way Pandora managed to revive life is what intrigued Angel the most of its ability and yearning for life on that unceasingly fascinating planet. He thought, "If Pandora itself could be a living, thinking creature?" All he knew was that Pandora existed before his Creators.

"I can hear my inmates; they taunt me. They tell me lies; they say that the Spark of Darkness whispers of its origins and its purpose, but I am strong, and I resist! They tell me I have a brother, but I know I'm the only child of the Seraph, and I was created for a purpose," the soliloquy comes to an end.

Joined by the rest of the council, Ifra begins, "I'll hear a report from all of you before we discuss the meeting's purpose." She indicated for Tawil to begin. At the council, all the eternal beings that were present were the beings of energy, and that is how they recognized each other and communicated with each other.

Tawil's energy was very stark. Everything is black and white about her personality. She is assigned to watch over the Shaitan in their prison, and she was also the closest to Ifra; they had a relationship built on trust. "The Shaitan has been very excited recently. I've sensed nothing from their spark. It hadn't given up any of its secrets, but I can tell that it has given them something, and this has got them worked up," said Tawil.

There was a flurry of apprehension around the council. While they were joined like this, something connected their energies, creating an empathic link between them. This joined state meant their emotions would bleed into each other, amplifying to reach a greater level of sentiment and emotion. They all could feel each other's energy. At times, the higher levels would become difficult to control and regulate, "Calm your minds, brothers and sisters." Ifra was the calmest and the strongest of the Seraph. She was always composed at times like these and made sure to never lose her cool.

This is what made Ifra the Supreme, her ability to sense sparks and synchronize them to instil life in others and impart universal knowledge. She saw all three sparks, The Spark of Light, The Spark of Darkness, and in between, there was The Spark of Balance. Ifra was meant to lead the rest, and she was strengthened with a more purposeful personality. Ifra's attachment to her kins was like that of a mother, and she still remembers the moment her brother and sisters were made aware of their various abilities.

Ifra soothed them. "Be calm, my kin; I already love you. Be still and listen. They have given me the words to speak." a gust of energy came forward.

"I am Abbud, the second-born, and we were created to listen to the words you speak," he reiterated.

There seemed to be a ceremony developing, and the others followed suit, instinctively declaring their names in the order of their birth after, starting after Abbud. "Tawil, Washma, Malak, Sheikh, Daoud, Nazmin, Raiya, Salameh, Fawaz, and Jaber." There were 12 of the Seraphs on the council, and all had the duty to look towards the planet. Ifra began, "We are the custodians of this planet; our duty is to ensure that it flourishes and is protected at all costs. The sparks created us, but before that, they created this land and named it Pandora. Life has already been seeding and prospering here; we are here to watch and protect."

However, things were different now, Ifra was still the Supreme, but now she only led the six of them. She looked to Washma for her report, "The humans are scared of the dark; their instincts for a long time have told them something is lurking in the shadows. I've been warning this council for long enough that something wasn't right."

Washma was assigned to watch over Pandora, but mainly to oversee the interactions the Shaitan has with the humans. They needed to find out how they have influenced and interacted with humans from their prison.

Washma has seen the evil and faced it more than any other Seraph, and it had left lifelong scars on her. "There is a creature in the dark; it seems to be made of thought but can only exist in the shadows. It lurks in the dark and fears none. I believe it has something to do with how Angel was created. As you know, with each destruction caused by the Shaitan, there was residual energy building upon the planet's surface. We harvested the energy and shaped it into Angel, but we left behind a bi-product expecting it to degrade. A doltish act, indeed. It seems that it has combined and formed a conscious being. However, there is no sign of intelligent thought.

It is primordial by nature." Washma presented the supreme one with a strong theory.

"Our war has had yet another unexpected consequence for Pandora in the form of this creature." Collectively they thought back to how all of this started.

Discovering that the sparks remained mainly dormant, they could extend their own will over Pandora without interference. At a young age, Pandora was a great playground for those who wanted to learn and explore.

They particularly enjoyed creating life. Ifra found that Abbud was very quick to pick things from her and quickly became an accomplished teacher himself. She decided to split the Seraph into two classes. Ifra took Tawil, Washma; Malak' Radiya, Salameh; and Abud was left with Nazmin, Sheikh, Daoud, Fawaz, and Jaber. They explored every part of the planet, from the highest mountains to its deepest oceans-- creating life, turning it to ashes, and altering it where they deemed fit.

They were young, and it amused them; they wanted to play. Abbud observed Ifra and her class closely, and an unlikely thought crept across his mind... He felt pride when he noticed his students creating better creatures, and so he felt the need to boast, "Why to create tiny little snakes and lizards? We have the mighty giant lizards over here," and as he said that, he entered the mind of one of his creatures in an attempt to control it. The pride took the best of him, and he commanded the gigantic creature to destroy as many of the smaller creatures as it could.

Upon this, Ifra tried to call off things at once. "Abbud! Return to your pupils and think about the example you're going to set for the entire planet!"

Ifra was enraged, she sensed the change in Abbud's behaviour, and she could see the trouble unfolding.

Abbud realized that he took control of the creature by commanding it and controlling its mind. However, he still feared his actions, and that fear remained in him even now. From that point on, he taught his pupils to devise creatures that would worship them and would remain subservient to them. This way, they will be gods to the creatures they create and control those creatures to fulfil their own agenda.

Back in the council, the other members raised concerns regarding what had happened with Abbud and his pupils. Flashbacks from that day still haunted Ifra as she sat on the council.

"Before we make our decision today, we need to understand our past. We need to understand the actions that have brought us to this moment before making any further decisions." Ifra insisted.

"What decisions?" Tawil asked.

Ifra ignored the question asked by Tawil and continued, "Radiya, your report?"

Radiya is far more reserved than the rest of the people on the council, he doesn't like to waste his energy on meaningless conversations, and so,

he keeps it to the point. The persona is befitting to the gravity of responsibility he is entrusted with. His life revolves around science and understanding Pandora as an entity and the spark of light, trying to unlock its deepest secrets.

"My studies seem to show that Pandora is alive and well with its problem-solving intelligence. It created the humans, and it created tunnel networks lined with a crystalline substance that prevents us from seeing the past. The planet has developed defences against us, which don't surprise me at all; if it is sentient, then it would see us as a threat?" Radiya explained.

Once again, the council was reminiscing the past. And while they did that, the nonpareil abilities to create and destroy life got stronger with every new creation.

On the other hand, Abbud was worried due to the inability of his class to interfere with the life of their creation. What is godliness without any control over the creations? Abbud's class became obsessed, and their main goal was to influence their creations. By the time Ifra realized that they were feeding off the control they had over their creatures, it was too late. Abbud and his class had already thrown off the balance of Pandora. An unstoppable and irrevocable chain of events was initiated. What was to come after was disastrous. The planet shook; parts of it exploded and turned into ash, a bright red molten lava.

At one point, the entire surface looked like it was ablaze. Ifra and her class were distraught. For the first time, they felt the energy, the energy that was brimming with sheer negativity. Before now, they just saw physical creatures but couldn't feel them this way. Ifra realized that these playthings were miniature versions of themselves. These creatures had skin but were energy, just like the Seraphs, and they just wiped all the weaker beings out. "Abbud, what have you done?" Ifra confronted him.

Abbud was silent, and he was in a trance-like state. Ifra realized that Abbud was drunk on power, and his pupils were absorbing the planets' positive energy. The creatures that were killed, even their energy was still not at peace. They cannibalized them! Will this be the reason for the ultimate destruction of the planet? Only fate would tell but, Ifra could sense the danger.

The council stayed silent at the memory of Pandora's first destruction. Unfortunately, it wasn't the last disaster caused by the Shaitan.

"Salameh, how goes your report?" Ifra inquired. Salameh was probably the hermit of the group, not very friendly and straight to the point.

"We have been distracted long enough, and we have done enough damage to the planet we were supposed to protect! I know what you are about to propose, and I'm in agreement." Salameh replied enthusiastically.

Ifra simply said, "You know the plan, but you don't know the decision that it would mean!" Ifra brings their attention to the final memory.

It was the first council of the six, and they were the ones who decided on the banishment of the others. They were to be shunned and, from that point on, be known as Shaitan, The Whispers. The six were still sworn to protect Pandora as it re-birthed itself, but the Shaitan was set on its power. Eventually, this will be known as the Eternal war.

Angels creators were locked in battle with the Shaitan. For aeons, they were in deadlock. They fought over Pandora's dominion; if they won, the Shaitan would enslave all creation within it. The problem was that the light sparks and the dark sparks equalled each other in power. One can't exist without the other, and neither can be destroyed. What the Eternals didn't realize was they wouldn't wield the final blows in the war; it would be a human, in fact, a woman who would decide the fate of Pandora. No one will predict what she does and whose side she would choose. The humans were something they couldn't control.

The Seraph only wanted to allow Pandora to flourish. It was still very primitive. Prosperity seemed like a far-off target. There were lands filled with large reptiles; the crawling and slithering creatures dominated most of the lands. As they grew in intelligence, they became more aware of beings lurking in the shadows. At first, it was just a whisper, but soon the giant creatures started killing for no reason. The killings were extraordinary, nothing like before. It got the attention of the Seraph; they could see the Shaitan grow in power. As the indigenous life forms grew in intelligence and developed more into powerful beings, the more, they were corrupted. The deadlock in this war would be broken soon, and soon the Shaitan would have gained enough power to destroy or imprison the Seraph.

They had to make their move, or they would lose everything.

When it comes to saving the least of what remains, the unusual ways become the first options. They did something they swore they would never do; they revealed themselves to the inhabitants. They gave them access to the secrets of the universe, protecting them from the Shaitan's influence. The Shaitan resented this interference, and in retaliation, they unleashed their wrath; they aimed it at the Wise One's beloved life-forms and wiped them out.

The shock wave killed everything on the entire planet. They destroyed everything in one blow. They knew this would have no effect on the Seraph's power, but they were angry, and this tormented the Seraph in unthinkable ways.

They were distraught at this destruction. They have been observing Pandora and the life-forms they created, watching them grow, watching the inhabitants become the dominant species and become intelligent. They wanted to save them from the torment that the Shaitan would inflict, but they only brought destruction. Pandora experienced the re-birth of life. Neither faction could understand how life could be created, but Pandora survived. This could only happen with The Spark of Balance. It must still be close by for Pandora to survive.

First, it was just volcanoes, and then out of the ash came plant life. Pandora was flourishing, and the Shaitan waited once again. They knew they would try again, and they did. The cycle repeated several times; the survival and destruction took place several times. They were in deadlock again; neither faction gained ground. They were both equal in power, destined to fight for eternity. They both retreated from Pandora into other dimensions of their own creation. They created their bases and continued the war entrenched in their own domains.

While the Shaitan spent their time plotting, the Seraph spent their time meditating and watching life and its existence. They were great philosophers trying to understand their own existence since the sparks had created them, and they desired to know why and why they hadn't interfered in this war.

Over time, there were many theories as to why The Spark of Balance went missing and where things went wrong, but it will only make itself known when it's ready. It will be known only when the eternal beings are brought back into balance will it materialize again? What they don't know is how this rebalancing will happen. Their spark would give them prophecies. One of the prophecies predicted that the two remaining sparks were working together again to bring their sister back home.

They experimented with their own energy and their spark. Through the knowledge gained, the Seraph created Angel as a secret weapon. At first, Angel was confused. He wasn't born or created the conventional way, and they brought him into creation, using the residual energy from the Shaitan's wrath. He instantly knew why he existed from memory and thought transferred by his creators. Each time the Shaitan destroyed Pandora, a pocket of residual energy was created. The Seraph was harvesting the destructive energy, and they tried to experiment and growing knowledge of how to rework it. They would leave the by-products on Pandora to decay, something they would regret later.

Angel knew he had one purpose, and that was to destroy the Shaitan. Still, the thoughts would race through his head, and he would doubt his existence. Some thoughts he was sure wasn't even his own.

"I am here as a destroyer. I'm okay with that; it's all I know; it's all I am. Why? Though, why do I have to do this? Do I not have the right to exist? They design my energy to destroy theirs; it's not just death, its non-existence." Angel thought to himself. It was common for him to question his purpose like this.

Putting all his thoughts to one side, he set off, pushing through the dimensional barriers. The Shaitan felt him coming, and Angel could feel their fear. For the first time, they felt afraid, but soon that fear turned to anger.

However, the Shaitan was defending themselves, and in his fear, Angel felt a force against him; his thoughts froze, his energy vibrated. He felt terror; he realized that the Shaitan was amplifying it; he faltered, and he found himself trapped in the gateway between dimensions.

Angel became less of a destroyer; he was made to be a weapon but, now he is more of a gatekeeper for Pandora. By blocking the doorway between dimensions, he had stopped the Shaitan from crossing. He was able to stop most of their influence over Pandora, and although the Seraph weren't strong enough to attack the Shaitan, they were no longer under threat by Shaitan's negative energy.

As the world grew and plants and creatures sprang into life, it required the power of the sparks. The cycle of Pandora was directly linked to all three sparks; if the cycle loses any one of the sparks, the balance would be off. It would change the rigid dynamics of the world that seemed to be flourishing.

A new life-form appeared out of nowhere, a single male of the species and one female with long legs; they had hardbodies but different in some subtle and some not-so-subtle ways. The creatures were nothing like anything they had seen before. Neither Seraph nor Shaitan could have given rise to a creature so majestic yet complex.

The Seraph hadn't created them, and the Shaitan couldn't have from their prison. Pandora must have created a new life; for aeons, it was locked in a cycle of regenerating the life it was already seeded with, but this was something new. The seed was never planted for this species. Pandora must have created it. Or maybe it was just a fluke? But the Eternals realized that these creatures were capable of love and all that is good but also capable of atrocities and unimaginable evil.

The truth dawned on both factions, and they realized that the long-lost Spark of Balance that created them, they must hold both light and dark in

their hearts with the free will to choose which path they will walk. The new creatures couldn't contain the spark within them, but it has touched this species. They can't be influenced in the same ways but can be tempted and convinced.

The choices these creatures make in the coming days and then through the coming millennia will shape Pandora's future. The Shaitan rejoiced, they had a plan, and the new "Humans" would pave the way that would lead to their release.

The Seraph left the Humans to their own free will and watched the wonder of Pandora's own creation. They sensed the Spark of Balance within the humans and suspected that the spark had become embedded within Pandora itself. The reason remained unknown to them. With the Shaitan imprisoned, they returned to studying their spark and contemplating the surrounding universe.

They could sense their creator and could see its hand in events but couldn't even grasp it.

They knew that Angel had survived and was now guarding them and the planet against the Shaitan. The Seraph watched over Angel, feeling remorse for what they did. He was sentient. It had to be that way; the Shaitan was powerful enough to stop anything else. They would have just assumed that Angel was an ordinary creation that had lost its patience and has attacked them impulsively. By the time the Shaitan would have realized the danger Angel could be to them, it would be too late.

Every so often, they would sense an evil influence on Pandora. After some time, it turned out that the Shaitan learnt how to whisper to the creatures of Pandora, but it only amused the Seraph since the creatures couldn't understand them; they assumed that they were probably too primitive. What they didn't know was that when the Shaitan whispered to the Humans, first to Eve and then to Adam, the Humans understood.

The whispers made Eve feel cold and sick. They showed her pictures and invaded her thoughts, making her angry. They almost got into her head, and she heard noises in a pattern, but she couldn't understand it. It didn't sound like any animal or a voice she had heard before. The anger was building; she wanted to hunt; she wanted to kill. She resisted and refused to give in; in her core, she knew that life was precious. You kill to eat and cloth, not for any other reason. She couldn't understand where these thoughts were coming from. She didn't know the history of Pandora, and she didn't know who the Shaitan were. However, after a few days, Eve felt better, and the disturbing visions and thoughts stopped.

The Shaitan changed the plan and focused on Adam. They realized that Eve had impaired speech and was a weak target. Thus, they improvised, making her counterpart the next target. They learned their lessons from their encounters with Eve.

They showed Adam visions of the past, but from their twisted perspective. They spoke through their minds, polluting the thoughts and damaging the perspectives. They showed how they just wanted to be free, how creation was theirs and theirs to play with. Everything was made to serve; it was the purpose of life, to serve something greater.

They showed him how he was different and how he was made in the same way as that of the Shaitan by some unknown force, a creation of nature. He has been brought onto this land to rule it, but there were creatures that would stop him. The ones they fought since Pandora first came to be.

For the first time, Adam felt rage, something that he had never felt before; it was like a burning ball of fire inflating inside him. It grew and grew; he saw a rabbit and had a vision of twisting the life out of it. The thoughts urged him to do it. The vision made him feel the power he was bestowed with. He had the power to decide what lived and what died; he was the rightful ruler of this land.

The whispers were telling him to do these things. He had killed many rabbits before; he enjoyed their meat, but this was different. He picked up a rock, placed it inside his sling, and threw it; the rabbit tried to hop away, but it was too late; the rock hit it on the side of its light brown head. It wasn't dead, only stunned, but it gave Adam enough time to pick it up by the ears. A glint of excitement and amazement glowed in his eyes, witnessing the fear of the poor helpless creature. He slowly then crushed the left foot of the rabbit. But killing it wasn't enough; he wanted to hurt it. It let out a scream of anguish; it pierced through Adam's head, and he suddenly snapped out of his rage. Looking at the rabbit desperately trying to get free, he glided down his hands on his neck, and, in a single twist, he broke it. Adam felt relieved, like something that was choking him was lifted. The hatred made him feel strong, but he didn't know what he hated; he just felt it.

He didn't let Eve find out what he did or that he kept doing it, but when he found that rabbits didn't satisfy him anymore, he moved on to badgers, then deers. He would take his time with a deer, and he worked his art to perfection. He knew how to infuse suffering into the creature without allowing them to bleed to death too quickly; a remarkable hunting skill yet an inhuman behaviour.

It would amaze you how long something could live without certain parts. He relished in the pain and terror in their eyes. The Shaitan rejoiced that they had corrupted man; he was cruel and cold-hearted like them. They sensed the light in him diminishing and knew that soon that light wouldn't be there anymore. Soon the darkness in man would define the marvel of creation that Pandora took pride in. When the last bit of light would be eradicated and leave Adam, all there would be left in the darkness.

0

Chapter 3: Penny's Dream

With the classroom empty, the silence feels almost alien to Penny. The walls are anything but silent, full of artwork with themes. The artworks were from her class, but she arranged them on the wall herself. Everything had to look right. She couldn't stand other classrooms where artworks were all over the place and had no arrangement.

Her favourite art theme was always autumn, everything coming through in different shades. It had an order to it, the cycle of the seasons and how the spring turns into autumn. Looking at the autumn display always stirred something in her; she could almost smell the dry and wet leaves. Her Nana used to tell her, "The world works on balance; in order for plants and animals to survive, the previous ones need to die. They're nutrients that get absorbed by the ground and feed the next cycle of life."

A crack of thunder brought her out of the thoughts of her Nana. "Well, tonight's deliveries are going to be fun!" muttering under her breath. She checked her desk for the third and the final time, ensuring everything was in its correct place; she gathered her things and made her way to her car. She made a quick stop to get a sandwich for herself and then moved on to job number two. Because she has her needs and has got to pay her bills, somehow, being a teacher doesn't cover them. Then she got in the car, nibbled on her sandwich, and drove to the first takeaway to get done with the food delivery.

As soon as Penny reached her home and walked through her front door, she picked up all the latest bills and threw them away in a drawer. She'll get around to her credit cards one day, she thought, but not today; right now, she's just happy to have a roof. Her flat doesn't have much to look at, but it was enough for her. If you walk through the door, you will find yourself standing in the part-living and part-kitchen room. There are two more rooms, the bathroom, which is a shower room. The bedroom is so tiny that it can barely fit the bed and a wardrobe unless you're okay with opening the doors only halfway. She hasn't got around to decorating, so the walls are still magnolia, and there are worn-out red carpets. Penny loved it, though; at least it belonged to her.

She placed her coat and bag on the hook next to the door and sat in her second favourite seat. A yellow reclining chair, ugly as hell, but it was free, and it was comfy. Her favourite chair was a big cushioned armchair with a chunky lazy cat sprawled across it. She didn't particularly like cats, but this one appeared one day and decided never to leave.

Penny came to an arrangement with the cat that if it keeps away the mice, she'll never find an empty bowl. Penny knew better than to wake the cat up; she was a lazy piece of work, which wanted to be petted on its terms, and under no circumstances did it like to be removed from the chair. There were scars on Penny's hands to prove this cat's entitlement. Penny didn't own the cat; it was a squatter. If Penny forgot to put the food in her bowl on any given day, the cat knew where to look. It didn't need Penny to pet her; it just liked the comfort of her home. "So how was your day?" the ball of fluff just opens an eye before turning, stretching out, and going back to sleep. "Ok then!" She figured that sometimes, despite its ghastly personality, a part of her wanted its company.

After resting for a bit, Penny got up and fetched the bottle of wine from the fridge. She poured a glass and walked over to her bag, pulled out the leather-bound book, and examined it closely. She intended to return it before work in the morning. The leather was pale and very smooth. Penny remembered a Lecturer at her university who taught about ancient civilisations and that a part of their rituals was to bound books in leather made from human skin. The Ekoi people in Nigeria and Cameroon even used human skin to make leather masks, and they would use them as part of the funeral rituals. There was something about ancient and remote civilisations that intrigued Penny. She took extra classes learning about ancient culture; it fascinated her.

As Penny walked back towards the chairs, the cat jumped up and meowed at her, then clambered out the open window. "Your loss, mate," Penny shouted after him as she reclaimed her favourite chair, sinking into its fluffy cushions that were still warm from the cat. The book felt cold, and her hand turned icy at the touch of it. Penny could feel it up to her arm now and into her neck. As soon as the cold reached her right ear, she heard a raspy whisper, "We see you! We've found you!" Penny dropped the book incessantly, then picked it up and put it back in her bag before going to bed. She thought that she was tired and stressed out, that's all, and it could also be the wine.

#

Penny fell asleep. At first, she felt warm and comfortable, but then the whispering started. Penny couldn't figure out what was being said, but she walked down the hallway. There were hands from both sides trying to grab at her. On one side, the hands were white, and on the other, they were black. Penny was slightly jogging now, trying to find an end to the whispering and an exit from the hallway. She followed the smell of Lillies and reached a door; she opened the door with all her might and ran out of it.

Penny was a little girl again, panting and hearing Nana's humming until she knew where she was. She sees that her brother, Elliot is there with them. She feels a pang of pain upon seeing him, but she can't remember why. Penny settled down in Nana's lounge next to Elliot to listen to the story of Pandora. They were always amazing, stories of magical beings, a paradise, and the bad guys.

The fireplace was roaring, and the heat was intense. Nana's house was always roasting hot, but she always complained about the cold, and Penny never saw her out of that cream cardigan. Her hair was up and curled as always, not a hair out of place, and just enough makeup not to look pasty or plain but not to be too obvious either. But it was her smell that was so flowery and warm. She made Penny feel safe. She explained that Pandora was what ancient man called the Earth from a forgotten time. "Or not so much forgotten, just re-told so often and twisted that it no longer resembles the truth. Men ruled the world; it's always been that way, and they are the ones to write the history; that's the first lesson."

Penny noticed how her Nana sometimes got too passionate about her stories, almost sounding like a political statement.

Nana began her story, "The bible tells us that Eve committed the original sin by taking the apple that the serpent seduced her. It's all lies." Her stories never failed to keep the listeners entertained, even though her stories might sound opinionated and biased to many.

However, Penny wasn't with Nana anymore; she was a part of one of her Nana's stories. Penny's stomach turned upside down. How could she be there?

Soon enough, Penny seemed composed, and a calm settled on her. She realized that nobody could see her there. She was just an observer, and so she observed.

#

First, Penny watched Adam closely as he was out hunting. Adam seemed to smell his prey, hunting half with instinct and half with intellect-- crouching, wearing loose fur, and holding a spear. Adam was the spitting image of a caveman stereotype. They were in a forest; it was hot, and there

45

was a humid swamp smell as well. The tree canopy was covering the roof of the forest, blocking out the sun. Penny wondered how Adam could see so well in such dim light.

He threw his spear, and Penny followed it to its mark. A sharp yelp made it evident that the spear had hit its target; the animal was down as soon as the spear tore through its flesh. His aim was perfect. This isn't like something she had seen in the movies. The sight made her look away in fear. She couldn't bear to watch the poor thing in agony. Adam stood up and walked over to the animal; at first, Penny couldn't figure out what animal it was but then recognised that it was a Tiger. The orange and black stripes were visible even though he was covered in mud and his own blood. Then Penny sees the enormous teeth; it was a sabre-tooth tiger! The smell of dung hit her, and she realized that it had soiled itself. Penny felt her heart reaching out to it as if she could feel the pain, staring into its miserable eyes. She figured that for the tiger to survive, Adam had to put it out of its misery. She screamed at him about what to do next. Adam pulled out a large black pouch and opened it up; he had a lot of tools in there, apparently. Penny watched and begged through tears to a spectre who couldn't hear her.

Adam hoisted the tiger by its front paws from a nearby tree, and Penny could see the full underbelly of the giant cat. Witnessing all this made her feel like a squatter. Adam took a stone that was longer, sharper, and heavier. He put the long thin stone against one tooth like a chisel and, WHACK! The tiger's tooth was separated. Penny fell into a defeated silence. The tiger was in agony, and Adam was actually enjoying all this, letting out heavy breaths and relishing in its pain like it was ritualistic. He was muttering; in fact, it almost sounded like he was praying.

Penny found herself out in the open, and there was smoke and fire. She could see that Adam and Eve were both presented there. However, Penny could see that Eve was keeping her distance, and Penny could sense that something wasn't right. Looking at Adam and the way he looks at Eve, Penny could tell that the animals didn't satisfy him anymore. Penny became afraid for her. Eve was a good foot shorter than Adam and was slimmer. She was gaunt, unlike Adam since he had been taking the best of the food for himself and leaving Eve with scraps. Her long black hair reached her hips, covering her breasts and fur around her waist. Adam sat by the fire, sharpening his tools, preparing for his next prey. And Penny could see that even Eve could sense the danger now but still wasn't running.

Penny remembered back to her own relationship, how she was stuck with her abuser for so long. And even though she could sense that she was in an abusive relationship, she still couldn't let it go. So she completely understood the trap Eve was in, stuck in her relationship with Adam. Penny felt a bond with Eve and felt like it was her responsibility to look out for her. She shouted at the top of her lungs, but she was just a spectator; it was not in her hands to stop it.

With a quick manoeuvre, Adam sprang up and slashed Eve behind her ankles, cutting through her Achilles' tendons. He did this to prevent Eve from running away from his trap so he could take his time. He stood over what would be his greatest triumph. As Penny watched all this, she glanced over to the side, following Eve's desperate gaze. Penny's eyes laid on children of different ages, and for the first time, she saw the children of Adam and Eve. Laying there helplessly, Eve begged them to run. The children tried to escape, but Adam didn't seem to care about human flesh anymore. Something in his eyes changed, and the thirst Penny saw before just vanished; his eyes were now blank.

Penny begged herself to wake up; she didn't want to watch this monster win. However, Penny couldn't get to wake herself up from the nightmare and watched as Adam spent the rest of the afternoon taking his time with Eve. He took out Eve's kidney at one point and held it in front of her face, letting her be the witness of the agony inflicted. He had discovered from animals that everything has two of them and could live a while without one.

Unfortunately, Eve didn't survive Adam's dread. When she died, Adam sat there looking at Eve, or at least what was left of her was now burning in flames. Her flesh smelt sweet, for which Adam had built up an appetite. He took a stick and pulled out a round bit of her flesh that looked almost like an apple. He took a bite and swallowed it immediately. At that moment, the ground trembled, and the air crackled all around him. He seemed to emanate darkness, and his aura was pitch black. Everything he touched turned grim. He had triggered something in the planet, the gloominess grew, and Penny could feel something was coming. Whatever it was, she could feel that it was something evil. His eyes had no white in them anymore, and they looked just like black coal; Adam had committed the original sin.

As he sat there watching Eve blowing up in flames, he opened his mouth, and there were the whispers again. Over and over again, he could hear the whispers say, "We see you," "We see you," "We found you!" And at that time, all terrors and evils were being poured into the land out of Adam's mouth.

The Pandora's Box was unlatched, and evil was to take over. Penny woke up drenched in sweat. She was panting and had a hollow feeling in her chest that she always felt when she dreamt of her brother. She picked up the picture that she kept by her bed and tried to imagine the bond the two of them must have shared. She remembered the day the picture was taken; it was an abseiling trip when they were about 14 and too young to grasp the realities.

Elliot died in a car crash when he was high on something. When the doctors checked, his alcohol levels were off the charts. As far as Penny was concerned, her dad was responsible for it. If he had been a better father, then maybe it wouldn't have been that way. If he had been a better father, she might not have sneaked out to go to the Abbey. Penny shook her head and got up to get some water. She couldn't get the dream out of her head. It was so vivid, the colours, the smells, the fear. Funny though, she didn't remember Nana telling them stories like that. Sniggering to that thought, Penny poured water into a glass in the shower room; she looked up at the mirror and saw Eve standing behind her covered in blood. Penny shrieked and dropped the glass in fear.

50

Chapter 4:
The Day Everything
Changed

Looking at the picture of her and Elliot on the table next to it, she suddenly realises the date. "A whole year since the car crash, how did it pass so quickly?" Doubting, bitterly, that anyone else would realise what day it was. "Why did you drive that day?" she cursed herself, reminiscing on the unfortunate event. He drove his car the wrong way down the street, swerved, and hit a tree. The speed he was driving at, the tree just merged with the car into a metallic melted mass. "Miss Whyte, they ended up using his DNA to identify the dead body." The police had it on file from one of his many arrests.

Penny is jolted from her thoughts when her phone rings; she looks at it, and it's from the school, "Miss Whyte, is everything okay? You were supposed to be here 30 minutes ago," says a young voice on the phone.

Penny recognized immediately that it was Sarah, one of the school secretaries. Penny looks at the clock and swears under her breath, "Sarah, tell Ms Fox that I'm sorry, I'll be there as soon as possible. I don't know what happened."

Penny knew she had messed up. She figured that she woke up in her favourite chair feeling sick. As soon as she regained consciousness, she remembered everything. She could still smell Eve's burning flesh, looked over at the fat cat in the chair across from her, and shook her head.

"Well, you do burn the candle at both ends, your class is covered for the rest of the week, and you are expected in Ms Fox's office ASAP. Something has happened!" Penny could feel the sarcasm at this point, and at that, Sarah hung up. Sarah is young, and her attitude matches her personality. Penny could almost hear her filing her nails while talking to her over the phone.

It was quite certain that this meant she was getting fired; Penny got to school in thirty minutes, realising as she got there that the book was still in her bag and she was supposed to drop it off.

As soon as Penny reached school, she rushed to Ms Fox's office. The room was large, and she had a big desk at one end with shelving and display cases down either side. The display cabinets had her many trophies and medals, not the school ones, her own. She was in her fifties, and judging from the medals, she apparently is very good at everything, but particularly, she is good at snooker. 'Snooker, not Pool', she would say in a loud projected voice whenever someone made the mistake of asking about her 'pool' trophies.

She was sat on one of the two couches by the entrance to her office, both green matching the power suit she always wore, like a predator's camouflage. Penny nervously sat on the other one, Ms Fox had a very sullen but determined look on her face, and Penny just knew she was done for.

"There's no easy way to tell you this," Ms Fox began. "There's been an incident; Mark Abbott's house has burned down." Her voice softened uncharacteristically, "I'm sorry, Penny, no one survived."

All the air suddenly left her lungs, and the room felt suffocating. She couldn't breathe, her stomach went into spasms, and her mouth felt dry. A plain-clothed police officer entered the room, but Penny barely noticed her as she was still reeling from the news and feeling around for a bucket. The massive room suddenly felt like it was a broom closet. Getting up and going for the door, Penny felt the ground move, but not the way she had expected it to, and then she felt the rough carpet hit her cheek.

Penny wakes up with two women standing over her, "Here, I got you some water," it was the police officer. Penny noticed her eyes first; they were green like grass. She was beautiful, "Are you okay, Miss Whyte?" Her voice was kind, not like Ms Fox. "Yes, s..s..sorry, I'm fine." Penny let her help her to the couch; she smelt amazing. Ms Fox sat with a glum expression the whole time staring; she seemed unfazed. She was an amazing teacher; the kids loved her as she would inspire them and make them laugh. She wasn't so good with other adults; it's like she learnt how to interact with kids but forgot how to do the same with her peers.

The officer introduces herself, "Miss Whyte, My name is Katy Digby, and I'm the family liaison officer attached to this case. I'm sorry to throw so much at you at once, but we need to investigate this as quickly as possible. We believe it was arson."

Penny reaches for the bin again as her head starts spinning again. "Can I call you Penny?" Penny manages a nod. "Penny, the house was broken into. They are searching for something but with no residents to ask; we don't know if anything is missing."

Penny told Katy about her suspicions around Mark's dad, "Maybe he had been involved in something, and my instincts were correct? Why didn't I say anything?" Penny put her head between her knees, but it was no use she filled Ms Fox's paper bin.

"Penny, how was Mark in class?" Penny was confused. "I just told you everything; he was quiet, he was also shy but a good student. He seemed to be distracted recently, and the incident with the book," Officer Digby's interest seemed to have been prodded "what book?"

Penny realized that she had given away something important, and now she was up for an explanation. She told them about the school trip and the book that Mark had stolen. She reached into her bag to get it out, but it wasn't there. "It's gone. It wasn't here when I arrived. How? Where?" They all looked at each other in confusion. Officer Digby carried on to say, almost unsurprised,

"Penny, it doesn't look as though the intruders caused the damage; they arrived after. They broke in through the police cordon and apparently expecting whatever they were looking for to somehow be safe and intact."

"So if not them, then who?" Penny's tone turned petulant, and she started to become suspicious of the questions about Mark.

She told the investigators that "Mark was quiet, had a tough time speaking to others." What Penny didn't tell them about Mark was the times he would struggle with his temper when something went wrong and often seem to lose his temper on the slightest of the inconveniences. It was like he was struggling with a mix of anger and fear.

There was a time they were studying molecules, and he built a prototypical framework of some water molecules in a box. He was walking to the front of the class to demonstrate what happens to molecules as a liquid either freezes or evaporates. He spent so much time on his project, built a frame to hang to molecules. He was going to show how the space between the molecules expand and contract depending on temperature. It would have been really impressive. However, as he was attaching the molecules to the frame, one of the hydrogen atoms refused to stay in place. Glancing from the project's framework to the sniggering class, Mark got flustered. He screamed and threw the whole thing at other people that were present there. That was when Penny tried to get to know him better. She made him take his lunch breaks in the classroom rather than the playground for the next two weeks. And she figured that he actually preferred that anyway; she wanted to know why he was so angry all the time. She would sit with him during recess to talk about the class, his classmates, and his interests in trains.

After spending enough time with him during recess, she realized that Mark would never talk about his family or shy away every time the topic was brought up. He completely avoided talking about his parents. And over time, Penny's suspicion intensified. The way his dad would act during the meetings, he was called to remind her of her own dad. He was always crunching extra strong mints and avoided eye contact, and when he did make eye contact, his eyes would be bloodshot. Although Mark didn't think she noticed, Penny felt him wince ever so often but wasn't confident about it yet.

Now he was dead; Penny wasn't feeling grief; she was feeling remorse and guilt; she should have pushed more and got to the bottom of things. Officer Digby pulled out a large file, and it had Mark Abbot written across the at its front.

It was his School file, containing all the information regarding his academics. And hit Penny, guess she already knows about Mark's outbursts.

"Penny," the officer begins, "We suspect Mark started the fire." Penny was confused, "You mean he set the house on fire?"

Officer Digby looked Penny in the eye; she had a hesitant look on her face. Penny knew, at that point, she hadn't heard the worst part yet. "Penny, Mark's parents, were found with their hands and feet tied with a rope; they had been beaten already with a heavy object we believe to be a baseball bat. And we have proof. Our team found a baseball bat in his room, which had bloodstains on it. And he could have left the place at any time, his window was wide open, and he wasn't bound. He could've left but, he chose to stay and die." Penny thought she would pass out again; the room was spinning faster than she could bear.

The officer continued, "We found a voicemail. He sent it on his grandparents' phone, and he was talking about these whispers, something like… they had set him free, and now that he had been cleansed, it was time to cleanse the house."

It all seemed too familiar to Penny, the whispering she had been hearing all come back to her at the moment. She feels like she's going to be sick, runs out of the room across the hall, and burst into the toilets. She locks herself into a cubicle and puts her head between her legs, trying to catch her breath. She instinctively started the breathing exercises she had learnt from her psychologist. Over time, she figured the breathing itself didn't help but concentrating on something like the timing of each breath helped focus her.

After doing a few sets of breathing exercises, Penny was able to calm her racy thoughts, and the erupting nauseous feeling alleviated. The room settled down, and Penny stood up, unlocked the cubicle, and walked over to the sinks. She ran cold water over her hands and looked into the mirror. She still couldn't get the vision of a bloodied Eve out of her mind and now Mark's burnt body. She splashed water on her face and dried it off before leaving.

Ms Fox was waiting outside for her. When she saw Penny come out of the washroom, she said, "Penny, go home, take the week off; you can't teach like this. The officer will be in touch with you."

Penny headed towards the door, but her mind was not in its place. She kept thinking about Mark, and she kept thinking about her dreams. What did it all mean? Was she losing her mind? She heard whispers, but they couldn't be the same whispers Mark heard. That book! It all seemed crazy, but deep down, Penny knew that book had something to do with it. They both touched it. But no, logical reasoning takes all over her, "I'm an educated person. I never believed in any superstition or paranormal myths."

But then again, it was such a tough time that she found it hard to maintain her faith. The worrisome part was the sudden disappearance of it; where did it go? It was in her bag when she went into the office. There was something freakish about it, something cold and cruel. Where could it go? Her brain kept repeating the same question all over again. Shrugging off the worries of safekeeping of that book, Penny distracted herself by thinking about having wine.

Penny headed for her car, but she was distracted by the smell of Lilies; they always reminded her of her mother. The smell had a soothing effect on her mind, but it also brought pain with it. She looked here and there, and her eyes caught the sight of the path that leads out of the school and straight up the hill to Beachwood Road. The sight felt peculiar, and she felt like it was pulling her. I grew up there; I need answers. Where did my mother go? All the questions started to race through her mind. The smell got stronger, even though there weren't any plants in sight. This was the moment when Penny decided that she wanted answers for herself. Her mother vanished somewhere, and only that bastard knew why or where, and he must tell her!

Chapter 5:
Old Memories

Falling to the ground, Penny curses the pavement's uneven surface. She puts her hand onto the chicken wire fence that borders the slabbed path to steady herself. Penny tried to gather herself by ensuring herself that it was her head that was erratic. Penny needed to control her breathing; three seconds out, two seconds in, three out, two in, three, two, three, and two. It was getting really hard for her, but she managed to put herself together. The ground slowed, and she got her bearings. The thought that her school was close to the place where she grew up made her feel a lot better.

Something still resounded in her. She couldn't stop thinking about her mother. Penny hadn't thought about her in years. Isobel abandoned them when Penny was just a small girl. One day she was with them, and the next, something went terribly wrong. Penny was young at that time, but she vividly remembers how cagey her mother became in her last few days with them. She became distant, arguing with her Dad, James. And then one day, there was nothing, not a word, she was just gone!

That's when her dad started drinking, which made him just as inaccessible as her mother. She never wanted things to go this way, but fate had other plans. One particular Saturday, Penny, who had just turned 7, was thinking of ways to fix her dad's drinking problem. At this point, he had spent most nights smelling of cheap wine. If it wasn't for Elliot making dinner and taking care of her, Penny probably would have starved or burned the house down trying to cook.

James spent his days in the pub, and Penny and Elliot spent the day at school before returning to an empty home.

"Elliot, let's bake a cake!" I bet dad will like that, said Penny getting all excited.

Little Penny thought that if she would bake for her dad, he'd read to her or let her sit on his lap for a while.

Elliot scrubbed Penny's school uniform with a Duff soap bar he stole from the corner shop. "Grow up, Penny! Dad doesn't even remember that we exist!" said Elliot.

Elliot was ten at that time, and he was just starting to see the world more like a man. Still too young to be understanding the things he needed to understand; but he had a sister to look after.

"Please, Elliot, he'll definitely remember when we give him a surprise; he'll be so pleased that we still love him!" Penny insisted.

Elliot threw the bar of the soap he had in his hand off the wall behind Penny. He didn't aim at her but wanted to scare her. He resigned himself to the fact that she would win. Because she always did.

"You finished your readings? And your maths homework?" Penny smiled and ran straight into the kitchen without another word and began to prepare things they needed to bake.

Later that night, she put on her loveliest dress, crawled into her dad's bedroom. The room was dark, with a scent of stale sweat and wine. Penny started going through the drawers curiously. She needed a particular item, the one that intrigued her the most as per her inclinations. She got so excited to make her dad happy; she found her prize, but then pain ran up her arm, and she shrieked!

Elliot ran through to see what had happened, "what the hell are you doing!" only to see Penny with blood everywhere and a knife sitting in the drawer. Elliot immediately realised what happened. The cut was not too deep but ran about an inch and a half. However, to avoid any infections, Elliot cleaned and dressed the cut without noticing what she took from the drawer.

Later that night, Penny sat in the living room, proudly holding her creation. Elliot took himself to bed with no interest in his Dad's whereabouts. While Penny was waiting for her father to return, she took the stolen artefact out of her pocket and pulled a mirror across the sparsely furnished room. Penny looked at her prize, and she remembered her mother wearing it often. There was also a lipstick lying in the drawer; Penny opened it and applied it to her own lips. She waited and waited the entire night with the cake sitting on the table beside her and eventually fell asleep. BANG! A loud noise was heard in the middle of the night. Penny screamed in fear, not knowing that it was her dad that finally came home, knocked the cake off the table and onto the floor. He looked up at her and saw as her face softened for a moment.

"Dad, I made you a cake, but it's."

His face turned to anger, "You made a mess; that's what you've done, sitting here in the dark, waiting to trip me up. Are you wearing lipstick? Is that your mum's! Well, it made her look like a whore and made you look like one too. Wash your face; I don't want to see it again tonight!"

Elliot burst through the door just in time and heard his sister being called a whore. Elliot launched at his Dad in anger but easily got knocked to the ground, and he was obviously no match for him. Even though his dad was drunk, he still managed a kick to the ribs for good measure and threw Elliot on the floor.

Penny shudders at the memory; that's the point, that's... the point when my world stopped functioning well. The next day she walked to school on her own, walked up to her usual group of friends, talking about dolls and comics like nothing ever happened.

"Mummy taught me how to style dolly's hair, and we had such a great time." Another two debating comics; "Dandy is amazing; he's the strongest man alive and eats nothing but cow pie!" Her friend's counter felt just as pointless "well, The Beano has Dennis, and he gets up to all kinds of mischief with his dog Nesher!" Penny counted; she wasn't counting her breaths this time. One, two, three, four, five. She stood there and counted her friends. Things were getting more worrisome and distressing for her at that time. She had five friends standing there, all talking. They were talking about things that Penny had no interest in talking about. She felt like she wasn't a part of their conversations anymore. She had learnt a lesson from the previous night. She learnt that people are in your life temporarily; they always leave when they want to. Sure, they serve a purpose in your life, but when that is done, they're out of the picture.

Soon, Penny's quietness and detachment from others alienated her from her own friends and classmates, and as they grew older, she was heavily ignored. It was like she didn't exist for other people. But that's how Penny liked it, though. Whatever was going at that time made things only worse for Penny, but she ignored them, and they ignored her. She was a square peg, and the world was a round hole; she just didn't fit in it anymore.

Even in her present life as a teacher, she didn't speak with the other teachers much; but she liked the kids because children tend to accept people and things at face value. They don't judge off the cuff; that's taught later; hatred and bigotry are introduced later in life.

Once, Penny's therapist explained to her that her emotional self had stopped maturing at a certain point of trauma. And this is what makes Penny so comfortable with children of primary school and not adults because that's where her emotional maturity stand. They told her that years of trauma had stunted her emotional growth.

At that point, the only thing that mattered to her was to save these young minds from the imbroglio she had faced already. Apparently, her trauma got a fancy long name and lots of recommended therapies that would come with a very long bill attached; thus, that was the last time Penny had seen her therapist.

I'm going to go see Dad, Penny thought to herself. She made her way out of the car park, up the path leading to Beachwood Road. She was moving towards her former house, the one where she spent her childhood. The house she grew up in came into view in only a few brief minutes. It was at the top of the hill and hadn't changed a bit, except the closer she got, the more dirt around the windows was visible.

Penny let herself in; the stench hit her straight away; it was vile. There were flies everywhere, and the sound of their buzzing echoed in the entire building. "Dad? Dad!" Penny walked into the living room only to discover a horrific scene. She was not sure if she wanted to go in there because of the fear of what she might see, but she knew she had to. She didn't come this far only to turn away.

As she entered the room, Penny slipped on something slimey and landed in a puddle of congealed blood. Peering over, she could see the source of where the bloodstream was coming from; there was a rigid figure on the floor. It was almost skeletal, wearing a bloodied, dirty white shirt and a pair of boxers. She barely noticed the TV in the background as she gradually got up.

Fumbling with her back pocket, Penny carefully pulled her phone out. Her hands were shaking as she tried to wake the screen. There was so much blood on her hands now that it was impossible to unlock her phone. Panic was setting in. She wanted to run from the room, but she needed to know. Who was lying on the floor? She knew the answer; as soon as she entered the room, but she refused to believe it until she saw his face; three in, two out, three, two, three, and two. She continued her breathing exercise.

Penny looked around the room and saw that their family portrait had a bloodied handprint on it. She was almost numb when she saw that picture because it had a lot of emotional attachment. Someone picked it up after killing the man lying in the room. She looked down at the body carefully once again. She figured that the man's face was badly beaten, it was so disfigured that Penny couldn't identify him, but then she looked back at his hands. It was a horrific scenario, and she wasn't sure how to overcome these things. The rings, those were her dad's rings. It was him. Her dad was dead!

When Penny finally came to terms with the truth, she realized the noise in the background; she realised that the TV was on, and for how long, she had no clue. Penny moved further close to the TV to pull the plug away from the wall, leaving a bloody print. As soon as the TV volume went off, The sound of an engine from outside could be clearly heard.

Penny peeked outside the window only to see a police car parked in the driveway; they were getting out and checked the house from outside. Penny looked at the body on the ground, her hands, and the prints she had left everywhere. "No! It wasn't me!" Penny was shouting through the window at the police walking up the driveway. She was anxious about what was going on.

As soon as they had come into the room, they took one glance and commanded Penny to walk towards them slowly with her hands in front of her. The scenario made her look guilty. The police immediately cuffed her, "I am arresting you on suspicion of murder, you do not have to say anything before you get your lawyer, but it may harm your case further if you do not respond when questioned. Anything you do or say could be used as evidence."

They escorted Penny down the driveway, with an officer on either side of her and one behind her to watch all her movements closely. There was a police van now behind the car and a black unmarked van right behind that. "Who parked that van there?" The officer on the left was getting nervous. "Just some dick parking where they want; there's always one."

Penny was so numb that she barely heard the conversation. How could they think that she's guilty of her father's murder? It must be some animal! It had to be a monster for the way they smashed his face. In her head, Penny was eagerly trying to untangle the murder of her father. She was so consumed that she didn't realize that all three officers were floored within seconds. She only heard someone shouting at her, but she couldn't understand a word as she was in a daze. The officers were bleeding on the ground; that's all she saw, and then she felt someone grabbing at her. There was a sudden sharp thud at the back of her head, and then there was darkness all around.

Chapter 6: Forbidden Fruit

Penny was standing in front of Adam; she looked around and realized that she was back in Pandora. His eyes disappeared in the darkness, Penny could hear him talk, but she couldn't see who and couldn't understand a word being said. The situation perplexed Penny a lot, but she could not do anything about it. She tried to listen closely to what was being said, but nothing could be heard clearly. It was all very confusing for Penny.

She had nothing but hatred for Adam, and the feeling was still fresh from what she witnessed. Penny moved closer in the direction of Adam, very aggressively, her hands were tightened to form fists, and Adam looked right in her eyes. His stare somehow completely disarmed Penny, and she felt powerless. She suddenly felt like a shrunken little girl standing against a giant. She could feel her stomach twisting in fear, her head trembling. He looks straight through her and moves his lips to say something, but it's that same harsh whispering from before that comes out "vetiti fructus". Penny listens to the words closely, and this time, she doesn't know how, but she knows it means the forbidden fruit.

Penny was well aware that Adam had crossed a line. He wasn't Adam anymore; in fact, there was something else emanating from him. It was darkness, and it pierced through whoever saw Adam. The darkness was spreading from him and into the world. Most humans feared in the night is the darkness that takes over and what hides therein, but Penny was facing both of them simultaneously. All the horrors of hell were surrounding her. And they consumed her energy.

Initially, Penny felt hatred and anger towards Adam. Why did he do it? She questioned herself. Adam had turned the order of the world upside down. Penny was aware, and it filled her with terror. Standing in Pandora, looking at Adam's unrestricted powers, the hatred and anger had passed from Penny. She wasn't even terrified anymore; looking at the superiority of Adam's strength, she was now jealous of his power. Her skin crawled at the thought of a man having all this power to himself. She coveted it for herself; she imagined herself in Adam's position, being the most powerful person in the world. No one would dare hurt her ever again.

Lost in her fantasies, Penny felt something touching her elbow. She immediately looked down with maddening eyes. A little girl was standing beside her, with her face almost glowing up with light. She smiled, and all the darkness seemed to fade away. Penny's stomach unknotted, her head stopped spinning, and she felt a little bit alive.

Penny gasped as she tried to catch her breath, regaining her senses. Thinking about the girl she saw, she thought it was one of Eve's children, and she must be around 12. The girl wore the same fur as her dad did and had the same long hair as Penny's mother. Penny realised it was the same long hair she used to have as a kid, unruly in that same way. She couldn't do much with it because they were thick and difficult to handle; she always ended up just growing her hair long and keeping them tied in a ponytail. That girl reminded Penny of herself, mainly because of the hair; they were somehow identical.

The child calmly walked up to the fire. She seemed immune to the corruption of the darkness spilling from her father, Adam. He looked into the girl's eyes; Penny could see strength building up between the two. Her eyes weren't glowing as such, but it was as if the light was flowing from them. She was beautiful, like a princess, a princess of the light. So much like her mother; brave and courageous. She walked up to Adam with confidence, and he turned around to face her for the first time. As soon as Adam came in direct contact with the girl, he seemed to wince and cower. His focus faltered, and the harsh whispers stopped.

His demeanour changed; the giant man was now shrunken so much that the twelve-year-old girl seemed to tower over him. He couldn't stand the light flowing out of his daughter, especially since he had given into the darkness. There was a look of evilness and cruelty in his eyes as he looked towards his daughter. Whatever amount of humanity left in him seemed to surface in him. His hands were holding his head as he crouched to the ground, a low growl coming from his mouth as he almost convulsed as he struggled.

His daughter shown her light and gave it to the world to balance the darkness. And to her father, she gave him the gift of forgiveness. It enraged Penny, though; how dare she forgave him after what he's done to Eve.

Penny was still not over the cruelty, and rightfully so. But then something happened, and in a breath, the darkness left Adam's eyes. Looking around, he threw himself to the ground, sobbing. He did have an idea of what he did while the evil power took over him; he was full of remorse. The darkness hadn't extinguished completely; it was overtaken by his light that was only shrouded with evil powers. His daughter brought back the good in him to the surface.

Having seen the situation, Penny knew what was about to happen at the back of her mind. Penny understood that if Adam had released the darkness and all the sin, then his daughter had delivered us redemption and forgiveness, but at what cost?

Adam couldn't live with what he had done. The guilt inside him drove him to stab a sharpened stone into his own throat. He cut himself too deep and was reaching his demise with every second passing by. He bled out next to the fire and turned to ash, and disappeared into the air. It had stopped the darkness that had been spilling out instantly. But, to Penny's realization, the order always balances itself. If there is light, there will be darkness. Just because Adam is not alive anymore to contain that darkness doesn't mean that it ceased to exist. It was soon evident to Penny that the darkness still existed in Pandora. It was true that it had escaped, and now it was out there somewhere, but it was uncontrolled and concerned Penny.

"What's happening?" Penny thought hard; all she could see was darkness, and her head hurt. The confusion was overbearing. She didn't know what was going on and that dream! She was instantly reminded of her dream. Something had changed inside her when she felt the girl's touch on her. It was just a dream, but Penny knew how impactful her dreams could be. She knew some parts of it, but she was unable to comprehend that dream in a way that could make sense to her.

Still groggy, she realised that they had now tied together both her feet and when she tried to move her hands, she was unable to move them without feeling the pain in her wrists from some restraints that she couldn't see. Penny remembered the car, the house, and the officers falling to the ground before everything faded into darkness. It was difficult to tell what had happened, whether her head was spinning in fear, whatever knocked her out of her consciousness; she couldn't comprehend whatever was happening. Why was she taken? Who were the people who took her? All these questions needed to be answered, for they were necessary for Penny's mental well-being and peace. She listened for a moment, trying to figure out where she was being held.

She was aware of the movement and could hear the sound of the traffic nearby. They came to a stop before she heard beeping from a pedestrian crossing the road. There must be other people close by. Penny sensed them outside. She wanted to cry out for help, but the rag in her mouth stopped her from doing anything other than attract her captor's attention. Someone placed an almost caring hand on her head and said, "shhh, it's ok," it was a calm and comforting whisper. The calmness in his voice was even more terrifying than the darkness Penny saw in Adam. The sensation of a hand on her head was almost too much. A sudden waft of vomit and Penny realised she had been sick.

It was intense and reminded her of the older men in the pub her dad would drag her to. The sickness left, and the fear returned; she did not understand what was happening or why. Penny realised the man asking her to stay calm was on the phone. He spoke to someone and realized that they were discussing a book, but it couldn't be the same one? "What is with this bloody book?" she thought. She remembered how it seemed to radiate up her arm and that strange leather made from human skin. What made things even more ferocious was that she got to hear something she did not expect at all. She heard the man say, "we searched for the boy's house, and we have the teacher. Neither has produced the book of Shaitan." There was a pause on the phone while the person on the phone spoke. Penny couldn't hear him. The man again replied, "No, the boy is dead; we believe it consumed him." Penny assumed he meant the fire, but the way the man said 'it,' she was almost frightened as if 'it' had a name that he wouldn't say in front of Penny. "We didn't set the fire, but at least we need not worry about him. We have to check her flat; it must be there" there was a pause while he listened to the other person speak. She can't tell who he's speaking to, but from the tension, he was someone to be afraid of.

Thinking about her past brings her immense pain. However, her recovery had given her insights and understanding of the events that happened in the past and the things that were happening now. It allowed her to understand people better, and she saw the guy almost shaking while talking on the phone. She can sense it in his voice. He was afraid of the person he was talking to. He hung up the phone, with the parting word "for The Clan". Another voice asked, "What does the Operator want us to do next?"

"We get rid of this…." He never finished his sentence. A sudden smash hit the car, and suddenly she felt like the car was spinning as she rolled inside it, getting thrown everywhere, and the darkness took over again.

All Penny heard was the ringing in her ears from banging her head. A pain in her side took her breath, but she couldn't reach to check. They tied Penny to something solid in the van, which saved her from something worse, but her body felt broken. Everything was motionless then; she couldn't get past the ringing in her ears to listen for her captors. And no idea if they survived. At least now, there might be a rescue by the police.

The thought struck her; she thought about the police. She had no idea if they were alive. It all came back to her;

she was arrested when they took her from her old house. They posed her for her dad's murder. She remembered being covered in his blood. Mark's dead. The voices. The dreams. One, Two, three... she started counting to maintain her focus.

Penny had managed to get rid of the spiral she was in, but she was scared to even now. Her fear hasn't gone away though, she was in pain, out of breath, tired, and she's had enough of today and that fucking book! It pissed her off now thinking about that book. Panic set in when she realised she couldn't catch her breath; something beside her was stopping her from fully exhaling.

She had a pair of hands grasp at her, and she tried to scream; it was too soon for it to be the police or fire brigade. She was exhausted and just had no fight left in her. It must be her captors. They are alive, she figured. The firm hands cut her free of her restraints.

At last! She could move her arms and legs again. She threw a punch but was winded by the pain; the punch turned into a nudge.

The sturdy hands lifted Penny up and away from the crash. He put Penny into the back of a car and shut the door. The driver gets in, starts the engine, and drives off. Penny reaches up and pulls the hood off her head and the rag out of her mouth. She peeked from the backseat to see who the driver was. She saw his face, but she couldn't manage to speak. She was constantly trying to utter some words and call for help, but she could not do so. She mumbles, "It can't be you; you left us; why did you leave?" with the blood loss and trauma of the day, Penny passes out, muttering, "Where?"

#

In the mid-90s ford, Ibiza made its way north, not in a hurry to attract attention but purposefully. The late summer sun was still high, being mid-afternoon. He had to create some distance between them and the crash. He hadn't checked on Penny's captors, so he didn't know if they were alive to check in with The Clan and report him.

Before they would reach their destination, they would need to stop somewhere safe, so Penny's rescuer could assess her injuries and treat them. He looked at her face, wondering how it could change so much. For a moment, he thought he had picked up his sister. He was confused and wanted to sort things out in a better way. Shug couldn't believe how much Penny resembled their mother. Determination crossed his scarred face. He wouldn't fail Penny the way he failed their mother. He wanted to make things better. The thought of him failing Penny brought only regret. He didn't have the capacity for anything else anymore.

Ten years ago, he returned to check on them and came face to face with his brother-in-law. The man couldn't stand it; he was so drunk he barely recognised him. Shug was short but stood like a man of much higher stature, very sure of himself at that time. He had broad shoulders and knew how to carry himself.

When James got up to his feet, he towered over Shug. It was a remarkable scenario, the one that could give everyone goosebumps. If you were to witness the scene, you would think the roles were reversed. Shug seemed to tower over the drunk Jame.

"Get out of my house; you abandoned us as she did!" It was almost a sob. The man was pathetic. Too drunk to be angry and too unsteady to square up to Shug. There were no words left to speak, and Shug understood and left. Both the children were at school, and he watched them from a distance before continuing his search for The Tribe. It was one way for him to get answers. One light bearer and one protector, both born in each generation, joined by the work of fate. Something took her from him. Something happened to her; she wouldn't think of just leaving everything behind. He needed answers, and The Tribe was his people. Even though they were never a part of his life, he trusted them to get all the answers.

Shug shook all the memories away and looked back at Penny. I wish I had taken both of you that day with me; Elliot wouldn't have died and would have kept you safe. I kept failing her. But not again, and not this time, especially since you've been activated!

Chapter 7: The Operator

Their entire life, Elliot and Penny looked out for each other. When their mother left, their dad hit the bottle. He disappeared from their lives. It was as if he had nothing to do with his kids.

Their Nana had died when they were still in primary school. She held a massive place in their hearts: She was a good woman who treated both kids with affection, there were so many stories she told them, and they had so many memories with that woman. When Nana told stories, she told them like they were real; she described everything as if she were a part of it. By the time Elliot and Penny had heard all the stories, they felt like they knew every detail about Pandora. When dad was on a bender, they would retreat to Pandora.

Growing up, they had heard so many stories. They would sit up at night for hours, making up their own stories. Elliot liked scary stories about the shadow creature, but Penny enjoyed talking about the tribes of a man living in a complex tunnel network. It was like the imagery of another world in their minds, the one that intrigued them more than the world they lived in. The world in their head seemed like a safe place to be. It fascinated Penny to create stories about the council of elders and their wise leadership. She loved how they managed and led things mostly in peace until the darkness fell.

They heard stories of mysterious children who appeared one day and the girl born to lead them and hold back the dark. Penny was delighted to know about a girl leading many tribes; and how she brought them all together in unity and held her seat.

There was only one tribe refusing to join, calling themselves The Clan. They became a splinter group of men, and they were originally the fishing tribe. Fishing was not only their identity and originality but also a source of their income and livelihood. A mysterious man led them; no one knew of him before he joined the tribe. He wasn't born in the tribe but joined it later and rose through the ranks. That same man convinced The Clan to follow another path and refused to follow the girl who led the other tribes.

Before the girl brought them together, the tribes had broken apart into factions, squabbling over resources and food. Then the girl named Jasmin, the eldest of Eve's daughters, united the tribes.

The tribes weren't always fighting; there was peace at the start. They shared what they had and loved each other. Then day became night, and the air sounded like a screaming storm. Suddenly after it, all subsided a group of children arrived at the cave entrance. The Tribe took them in because their hearts were full of love. Except one of them suddenly felt something else as if the darkness that had subsided had somehow penetrated his skin. He felt suspicion. Who were these children, who were riding in on a storm of screams? What trouble do they bring?

The darkness didn't subside; it only hid in the shadows and penetrated the hearts of all creatures. The previously harmonious tribes slowly became fractured; jealousy, hate, and anger ruled them. One faction was always suspicious of others' intentions. Things had changed quite a lot, and there was a drastic change in the proceedings within the tribe—all of this coincided with the children's appearance.

Even then, some blamed the children for the fighting. The different factions only emerged after the children arrived. It was like they brought a curse with them. No one understood what had happened outside of the caves. Before all this, there was never jealousy or hatred amongst the tribes. But now people hoarded crops, brother fought brother, for the first time man paid attention to their differences, their disagreements were based upon how they looked or spoke, and the things they believed in.

For the first time, something was lurking in the shadows, and it was waiting, the patient always watching. They became afraid. The tribes had felt this for a long time, a shroud had fallen, and the heart of man was never the same. The more time they spent outside of the caves, the worse they felt. Soon they learned not to go out at night, or else the shadows would somehow attack them. Creatures with hands grabbing at them, long spindly fingers scratching at their skin.

Humankind was doomed; there was no way for them to stay safe. Then Jasmin worked as a saviour who helped them. She spoke of the eternal beings and the light. She told the man how the light existed in everyone and everything. The crystals in the caves gave protection to humankind; however, one must know how to use them. Jasmin showed them how to make protective amulets and bracelets from the crystal. It took some time, but ultimately the humankind understood how it was created. Soon the protective charms and bracelets allowed men to come out of their fear of the shadows, and it gave them the power to resist the darkness. Through Jasmin, humankind learned many virtues that were missing in their lives, virtues like being fearless, patient, and tolerant.

During his teenage years, Elliot fell in with the wrong crowd. He stopped telling stories to Penny because he was so occupied with himself. It was Saturday night, and at that time, both Penny and Elliot were pretty young, with Elliot being 15 and Penny was 13. She was hoping to spend quality time with her brother on a Saturday night, and so she said, "Elliot, stay in and watch a movie with me?" Penny was desperate for her brother's attention, especially now that she did not have her mother or father around. But at that time, Elliot didn't know any better because he was a reckless teenager, so he ignored Penny's request.

But Penny being a needy teenager, jokingly hugged his leg in a mocking 5-year-old kind of way. What came next was a horrible response from her brother that still scared her. He grabbed her by the hair and pulled her off, throwing her away. He wasn't recognisable anymore. He was definitely not the brother Penny had spent so much time with making and telling stories under their blanket fort as kids. He was a whole different person, someone who was frustrated and abusive. Through teary eyes, she couldn't recognise the boy in front of her. He was so full of anger; he left the room, instantly shutting the door behind him, leaving Penny alone and scared, wondering what was happening to her brother? She felt isolated; there was nothing but solitude around her. The worst part of all this was that the further he drifted away, the more desperate Penny became for his attention.

With her dad always drunk and sometimes violent, Penny was always filled with fear. Things were difficult for her, and the bad part was that she could not do anything about it. Her dad never hit her, but he would hit Elliot in front of Penny; he punched drywall and countertops in anger. Penny saw it all, and she was scared that one day she'd be at the receiving end of those punches. One night her father slammed his foot through the TV because the electricity got cut off. Of course, he hadn't paid the bill, but that was the TV's fault or the electricity company, or maybe the world
– but he refused to acknowledge his faults.

Penny mostly blamed her dad for Elliot's anger. She was angry too, but more than anything, she was scared and isolated, like she was on an island surrounded by drunk and angry sharks. She knew where to channelize her anger; she used to draw, read books and do anything along the lines of creativity that made her feel better. Penny had seen the violence caused by her brother and her father, and she promised herself never to be like them.

After a couple of years, Elliot finally came off the drugs, but he was still not done with his drinking problem. At least his temper had cooled down, and she recognised her brother again. So, when Elliot told Penny he was sneaking out and going to the Abbey with his friends, she begged to come along. Because she stayed most of the time indoors, she wouldn't miss a single opportunity to get out of the house. At first, Elliot refused it because they were going there to get drunk, and she was only fifteen. "Penny, you're too young; I just need to get out of here; I can't look after you all the time."

Penny felt the rejection hard, but she knew what she needed to do. Penny looked him square in the eyes and said, "Ok, I'll go tell dad what you're doing and that you have a bottle in your bag."

Penny knew that their dad wouldn't give a shit about him sneaking out. But she knew he would care about Elliot stealing his drink. It was a smart move on Penny's part. After hearing this, Elliot raised his arm in the window's direction and stepped to the side in an exaggerated beckoning for her to go ahead. Elliot took Penny to meet with his friends; that night, Penny also met David, the man who later that night would rape her.

Elliot never knew until weeks later what had happened, but when he found out he was in a rage, Penny had never seen him like that. For Penny, it was like a nightmare, seeing a person in the state of mind you never even imagined. She thought the abusive Elliot had returned and blamed herself for it. Penny did not know Elliot could be this way; He looked just like their dad when he threw a fit. Elliot spent days trying to find David; he asked all his friends from the bar and the guys who supplied him drugs. Elliot tried his best to get his hands on David, and when Elliot finally found David, he beat him so violently that he went into a coma. The injuries he inflicted upon David were so bad that he could have died the police had not turned up in time.

Elliot stayed some nights in jail. However, his notorious friends found a way around the legal system to get him bailed. The night when Elliot was finally free, he went partying with his friends and got wasted; the need for more drink rose in him, and he felt there were ants under his skin. The walls were getting closer and closer until he couldn't take it anymore. He was hurt, but he kept going until he found the escape route. He made his way out to the car but never made it there; someone grabbed him and bundled him into the back of a van. He could feel his stomach burst into a fire as the rage rose; the police were there so quick. Tied up there, Elliot tried to fight them but struggled and failed. Then the police did something odd; he remembered being hit on the back of the head – maybe by the police, he couldn't see who it was.

#

Elliot woke up in a metal room with no furniture, just silver steel walls, floor, and roof. He rustled when he moved.

Someone had taken his clothes and dressed him in a white paper boiler suit. He had no clue how long he had been in here. Laying in the same position, he caught a whiff of something. He tried to look down, but the way he was tied made any movements difficult; however, Elliot soon realised he had shit himself.

He did not understand what was going on; it was like something straight out of a 'saw' movie; he desperately needed a drink. The scene was so scary and horrific that he was feeling goose-bumps. His insides were twisting with dread but not at the room; it was withdrawal. The stomach cramps would come soon, and he also felt the retching. He could feel his organs trembling along with his hands and arms. That's when he saw the spiders coming; they were bleeding through the walls. He knew from experience that they weren't real, but the fear he felt looking at them was genuine. What he was going through at that time had a severe impact on his mind, and despite it not being real, all he could do was hold on while the room spun.

Once before, something similar happened to him. When Elliot had decided he would not be like his dad and would give up on drinking. He refused to go partying and buy a drink with his friends, and everything went smooth at first. But then the spiders came; again, they were bleeding through everywhere, and he lost his nerve. Elliot had downed half a bottle of vodka right there at the counter of the shop. He didn't even notice the family staring at him or the shopkeeper shouting at him to get out. He just wanted the spiders to go away.

Chapter 8:
Angel

Angel now exists between the worlds, worlds that have become a vacuum of nothingness, no one's meant to live here.

"I don't know how to stay here. I haven't heard another voice since coming here; I don't remember what my creators sound like anymore. It feels like it has been centuries, They wanted me to end the war, and I served my purpose, but now I'm forgotten! As if that was the only reason for my existence. My charge is important to keep the dark ones at bay, but sometimes I feel almost as much a prisoner as a guard," Angel talked to his old friend, Pandora. Frightened that the Seraph would hear him, he stopped talking aloud.

However, Angel was always free to leave only at the expense of his prisoners escaping, and he couldn't bring himself to do so. He couldn't defy his loyalties to the Seraph. Suddenly, his energy fluctuated somewhat defiantly. It wasn't for the first time; it would come and go. He was groaning in pain, pulling his energy back together and in harmony, but something inside him was trying to break free. He felt anger, defiance, and rage intensifying, but he controlled himself to bring his energy back to its centre. It caught the attention of his captors, he figured.

Soon, Angel realised after trapping the Shaitan that they watched all his movements; and they studied him closely. They looked for weaknesses and opportunities, but they wouldn't find any, Angel assured himself.

The Seraph seemed happy with the arrangements, and Angel just wanted to please his creators. He took pride in the fact that his creators were satisfied with what he was doing. Angel watched over Pandora and noticed the new species that had appeared. However, he didn't know how many of them were there. He found it hard to keep track and to get an idea of their numbers. Looking at the new species reminded him of moles disappearing through holes, living in a network of tunnels, the only place on the planet that Angel couldn't see. He couldn't understand why. He had one foot in Pandora and one in the dark dimension with Shaitan. Angel experienced time, but he was also aware of the concept of eternity

Angel watched the humans doing well, they were intelligent and organised, and they lived according to a hierarchy. They amused him more than any other creature. To him, humans seemed peculiar, like tiny but intelligent ants. He's not sure how much time has passed down there. It was beginning to feel like a curse being aware of the time that had passed. The Seraph hadn't come to him since the humans had arrived; they seem to have something shiny and new to watch over.

Angel felt resentful; it didn't sit well with him that the Seraph was busy looking over something else. He tried many times to let the feeling of envy go, but he failed each time. Consumed by his jealousy, Angel heard the whispers in his ear say, "You're a fool; that's what they are saying about you, hidden away in their safe dimension." Shaitan smelt his resentment instantly, like a shark smelling blood, stirring up a frenzy. Of course, their plan worked, and Angel seemed to be influenced by the whispers.

Shaitan continued to whisper. Angel ignored the whispers initially. He pretended like he had no interest in what they had to say. However, as time passed, Angel's energy became more unstable. "You are the only prisoner here, Angel, tricked into this by his own creators."

Angel ignored but could feel his energy swirling in the opposite direction, but he tried to ignore that too. But, he kept hearing the whispers say, "The Seraph! Humph! They mock us! Judge us! Why do we serve them?"

Angel was constantly ignoring each word as best he could, always the loyal servant of the Seraph, no matter how his creators had ignored him. However, the last sentence struck him hard. He thought about the whispering voice and what it had said. "Why do we serve them?" It said, "We." Angel's energy was racing, but his thoughts were suddenly clear. He looked towards the Shaitan and saw they weren't anywhere near him.

Who was speaking to him? Angel couldn't figure it out at first, and then he turned to face his own energy. What he saw next shocked him to his core; he realised it was him who was speaking. It was his own energy that was whispering to him. It was the part of him that he had been resisting for a long time, trying to fight it away, but now it had become something else. Now, it speaks to him. It grew so bigger in power that it could get in his head and say things that he had been trying to avoid. It doesn't whisper but talks in his own voice.

"Now that we understand each other, what do we do next?" another whisper was heard.

#

Ifra had noticed something wasn't right. The barrier was fluctuating, and she was concerned about Angel. Something wasn't right; she could feel it. Closing her eyes, she tried to communicate to Angel, and she instantly realised the madness in Angel's head. She knew that he had forgotten what he was doing and what his purpose was. After all this time, the Seraph has uncovered more truths about the sparks and more ways to use them. Recalling the previous council of the 6, they discussed Angel.

"Angel wasn't designed to be a permanent barrier like he has become; nothing sentient could withstand what he is going through and have their sanity intact!" Ifra announced. There had been a unanimous agreement.

Radiya explained to the council what he had learned from the spark of light, "We now have the knowledge to create a barrier of energy similar to Angels, but I think something like this should be created without thought. We can release Angel from the void between dimensions and still keep the Shaitan."

Washma pushed her way in. "Wait, what do we do with Angel? We can't release him onto Pandora; the creature down there is somehow linked to his creation. We don't know what will happen if they came into contact with each other!"

Salameh stayed quiet but listened to what everyone was saying, and Tawil asked for calm consideration. Ifra had made up her mind; if the council didn't reach an agreement, she would make the decision without the consent of the council.

Every time Pandora had rotated around the sun, she had thought about Angel at least once. Tawil and the rest of the council sensed this from her energy. Realising what Ifra's intentions were, Washma instantly went into action,

"I demand Ifra be removed from this council," Washma announced.

There was instant pain across the council as they all felt what Ifra did, the pain of betrayal. Salameh spoke for the first time, "I think we need to stand behind our leader and support her in this, I hear your caution, Washma, and I feel your concern, but we need to the right this wrong, together."

The council became silent, and the discussion was over; it was clear by the end of the meeting that Washma's motion had no support. And now that the meeting was over, the next task was to work on freeing Angel. The plan was to give him life as one of them, to give him the position as a Seraph, but keep him from setting foot on Pandora because he must never know about the creature lurking in the shadows.

#

The Seraph came to Angel and explained their plan, that they were skilled enough to create an additional barrier that would release him from his duties. For the first time in aeons, Angel will have a choice to make and decide his own fate. Angel couldn't believe he had been remembered and was finally being rescued.

Apparently, Angel seemed beyond happy, but his alter-ego was still very vocal and didn't trust the motives of the Seraph and their sudden willingness to rescue him. In his head, Angel could still hear the whispers say, "You're just being moved around, you'll be a slave somewhere else, and your true allies are the Shaitan."

He ignored the voice and obliged loyally, accepting his reward for his loyal service. "Fool!" again, the voice disrupted his thoughts. It was like an anchor holding him in place. "I won't let you destroy us," the angry part of him was holding onto the void, and Angel's expressions were now different. The Seraph was starting to seem concerned.

#

"Ifra! Somethings wrong, this was supposed to be seamless, but he's resisting coming back to us. He's arguing… he's arguing with himself. He's lost his mind!" Salameh exclaimed.

The Seraph had to act fast because the Shaitan were taking advantage of Angel's vulnerability. Through Angel, they were trying to build an escape. Darkness was spilling onto Pandora, and they were trying to force a wedge in the void, trying to create a doorway to their freedom.

Now that the Seraph had entered the void, they had no choice left but to take Angel back with them. The Shaitan retreated back in shock of the sudden brazen move. The Seraph took hold of Angel and forced him back to their own dimension.

"Washma, report!" Ifra wasn't in the mood for pleasantries. And in an instant, Washma reported, "Angel is unconscious; he's been driven insane with dual personalities. This caused conflict during the transition. Although the new barrier is in place, the Shaitan managed to create enough of a wedge in the barrier to have a greater influence than before, how much, I can't say."

Ifra thought for a moment and then said, "It's settled then, we need to have someone on Pandora, and we need someone to fix this!"

Their plans for Angel changed, and his freedom to choose his own purpose of life was taken away again. If the darkness rises on Pandora, they need a prophet – someone with enough strength to lead the humans. The decision was made while Angel was still unconscious, and before he could object, they cleared his mind of all the doubts.

The Seraph took away his memories of himself, hoping it would protect him from his own negative thoughts.

They gave him a body, then used the spark's energy to transform him into their Prophet. The Seraph thought everything went smooth. However, they later realised that something had gone wrong.

Angel's madness and the darkness that had entered his heart had an unexpected result. They subdued the angel successfully, but not once did they thought about the other personality that took birth in him.

"I will protect us even if he won't!" He reached out and touched the spark of light and vanished. He then broke through the new barrier and touched the dark spark, then vanished with that too. None of the Eternals understood what happened or what gave Angel the power to do that. It was a long time before any Eternal realised where Angel was. While Ifra and Tawil tried to work out the problem, Washma watched on, learned, and waited for the opportunity that would lead to Ifra's downfall.

Later on, it was found that Angel was on Pandora, wandering the deserts. The Shaitan were furious about it but couldn't get past the barrier and couldn't understand how Angel took their spark. He now possessed the power of both sparks but was now wandering the desert, lost in his own thoughts.

It made little sense at that time, and the Eternals didn't stop him. Actually, they couldn't. In possession of both sparks, he was now more powerful than any of them. On the other hand, the Shaitan's work carried

on, Eve was an impossible task, but with what they had learned, they made excellent progress with Adam.

Chapter 9: Uncle Shug

Shug was Penny's maternal uncle; he played rough and would easily throw the two of them in the air like they were twigs. Shug would visit Penny and Elliot every day; he tried his best to see both the kids daily and to spend time playing with them.

Whenever Shug visited, things would always feel a little awkward. Penny would feel like the air was a little heavier in the room; the tension between her dad, James, and Shug was too apparent to ignore. And this discomfort persisted only because of an old tale, a bond between Penny's mum, Isobel, and Shug. A bond that was barely noticeable unless you observed a bit closer, only to find stolen glances and hidden smiles. Something there, but always left unsaid. They had this way of conversing, as if in code, that no one else could understand. as if a code no other could understand.

When Pennie's mum got a mysterious package, something shifted in her that caused her to leave everything behind and walk out on their family. He travelled the world to find her but failed and refused to come home. They came from an ancient line of travellers who held the belief that it was a great dishonour in abandoning your family, especially when there is so much to teach the coming generation about their responsibilities to the world and creation.

#

Shug had been travelling all these years searching for Isobel. He remembers their mother telling them stories and the history of their family; that fate bound them, two halves of the same power. They were twins. His job was to protect Isobel, and Isobel's was to care for the spark, the channel of energy that gave life to the universe. Shug glanced back at Penny and decided that he needed to pull over and deal with the chunk of metal sticking out of her side. He only hopes that she understands what he needs to tell her. Her dad wouldn't let him return, having refused Shug to explain Penny's heritage to her and the truth of who and what she is. She doesn't understand the danger she's in or the power that she has. With Elliot dead, who would be her protector, Shug needed to extract her, even if it was against the Elders' wishes.

#

Penny woke a few times through the makeshift stitching. Shug didn't do a pretty job, but it was enough to hold the bleeding at bay until he got her back to the cottage. He looks at her face trying to catches her eyes. She was fighting the drowsiness that threatened to overtake. Her body could only suffer so much until it reached its breaking point, and Penny succumbed to darkness. He bundles her back in the car, spooked by how much she looks like her mum, but that was always the way with the light bearers. They had the same hair, same eyes, and the same destiny.

#

Shug kept tabs on his family, even from far away. He knew about Penny's dad and Elliot following the same path. He was ashamed of staying away for so long, but the longer he stayed away, the harder it was to go back. Isobel was brave and stubborn. Growing up, they would explore the countryside, and they loved the old abandoned houses in the fields. Isobel always found the best treasure, old coins, or jewellery. She loved animals, and they loved her. Sometimes birds would even come and sit next to her on the grass.

When their mum told them stories about Pandora, they loved it, their imaginations going haywire; stories of the herds of animals across the green hills, the butterflies, and the crisp, clear waters of the rivers. It sounded magnificent but also diabolic. Then, the tone of the stories changed; their mum's stories felt more like history lessons and facts, not fiction. Entire species being wiped out as collateral damage as powerful beings had their wars. Then the stories became more specific, about Adam and Eve, their children. Although Adam and Eve were always the ones spoken about, they weren't the only humans; they had popped up all over the planet. The Eternals weren't aware of them to start with. The children that escaped Adam got to safety, and The Tribe came across them and took them in. They stayed hidden in the caves; Pandora had protected its children. A community was developed in the caves. In fact, there were caves all over the planet with developing communities.

#

In the start, Pandora was peaceful, then one day, something happened, a black cloud came from a hill-like volcano, it spread over everything they could see and then just as quick, the source flashed white and stopped. The darkness fell over everything like black snow; that's when the nightmares started. It was the first time the communities experienced crime. The animals had changed; the carnivores were hunting the humans and humans them for fun. Something had changed in the human heart, and it had revealed darkness. People became greedy, jealous, and they grew to hate. The communities fought with each other for the first time. This grew over the centuries into wars. In fact, mankind has never stopped fighting since.

There was one community that called the fishing tribes who refused to work with the others. They became more organized, more ruthless and determined, under an unexpected leader. They spent a lot more time outside, which seemed to be the reason for their extended exposure to the darkness outside. Inside the caves, things were more like the old times. Something about the caves gave them a sense of peace in their hearts, a shelter from the darkness. Modern-day man instinctively tried to replicate it with salt crystals and such. The fishing tribe's numbers grew; they didn't just fight over land and resources; they invaded other communities and enslaved their people, wanting dominion. They became known as The Clan, their hearts desired power, and their leader had the power of knowledge. No one ever saw him, as he stayed hidden, always pulling strings. The cleaning brainwashed the children and turned them into foot soldiers.

They soon became the superpower of ancient times, before the planet, before the tribes rose against them with their own powerful leader, Olivia. The war raged, but as often is the case, nature ended the war. The Clan should have won, but because of natural disasters, the planet itself fought back. There is a saying, 'history is written by the victors,' but with this war between men, the history was erased. The history of the First World War, the one that everyone forgot about. This was the severest punishment of the time; being erased from history, to have never existed, is the greatest shame.

The day she revealed the stories were real, that they weren't just stories, but history and told about their destinies. They both looked at each other and laughed. They refused to believe what they were being told. "You guys are ready for the truth, and I had the same look as you did when my mother told me," she led them downstairs into the basement. They had never been allowed down there, but today was different. There was an altar with a white book. It was beautiful and almost glowed. Their mother instructed them to put their hands on the book and close their eyes. They both looked at each other with smirks, thinking they were popes. They played along and put their hands on the book. As soon as they closed their eyes, they felt a warm burst of energy wash through them. They opened their eyes and found themselves in a white room. The room had nothing other than three chairs. They sat down, confused; what was happening? Have they been drugged? This can't be real. Then a woman in a white dress walked over to them, "Welcome, my name is Eve." From that moment on, nothing was the same.

#

When his sister left, he went after her, then went to look for The Tribe; Isobel's light never activated, and she never became a light bearer. He had never heard of that happening before and wanted answers. Their mum hadn't told them where to find The Tribe, and he had the feeling they didn't have signposts. It was several years before he found a rumour which panned out. They led him to a network of tunnels in Wales. He had walked through them, exploring for days. There was nothing apart from the odd symbol printed. These caves had been mine shafts and explored for well over a century, probably longer. Nothing was there. Then, one day, he sat in the caves with a bottle of whiskey, fed up with his efforts, ready to give up. He was chasing ghosts instead of facing his grief and the shame of not protecting his niece and nephew from their dad, but he was such a good man before Isobel died, Shug thought.

He heard voices in the tunnels and investigated, probably just kids. He walked towards where the noise had come from, but there was nothing there. He took another swig from the bottle, and as his gaze lowered, he felt a bang on the back of his head and stars. The next thing he was waking up with Trevor, hanging over him unapologetically, and the person tending to Shug's wound was giving Trevor a grilling that would have scared any grown man. After he explained where he came from and who he was, they let him stay, but he was an outsider and wasn't trusted with their secrets. Sometimes he would get glimpses of technology that he had never seen before and hear whispers of being somewhere other than Earth, but none of it made sense. He got frustrated; he wanted to speak to the Elders, but they wouldn't see him yet. He felt he was being watched the whole time to see what he did.

Finally, he went exploring, sneaked past some locals. There weren't any guards; there seemed to be a high level of trust with each other. It wasn't long before they noticed he had lost his stalkers. They seemed to track him at an impressive speed; he ran through the marketplace and into the first door he saw. Closed the door, turned round to see a crystal stand with a book. He blinked, not believing it; it was the book from all those years ago in Nana's basement when Eve spoke to them both. Just as Shug placed his hands on the book, two men burst into the room. Shug was thrown backwards against the wall due to the tremendous burst of energy. The men went to pick him up when an old man came in, wearing all white. He raised a hand, and everything stopped. "I'm Elder John, come with me; it's time we speak. I knew your mother."

Chapter 10:
Family History

Shug pulled the car up outside a cottage. They had driven for around five hours and were in the Highlands, somewhere outside of Dingwall. Penny had woken up around an hour ago, but words wouldn't form in her mouth. She couldn't find the source or the cause. Her Uncle could barely look at her. He felt the pain of losing his sister at every glance. She looked so much like her mum. They stopped just outside of Inverness, at a truck stop. Penny was able to get a change of clothes and a shower. Shug had disposed of her old clothes by the time she was finished. He never asked about the blood. She assumed he knew, and she was in no mood to explain to him, not even this. She owed him absolutely nothing, after all!

#

They got out of the car. The cottage was at least a century old, with stone walls sprawling across a relatively small space. There was also something t looked like an outside toilet. Penny cringed at the thought. Then she noticed something out of place. The roof had solar panels.

The absurdity of it boggled Penny's mind. You wouldn't think there was enough Sun in Scotland, but the owners thought it was a good idea.

"Is this the place where you've been hiding for 20 years?" A wave of disgust washed over Penny's face.

Shug winced at her tone. He doesn't know how to answer, "Penny, I can't make up for not being th…"

She cut him off, "You left us alone; with HIM!" It filled the air with painful silence. Shug could feel the anger emanating from her and something else, something familiar.

"We need to talk, and we both need to stay calm." Shug tried to negotiate. But alas, that only enraged an already upset Penny, "I have nothing to say to YOU!" she snarled. The ground rumbled, and one of the solar panels cracked and fell off the roof. "Penny, please, you don't understand. They'll see you if you don't calm down, they'll see you, and they'll know who you are!"

Penny felt the infectious coldness of the book again, "What did you say?" Penny's mind raced back to the whispers, telling her that they see her, hear her, and know her.

Shug looked at her with confusion etched on his face but repeated nonetheless, "They'll see you and know who you are if you don't calm down. There is so much to explain and not enough time."

Penny dropped to her knees. She felt like someone just knocked the wind out of her. Shug picked her up and said, "Hell of a hangover, isn't it? You'll get used to it!" He took her inside and laid Penny down on the couch. Inside was nice wooden floors with warm rugs, a solid wood dining table, and rows of wooden chairs along with a red cushioned sofa. There was an old rocking chair in the corner. It looked almost as old and dingy as the cottage. Shug put wood into the fireplace with paper, started the fire, and it soon warmed up. "It's as safe as it can get here. They made the walls from cave rock."

Penny looked at him with confused dismay. "I guess there's a lot to talk about. Did you do it?" Penny felt a fire being lit inside her stomach. Her anger demanded a victim on which to unleash itself, but Shug looked away at the stare she gave him. "Well, if you didn't, then we don't know who it was. He wasn't a target. It would create unwanted attention for The Clan. It doesn't make sense." Trevor was almost speaking to himself at that point. He must have been because Penny had no idea who or what he was talking about. There were four situations that became a forceful reality to her. Her dad was dead. The police think she did it. Three police officers were murdered in front of her. And she was being blamed for all of it! "Do you remember mother's stories?" Shug asked her with a light in his eyes. He must mean Nana's tales she used to tell. Penny nodded, and Shug continued, "Well, they're true!"

Penny rolled over the couch. She suddenly realised he rescued her from her kidnappers, but also the fact that he was a complete whack job. She was trying to stay calm, but that didn't stop her from looking around for a fire poker or something to use as a weapon. She still couldn't process everything around her. Every sense had been pushed to its minimum.

Every muscle was drained with the miseries of life. Why does she not feel anything? She should be terrified, she should be a mess, but she felt detached from it all. She shouldn't be surprised. This was the spiral where she was destined to go. When she was raped, when she was beaten by Gary, or everything else that happened, the spiral was her only destination – her only safe haven. Her safe detached space where emotion doesn't exist. She is protected from the world inside her own little bubble dimension, able to view and interact with the world but not a part of it.

#

The car keys were in his pocket. She looked at him as she started to plan the next set of actions she could undertake. She could hit him over the head, take the car keys from his pocket, and drive to safety. After the shock and anger of seeing him again wore off, Penny started realising her predicament. She had been kidnapped, then stumbled into a car crash, and if all of that wasn't enough, she was then kidnapped from the kidnappers by her uncle! Her eyes rolled in her head again, her head felt heavy, and darkness was closing in. Looking down, she realised things were even worse. She was bleeding through her stitches. Her top had been soaked in blood. She tried to say something, but it only came out a murmur into the darkness as she drifted into oblivion once she passed out.

Penny woke up slowly to a strange old woman tending to her wound. She groggily lifted her hand to get a good look at her. The woman declared that she had cauterised the wound and handed her two tablets, explaining to Penny that these were antibiotics to stop the infection from spreading inside her. Penny pretended to take them, but instead, she stashed them under her tongue until no one was watching. Once everyone was out of sight, she started to slip them into her pocket. Just as she looked down, Penny gasped loudly. That's when she realised that someone had cut her top off. She moved her head from side to side in disbelief. Her head goes straight back to the night at the Abbey.

Everything was perfect. She was excited about being with her brother and his friends. One boy kept glancing at her from time to time. Once he gathered courage, he approached Penny and paid her compliments. She was told how beautiful her hair and eyes were.

Penny was ecstatic. It had been so long since someone had wanted to know about her and spoke to her rather than about her. He had suggested they go for a walk. And that's when he did it. When they were far enough away, he took her hand and started kissing her. She loved it. He made her feel a warmth in her chest, butterflies in her stomach, and a heat between her legs. He pulled her gently to the ground, and she nervously laid down. Her nerves grew when he put his hands on her breasts. "You are so pretty. You like this?" she felt his hot breath as he whispered into her ear. She could feel his bulge through his jeans. At that point, her amusement rather turned to an instant surge of unhappiness. "Whoa, can we slow down a bit," she replied huskily, feeling desire waning from her body. He acted as though he never heard her, "Mmhmm," he moaned loudly.

"I don't want this!" she said as she removed his curls from her forehead. He was on top of her now, breathing heavily, kissing and licking her neck and face.

"Please stop." A whisper escaped her lips. Her fear had frozen her. He still had said nothing other than the occasional moans that his body produced. To her, it felt like she was just an object, and he had forgotten that she was a person. He tore away her top, wanting to get easy access to her breasts. He removed it off, leaving her in just her bra. Penny couldn't move. She was frozen. She just wasn't there anymore. She was in her safe bubble dimension. Then suddenly, it was all over, after what felt like an eternity. It was that simple for him. He got up and walked back over to his friends. But Penny took her time. She slowly got up, sobbing and holding herself, trying to console herself. She tried to stand but felt a sudden rush of pain between her legs. Blood started to seep down her leg. It didn't matter how much she wiped herself; with every step she took, she felt the pain, and she felt him; inside her. She didn't just feel dirty; she felt poisoned. She was toxic now. He had killed her. That's how she felt. He killed the child in her, took her innocence. Once she reached home, Penny walked past her unconscious dad and found him stinking of whiskey. Penny then climbed into the shower, sat down with the water running and cried, hugging her legs. She didn't know if the water could wash the impurity away from her. But she wished with all her heart that it could.

#

Back in the cottage, she thrashed, trying to punch anyone that came close to her. Somewhere she heard glass smashing and solar panels falling from the roof. Then a sharp scratch in the side of her neck stung her, and the darkness again overpowered.

Shug groaned in frustration, "Trevor, did we really need to do that? She just needed a few minutes to get her head together." Trevor shrugged his shoulders and just released a grunt before walking out of the cottage. Trevor was a burly man. Not fat, just a lot of muscle. He had red hair and a temperament to suit the stature. Everyone left him to himself. He was in charge of security and making sure that their home stayed hidden. He was good at his job, so people tolerated his attitude.

#

Trevor wasn't always this way. He used to be one of the most progressive members of the community; he wanted to explore the world and encouraged his wife and daughter to do the same. Over the years, he made his home his only sanctuary. Trevor only agreed to this trip to protect the elder.

#

He was one of the brightest minds, making leaps and bounds in botanical science, using their sacred crystals to fertilise the ground. This had a dramatic effect on the growth rate, the nutritional value increased tenfold, and the crops never failed. He was creative; he discovered how to complete a complex protein structure within the plant, which increased photosynthesis and reduced how much hydration the plant needed. This allowed them to grow crops inside the shade and security of the caves for the first time. On the outside, he discovered that it improved crop yields and allowed the plants to grow in the inhospitable ground. He theorised that if they applied this advance to the wider world, world hunger would be dealt with a massive blow. For the first time, they could grow any crop on any ground. All he needed to do was to train the outsiders, but the council of elders held him back.

#

The council was made up of one of the oldest and the wisest of the tribes, and they were their ruling group. They refused to share technology with the outsiders. All they do would turn advances into weapons. The tribe had grown to look at the world with disdain; they saw how dark the human soul had the potential to transform into when they watched Britain create their empire on the back of slaves, having superior technology. The Clan's influence in the world was evident, and The Operator's reach was ever-expanding.

The elder in the corner just shook her head and sighed, "Katy, she met you at the school, so it might take better to a familiar face. Can you gently take her through to the bedroom and make her comfortable? We can continue in the morning. We all need some sleep here." Katy Digby walked over and lifted Penny into her arms. She carried her through to the bedroom. Katy felt awkward in doing the act, but she had to remove the rest of Penny's clothes before the blood stank her entire existence and that of her surroundings. She dressed her in the white of the tribe elders as instructed. She wasn't sure how this would go down back home. The wearing of colours showed rank after all. White was for the leaders, which were traditionally their elders. When Elder Claire brought this over for Penny to wear, Katy didn't know what to say. She couldn't think straight or form any response. Her heart was palpitating, leaving her slightly breathless. She gave Penny a last glance as she lay on the bed and walked back out of the room. After closing the door, Katy leaned against it to catch her breath.

'God, she's beautiful,' Katy thinks to herself. She forgot from their brief first encounter the enrapturing beauty that always surrounded her. How long her hair was. How big and deep her eyes were, like pearls of wisdom lay deep within, too timid to come out.

#

Back in the living room, Shug was sitting in front of the fireplace warming his hands. The night was drawing in, and he was exhausted. The elder joined him and asked, "Hugh, what are you going to do if she rejects us? Will you return to Pandora or try to rebuild what you've lost with her?"

Shug realised there was no wrong answer, just a very complicated decision to make. They have pinned all their hopes on Penny. She is the Light Bearer. She's already been showing her power, even if she doesn't know she's doing it. The elder sat in deep contemplation among each other. They had to make choices, and the strongest choice presented itself as Penny since she was the most vigorous Light Bearer the elder has felt in generations, and without a guardian, that's almost as unusual as when her uncle showed up with a bearer.

#

It was a rule of the world. When a Light Bearer arrives, so does her guardian. The bearer is always the daughter, and the guardian is always the boy. It's been that way since Adam and Eve when Eve's protector and guardian turned on her. The original sin bonded the couple's offspring in more than kinship. They don't understand how it works or why, but the Light Bearer can read from the book. Sometimes there are clues given, and a little more is known, but there is still so much shrouded with mystery. Each light bearer is shown something different by the book, shown their own lessons. No one light bearer is given all knowledge. That power was bestowed on the Eternals, and they became corrupted.

#

Trevor came back in, wheeling a device the size of a table. He placed it in the room and flicked a switch. Sitting on the couch alone was the elder, deep in muddled thoughts.

He hesitated to interrupt her train of thoughts, yet his curiosity got the better of him. "What is it?" Trevor asked, inching closer to her.

Claire looked over the prophecy. "I was thinking about the prophecy. What if she is the last?" She said without looking up at him. Trevor sat on the floor with the wall behind his back; he exhaled loudly, "Well then, we had better get ready."

#

The mini generator created a field that protected them from what potentially came into the dark. They don't know exactly how they came to be or why they look the way they do, but they called them Phantoms because they weren't alive and they weren't dead. Neither were they microscopic, or else they would be called viruses. Instead, they were creatures or things of the dark. One can perceive them, how they would perceive the darkness growing many fingers. The phantoms grabbed people from the shadows and pulled them into the darkness. They're never seen again, and no one knows what happens to them. Just an endless scream in the void and then nothing. As if they assimilated into nothingness. The chattering started, like hundreds of joke false teeth. Katy looked all around her; they had surrounded the cottage. They shouldn't have even known they were there, but they always knew somehow. The Phantoms had circled the cottage. Katy looked to the elder for reassurance; the elder just smiled and went to sleep. She trusted the generated field. They had never tested the field generators against so many phantoms,xattacking at once. The fingers of the darkness were closing in, and Katy could feel it breathing down her neck. The whispering started, and she went through to Penny to sit by her bed and make sure she was safe. Her daughter Kim was sleeping on the floor next to her. It was Kim's bedroom, and she was letting the guests have the mattress.

Chapter 11:
The Tribe

Penny woke up in bed with a start. She was not sure how much time had passed but felt more rested than she had felt in a long time. The room was a child's room; pink walls with cuddly toys at the bed's foot, the covers showed a man dressed as a clown. It depicted the aura of a loving household.

Penny would have sat there watching the room until the sound of a soft voice came from the doorway. "That's Mr. Tumble. I told mum, you can sleep in my bed. It's the comfiest in the house," a girl of about 5 or 6 spoke, standing there, wearing a flowery dress, hair in pigtails.

"Well, thank you, and what's your name?" Penny swooned in relief, speaking to a child again. The girl turned around and left without saying a word. *That was weird.* Confused, Penny swung her legs around, stood up, stumbled for a moment but caught her balance.

\#

The floor was freezing under her feet. Hardwood floors and the highlands didn't mix. It chilled her to the bone.

Suddenly, she realised she was starving. Seeing the child made her feel mixed emotions. Penny paced hungrily around the room with relentless steps. She loved children dearly but was horrified she was witnessing this. Was she a prisoner like her? She felt her blood boil at this. She put a dressing gown around herself and straightened out her dress. Someone had left it on the back of the door. She then made her way down the corridor towards the voices. The voices of the men greeted her ears. They seemed to talk excitedly about the light bearer returning. She had heard of that term before but didn't exactly know what it was. She slowly walked into the room, not sure what to expect. She wasn't sure if the freedom that was afforded to her was transient or permanent. She felt odd to be allowed to walk around freely like this.

#

Shug sat at the table with four others. They were all jabbering, making plans to move forward.

"She's not ready. She doesn't even know who she is." The voices resounded in unison. No one seemed to notice her walk in and carried on their heated debate. The small angry-looking man carried on with his point, "She doesn't even know what she is." A small voice from the corner of the room cleared their throat. Penny looked and saw the little girl standing there, smirking at the group. Penny looked back at the table and found everyone staring at her.

The atmosphere was tense; they were waiting to see what she would do, and she was waiting for what they had to say. Both had expectations from each other that the other knew not how to fulfil. Finally, Shug broke the silence, "Penny, you must be starving, come, sit down." Penny walked over to the table, not saying a word. She just glared at everyone.

"My God, that's the exact same look your mother gave me when I came home after going walkabout for days."

A tall, slender woman said, "I remember when I was five, and I kicked Terry Evan's between the legs. She gave me that exact same look."

Penny was angry. *How dare they make fun of her?* But then suddenly it hit her. "You're Officer Digby, and you knew my mother?" She asked in a high-pitched voice brimming with excitement.

An elderly woman, rocking back a forth in the chair in the corner, spoke up, "My dear, we all knew her. She was one of us, as was your Nana."

"Then, why are you keeping me, prisoner? You're a police officer. They are not supposed to do that. They are supposed to protect their people," she pointed at Officer Digby.

Shug raised his hands, "You're free to go. All we ask is that you hear us out first, and this is Kate."

There was a long silence as they all stared at each other, unsure what Penny would do next.

"So, my mother has been with you this whole time?" She asked with a hint of annoyance.

Kate stood up and suggested they get some air, "You'll find some clothes in the top drawer of the room you woke up in. Meet me outside when you're ready." Kate left and headed outside; the little girl followed. She gave Penny a look as if she wanted to say something but didn't.

Penny found the clothes, a simple grey top and trousers. She quickly got dressed, hoping she would feel less vulnerable wearing something other than a dressing gown and underwear – she felt too naked in that. She walked out the room, down the hall, and paused as she watched everyone around the table. She caught the eye of the older lady on the rocking chair, who simply smiled at her like she already knew how everything would go. She stared at her with deep curiosity. Her eyes were brimming with wisdom and secrets.

#

The sun shone brilliantly in the cloudless sky. Penny made her way through the door leading to the front of the cottage. As she stepped outside, she saw a couple of men cleaning up broken solar panels. It wasn't a dream, there was some kind of earthquake, and she remembered the rumbling somewhere in the background, during the panic of the previous night. Kate was at the bottom of the garden talking to the little girl, picking some flowers. A soft breeze infused with the scent of wildflowers filled Penny's nostrils as she trekked the path. It was almost ideal with the highlands all around. Heather carpeted much of the ground, mostly a purple colour. There was a particularly strong smell of Lily's in the air, but Penny couldn't see any? There was a large flat mountain face behind the cottage; It was the most stunning part of the scenery. There was a lake at the bottom and a small waterfall running into it. There were burns running away from the lake and disappearing into the hills. There were a few scattered clouds visible here and there, but they didn't obscure her view of the mountain behind. Penny filled her lungs with the sweet fresh air.

As she approached Kate, the little girl stood up and smiled warmly at Penny.

"Kim," she said in a sweet voice.

Penny looked at her with confusion etched on her face.

"My name, you asked before. It's Kim," she completed. She marched forward, and very formally, offered Penny her hand. Penny almost burst out laughing at the seriousness of her face at that moment but took her hand nonetheless.

"Okay, Kim, it's time to go back in with your flowers," Kate demanded as she looked at the mingling duo.

Kim turned to look at her mother before she nodded. Holding the flowers, she gave Kate a kiss on the cheek. She turned, and to Penny's surprise, she asked her to bend down. Complying with her demands, Penny crouched and came close to Kim, after which she gave her a kiss too before running back to the cottage.

"So, you met my daughter? Sorry if she woke you up. I told her to leave you be," Kate said with a contrite tone.

Penny was so confused. She was out here in the middle of nowhere, and being held captive or not, but definitely without her consent. Her uncle was here but not her mother, and that was before even thinking about the previous couple of days. She had numerous questions, the list of which was too long to enumerate, but she didn't know where to start.

"Why don't we walk?" Kate beckons Penny to follow her as if reading her mind. "We should talk about the book, Mark, and who we are, but we shall start with the subject of your mother first."

#

"Isobel did come back to us for a short time, but she seemed unsure of herself. She had awoken much as you have."

She shook her head at Penny's confused look.

"We'll get to that. She kept telling us something was wrong. She didn't feel the way she was told she would. Then, one morning she was gone, no explanation, and there had been no trace of her ever since."

#

They walked along a dirt path that followed one of the lakes. Penny acted like she wasn't interested in this new bit of information. Her mind instructed her to know first about her current situation. "I think you better tell me who you are, where I am, and why you have taken me," Penny tried to sound insistent.

"Well, a simple answer to why we took you is to stop 'The Clan' from killing you," she said, with surprising ease that made Penny feel as though it isn't the first time Kate's done this. It came so naturally to her. Kate continued, "We are the tribe. We are your people. Your Dad never told you about us?"

Penny simply shook her head. She wasn't ready to start talking back.

She needed to know more before she could form an opinion.

"We are an ancient order, descendants from the first tribes of man, dating back to Pandora."

Penny's first thought stumbled over the possibility of her being taken by a cult. Her legs wanted to run, but she knew she had to take in all the information first.

"We took you because The Clan had kidnapped you, and we had to make sure they wouldn't get your light."

Instantly, Kate looked regretful at the last sentence, like she had said too much too soon. Penny's knitted eyebrows further confirmed her suspicions. They had reached the waterfall, and Kate sat down on a bolder. Penny continued to stand but now had her arms crossed. For some reason, Penny couldn't hold Katie's gaze. But she waited for her to say more.

"This is one of our most sacred sights. In ancient times, we used the tunnel networks to travel, and this is the site of one of the caves, which used to be an entrance."

"We used some of the caves rock to build that cottage. It keeps them from seeing us."

Penny realized everyone was crazy, and the cottage was their foil hat.

Penny didn't like this. She was starting to worry about Kim. This poor child was caught up in something her mind wasn't mature enough to know the consequences of.

"I took Mark's case because it was much like what we have seen through history and within touching distance of you," Kate sat down in the cool grass, then motioned Penny to join her.

She lingered there for a minute, but Penny finally sat down. The grief and pain were still raw at what had happened. She still couldn't understand how or why Mark did it.

Slowly but surely, Penny started to think about the whispers but chose not to say anything. Maybe she was going as crazy as these people. She began to wonder if the keys would still be in her uncle's pockets and whether she should try to grab Kim. She was certain Kim was in danger here. If Katie couldn't see it, that was her problem. But Penny needed to save her as much as she needed to save herself. Suddenly, Penny caught Katie's eyes. The morning light was hitting the waterfall behind her, almost reflecting against the water in the lake. Kate was pretty with beautiful eyes that glowed with unnatural vitality. They were grey, and when Penny looked into them, she felt calm, like she could almost believe anything Kate would say. Her hair was tied back in a short ponytail, and she wore clothes that served function rather than fashion. Combat trousers, but a green top, it reminded Penny of Lara Croft. Penny's mind drifted back to the times when she would play Tomb Raider games. It was during that time as she watched Lara when realised that she was becoming aroused. She had spent many years trying to figure out whether she was straight or gay but gave up on labels and decided love was love. It was wild, young, and dangerous, as beguiling and deadly as the ocean, unpredictable, unknowable, and yet inevitable. She didn't think she could trust a man again, but a woman could be an exception. Her thoughts were brought back to the present when she saw Kate smiling at her.

"What is it? Is it something on my face? I think it's the first time I've seen you smile."

Penny suddenly straightened herself up and looked away, angry and ashamed at herself.

"No, don't look away. You should smile more. I liked it."

Penny felt her face getting warm. The sincerity in her face caused her to blush. Her pulse quickened, and her breath came faster. She looked away and didn't look back for a few minutes, hoping she wouldn't see the effect she had on her, pretended to look at the lake. It was large. The wind made tiny waves ripple across its surface, lapping against the banks. It felt like an oasis. Life seemed to be drawn to it. At the far side, she could see a family of deer, and all around her, she could hear the frogs. In another life, she could be happy here, isolated from the world that she distrusted so much, safe. Why did she suddenly feel safe here in her presence? She started getting angry at herself. She should be scared. She should be angry. She should scream at them. She should run away. She should do *something*. They drugged her, and these people were crazy. Perhaps she still has the drug in her system. Maybe that's why everything seems to be a tad bit more beautiful. It's almost like she can feel the ground and the animals, even the water, like it was all connected to her soul in some way. She could smell the colours and taste the air; yes, she was still stoned!

Penny was watching the waterfall carefully when Kate asked if she would like to go into the cave. Penny couldn't see the cave, but watching Kate get up and walk somehow made Penny do the same. She got up and followed her, and soon, hidden behind the waterfall, she noticed a cave. The entrance didn't look spectacular, but it strangely pulled Penny. There was something inside that felt like a rope around her, she wanted to go in there, and it felt right to go in there. This was brand new, and Penny didn't know what to make of it. It felt like a shelter she so desperately needed. She could see some movement inside and hear faint whispers emanated. Unlike before, these whispers were warm, similar to when a grandparent speaks gently to a child. This must be what it feels like for a month to see a flame. Penny wondered if she was about to burn as well.

Kate stopped midway in her tracks. She turned and, with a solemnity new to Penny, said, "You need to do this on your own, and the Seraph will take it from here." Penny wanted to ask who the Seraph were, but it was too late, the world around her faded slightly, and she could only focus on the cave. Her feet started to move towards the cave involuntarily as if her body was being run on instincts only. She started walking towards the cave, towards the whispers, towards the dark figures moving around inside and towards the Seraph.

Did they burn Mark like a moth to a flame, and was that the plan for her?

Chapter 12:
The Prophet

There was a strange man who lived in Pandora, who later lived like a hermit. This man appeared from nowhere – a bit like the mysterious children. He had amnesia and was just wandering through the desert without any idea of where he was going. He had white cloud-like hair and a long beard; his eyes were a striking shade of blue, and the only bit of knowledge he had was his name, Angel.

Angel got strange flashbacks of an earlier life that confused him. He felt as if these flashbacks would slowly drive him insane. His overall possession consisted of two books, one black and one white. When the Tribe tried to read the books, the words just moved and dropped out of focus. 'The books must be cursed.' They assumed.

The Tribe didn't trust him because of these possessed books. They shunned him from the very start; they gave him food and shelter as this was their way, but they didn't have anything more to do with him.

Angel became obsessed with his work. This comprised of making sense of his flashbacks and trying to understand both of the books. The flashbacks felt as if they were taking root in his brain; they were memories just out of his reach. He got food one day when he saw two children playing with the crystals in the shape of animals. "Can I look at that?" The children didn't answer. Their parents had warned them to stay away from Angel, and they didn't want to be in trouble. Angel reached out and picked up two of the crystals, brought them back to his workshop, and experimented on them. He had even forgotten his hunger; something else was in control.

The next morning, he emerged and went to the council of elders. They were always polite to him, but Angel knew he wasn't taken seriously. "Is that the toys you took from my boys?" Angel turned to the Elder that spoke and didn't blink at the statement.

"These aren't children's toys! These are gifts. Let me show you". He picked up a sack and took a pinch of a powder out, placed it on the ground. He took two flint stones from his pockets and set them spark-free onto the pile. What happened next made everyone in the room jump up onto their feet. There was a loud bang, a short blue flame, leaving a scorch mark a fire would make. Angel called it 'Crystal Powder', and this one discovery will change everything, from how they hunt to how they set fires. Later it'll prove useful when they look at more efficient ways of killing each other.

The eldest of Eve's children, Olivia, was present and saw the demonstration. She liked Angel. When the children arrived, they also shunned them due to how things in Pandora had changed after they arrived. The Tribe had blamed them, but Olivia said nothing. However, she felt responsible for it. Olivia never told anyone that her dad brought on the darkness.

Olivia walked into Angel's workshop accomplishment when she saw something.

to congratulate him on his There was a table against the wall, which was usually covered by animal skin. Today, it was uncovered, and for the first time, Eve had seen Angel's books. She had heard stories of it but had never seen them.

She walked over and hovered her hand over the black book and felt cold. She didn't like it, but something spoke to her, and she felt a tremendous pull to open it. Angel was watching all of it curiously. He thought of telling her to leave them alone but wanted to see what would happen; she seemed entranced. Olivia cast her gaze over the white book, it felt warm and welcoming, but when she looked, her hand had taken it upon itself to pick up the black book. Instantly, she felt like being the most powerful person in Pandora and felt as if she could do anything.

In her mania, she started thinking about how everyone shunned her and her siblings. The resentment and anger were boiling over; the room started to shake. Then she saw her little sister standing in the doorway, looking afraid, and it brought her back to Adam, how she looked onto him losing his mind. She snapped out of it and dropped the book. Her senses came back to her, and the room settled again. In just a few moments, she was able to still her mind.

She looked back at the white book, cautious now, not sure what had just happened. The white book felt so warm and welcoming; she felt safe with it. She got the feeling of coming back home. She picked it up and felt better and powerful, but in a more balanced way; she was in control of it.

There was a massive energy burst from the book, and it sent Olivia flying backwards in a wall. She dropped the book, and it flipped open to a random page. Olivia picked herself up and looked over to Angel. Angel just stared, mouth open; he knew that the books were unusual, but they had never done this. Olivia walked over to the open pages. It talked of Eternal beings who created Pandora, and it's the creatures; it was history; not just a history of Pandora, but before.

"Who could have written this?" Olivia asks.

However, Angel has no clue where he got the book. He only remembered that he had them when they found him. Olivia picked the book up.

Angel looked thoughtful. "Olivia, something tells me you should take the book". She motioned to thank him.

"Don't thank me, I don't think I gave the book to you; I believe I gave 'you to the book." He commented.

Angel's last words rang in her head, "He gave her to the book?" What could that mean? The worry left her when she sat and opened the book. Straight away, she felt warm inside and energized. She read that the Eternal beings created Pandora and their war after. Also, they were the ones who had put the evil Shaitan into prison. As she read, she reflected on her father; "Was it the Shaitan that spoke to him?"

At that thought, she felt something inside her rising with her anger; her skin glowed, and the floor rumbled. It wasn't anything like before, but she felt in control. She felt the power within her, and she wanted to use it for the right cause. Olivia went to the Elders and read from the book. When they scoffed, she gave them proof. Glowed like crystals, they were stunned by her beauty. Whoever the light touched became at peace; their souls felt cleansed. From this point, she became the prophet the Seraph wanted Angel to be. As powerful as they were, that events were out of their control, that something even greater than them was watching, perhaps a plan put in motion by their creators, but who created the sparks?.

She regularly met the Elders and read from the book, telling them of the Eternals and the history of Pandora. Over time, people worshipped the Seraph and feared the Shaitan. The Book of Light, as it became known, made it clear they were protected. People around Olivia still shunned her, but out of fear of her new position. She was the spiritual leader of the entire Tribe Nation.

The only ones who didn't follow her were the fishing tribe. They stayed out of the cave and lived by the coast. Fishing tribesmen never interacted with the others; they only kept themselves to themselves.

Olivia missed her friend, Angel. She hadn't seen him in some time as he was busy in his workshop. She decided to visit him later that day. When she went to visit him, she was horrified to see the situation. He had been drawing over the walls. It looked like some instructions, but she couldn't even fathom what these things were about; massive flying machines that carried people and weapons.

When Olivia saw it, he had figured out how to create crystal projectiles and how he could use exorbitant amounts of crystal powder to create explosions. "I have seen the truth Olivia," Angel turned to face her, "I opened the black book, and it showed me who I am, restored my memories, the memories of their betrayal."

Angel became angry, "I sacrificed everything for them, laid down my existence, and they betray ME!" The crystals around him dimmed; they were rotting. Olivia ran, not knowing what to do. She went straight to the elders and asked for their council and to warn them. They nodded, "It is news to us that Angel has regained his memories. We are also aware of the weapons; there may come a day that we need to defend ourselves."

Olivia couldn't understand who they needed defence from. The book told her there aren't any other tribes apart from the known ones. Olivia was struggling with the thought of the Seraph betraying. They kinda loved only guiding, and she needed to learn more.

After reflection, Olivia decided that she needed to find meaning. She had failed her tribe. They were giving in to their fears, and Angel had lost his mind. She needed to figure out what it meant; she needed to finish studying the book before she could lead to anything. "I was naive to try to lead without finishing my study of the book." She thought.

In Olivia's absence, people started writing out chapter after chapter of what she said in their attempt to remember what was said from the book. They all remembered it differently. The result was everyone having the same beliefs but arguing over the differences. Then the whispers started. They had to leave the cave to hunt, leaving themselves vulnerable to the Shaitan.

They became paranoid, fought over food, created territories within the cave network. Even the fishing tribe fought since they no longer were the only fisherman. Then they started crafting the weapons from the crystals, using blueprints from Angel, building explosives, until someone made the first move and there was all-out war. They claimed it was over-worshipping in the correct way or spreading their version of the 'word', but it was just greed and power.

Angel was working on blueprints for more weapons. He wasn't even aware of what was happening outside of his workshop. The black book was telling him what to design' they promised him revenge; they promised to make him their prophet on Pandora. Making him believe that he would never die; he would outlive Olivia and would create his world. He saw all possible futures and manipulations to mould humanity how he saw fit. He would lead, not Olivia.

Angel saw his future and knew what to do to make it happen; the book told him. He placed his hands on the book and absorbed its energy into himself in the same way Olivia did with the Book of Light. He felt its

power and saw his future. He now had the plan; he would become the Operator.

Chapter 13:
The cave

Penny took one last look over to Katy. The light hit her just at the right angle, making her look almost angelic. Shaking it off, Penny moved further into the cave. She needed answers, and something feels different in here. She felt safe; that scraping feeling she had since touching that book had disappeared. The cave somehow lit, Penny couldn't see any lights or fires, but the light wasn't sunlight but didn't seem to be artificial either. Penny realized with a gasp that the cave was littered with crystals that glowed slightly, and their combined light was enough to see around the cave.

Walking through a short tunnel, she entered a dome-shaped room. There was something on the far side that looked like it used to lead somewhere; now, it's just caved in and a wall. Elder Claire was there as well somehow. She sat on a chair made out of rock and crystal. It had a high back and rests for her arms. Sitting in the chair, she looked like a queen, sitting on her throne. Walking up to Claire, Penny began to ask questions, "How did you…."

She stopped as the elder put her hand in the air. "I'm not the person you see, child," her voice was warm and calm.

Penny became confused at that; were they making fun of her now? "What do you mean? How can you not be you?"

The elder continued, "There is much you don't know yet, Penny. I have so much to tell you. Your father failed in his duties as men quite often do, he should have prepared you for the truth, but instead, he hid you and drank."

Penny took a step back. She wasn't prepared to talk about her father; that is a box she wouldn't open. The pain that man caused to her brother and the way he died because of her dad, "I won't discuss him!" All she could see was him lying dead on the floor, in a puddle of his blood. How she slipped in it, and she can still feel how sticky it was against her clothes and skin.

Penny was getting angry, and the glow from the crystals was increasing along with it. The elder just smiled, watching the show. She wasn't concerned or scared of what was happening. In fact, she didn't look surprised at all.

"Come sit, my child, let's discuss the past and the future. We must play our parts in what's coming."

Suddenly, when Penny turned around, there was an identical chair, "Okay, where the hell did that come from?" The elder looked unfazed, "The ground, of course."

Penny was ready to just walk out at that point; she had enough. The past couple of days had been something out of a movie, and she was ready to wake up and see a psychiatrist. Before she made it back to the tunnel, the elder asked her, "What do the whispers tell you?"

Penny stopped dead in her tracks, "They've seen you and are coming? You need the answers you came in here for."

Penny slowly went over to the seat and sat down. Penny starts first, "Who are you?" The elder just looked disappointed.

"After everything of the last two days, what you have witnessed all around you and heard in your head, this is your first question, child?" Penny took aback., It's the first time the elder sounded anything but patient. "I can feel your pain, child. The darkness of your life has stained you, but you are the light bearer. You carry our light forward to hold off the darkness."

Penny looked baffled at that, "What's a light-bearer? I've heard the others say it as well." The elder stood up and started walking around; she mused allowed, "it's been so long since I've had legs, I very nearly came here as a man, but the others thought you would be more comfortable with this form."

Penny wasn't sure if the old woman thought she was some sort of god, which would mean she was insane, or this whole thing was a hallucination which meant she was insane. The old woman walked over to her, "I'm always amazed how over the millennia, the face has never changed, ever since the first."

Penny said she needed to get some air, but the elder wouldn't let her leave, "We have all the time in the world in here, but when you leave, I will be gone too, and with it, your chance for getting the answers you want."

Penny looked her directly in the eyes, stood up, and said, "Tell me everything!" The elder smiled, "Finally, something I can do."

At that, the old woman sprang forward like someone a fraction of her age and put her hand on Penny's forehead. Suddenly, they weren't in the cave anymore; they were somewhere else. Penny suddenly recognized the place as Pandora from her dreams. The elder had taken her back.

She saw Adam, releasing the darkness as she saw in her dream. Then out of nowhere, there was a flash, and he fell to the ground. The darkness had stopped, but she could tell if it had been released. She saw it fall like dark snow as far as she could see. The wind had a strange sound to it, like it was carrying howls and screeches, but just out of earshot.

Penny looked around, alarmed. She felt threatened but couldn't see any danger. The Elder stood next to her and just smiled.

"You're safe, child. We are just observers of what's already been", it didn't make Penny relax more. Suddenly, it was nighttime, and Penny saw Adam slowly come to his feet. His features had changed, his hair was white, and he had bright blue eyes, then realised this wasn't Adam, it was someone else, someone new. "This is Angel, and he is our child and our betrayer".

He had something in his arms that Penny didn't see before, she couldn't understand where he came from, but he was carrying two books. The two books she herself had encountered over the past few days.

He looked as confused as she did, looking around in the darkness. The fire was out, and the only light was the moonlight. Penny noticed a glow coming from the white book, and it got brighter over time. It was reacting to something that she couldn't see. Then she saw them, black skeletons; they looked as though they were made from the shadows. The skeletons didn't arrive; they materialized from the darkness. When you looked at the space where the face should be, they were no faces.

It reminded Penny of a black hole, sucking in all the light. It had an event horizon around the skulls that seemed to shimmer. Angel started to spin around. When he saw these creatures moving towards him, some of them had gone in all fours, reminiscent of a crab or spider. They produced a chittering noise as if from some invisible teeth.

When they came across the light from the book, the chittering increased, and they retreated slightly. They seemed unsure of what to do. The book was definitely reacting to the skeletons, and it seemed to have the power to keep them at bay. Turning to the Elder, "What the hell are those?"

For the first time, the Elder had a disturbed look. "Something born on this day, out of the darkness. You see, the darkness that was released here on this day was free. With its freedom, it became aware, conscious; it has its own power, it can't directly interfere with humans; only whisper for our fallen brethren. But, whoever comes into contact with a book, a light-bearer or artefact shifts their sense of reality slightly."

Penny picked up on the word brethren, and the realization hit her. This wasn't a spirit or person; this was actually one of the Seraph in front of her. "It's enough for the darkness to become aware of them as a threat to be removed; that's when it starts to take its physical forms. These are what your new friends have called Phantoms, although they have been known by many names throughout time. They are the first wave."

Looking confused, Penny asked, "What do you mean the first wave?"

The Elder looked thoughtful, "Think of the darkness as being the hand of the Shaitan. The Phantoms are its fingers, probing into the light. But there is also a palm and finally a fist."

Watching the scene in front of her, she could see the conflict between the man and the Phantoms. He was shouting at them like a raving, terrified lunatic. He clung to both books and suddenly sat down. He seemed to realize that the white book was holding them back with its glow, but there was a sense that the second book, the dark one, was what was drawing them out. The Phantoms, after some time left, had given up, and the man fell asleep clutching the books.

Suddenly they were in a desert. The man did look well. He was walking and muttering, closing to death. That's when they found him and took him to the caves. She saw his life, saw the tribes fall into war. Then she saw the women leading them.

To start with, she was lost in the fight, watching the men battle seeing flashes of blue light. Penny had never seen weapons like these. A man threw an object that looked to be crystals wrapped in flint rocks. "Was it a grenade?"

Her question was answered when there was a massive blue explosion. It gave her several new temporary blind spots in her eyes. Then, where that object fell, there was nothing. It had vaporized everything and everyone.

This knowledge and technology had never existed; this was impossible. She knew this couldn't have happened. Humans, at this stage of development, had rocks and sticks and had barely mastered fire.

The Elder beckoned her to just watch. That's when Penny noticed them. As the men fought, the darkness rose around them. The spilt blood was like fertilizer, creating a breeding ground for more. She could see strands of darkness entering the head of each person as if they were puppets. Penny realized this was why the girl couldn't stop the fighting; the darkness was using them to feed itself.

Then every weapon and every crystal started to glow. She didn't know why but like how from the book, and it banished the darkness freeing the men. It was Olivia; she was chanting with the book of light, banishing the darkness.

Penny noticed then it was Angel that led the men that attacked; he wasn't affected. In fact, she was enraged all the more. He called the retreat, and the battle was over.

The Elder brought things forward a few years to show Penny what happened next. She saw the girl with great power. She taught the children, led the men in prayer, and taught the women how to lead alongside the men. She faced the creatures that were in the night, that hid in shadows; she was able to destroy them.

Penny started to feel tired. She was suddenly unsure; none of this could be real, her dreams, whatever this was. They must have drugged her at some point before she entered the cave.

The Elder looked at her, looking a bit disappointed, "Alas! Our time here is done, my child. It serves us well, and your friends will tell you more when you are ready, but it is your job to protect them to protect everyone."

With this, Penny woke up at the mouth of the cave, just under the waterfall. She had a hell of a headache and felt like she had a three-day drinking session, and now she was suffering the consequences. Looking around, Penny realized it was dark. 'How much time had passed?' she thought.

Standing up, Penny made her way out of the cave. She heard them before she saw them, a chittering in the wind, a dark pull on her soul like she was being pulled to a black hole. Down by the cottage, she could hear them shouting in terror.

The Phantoms were attacking the cottage. Something was holding them back. In the distance, she could see the crystals glowing. Then she heard something that made her stomach flip.

Katy was shouting, "It has Kim, It has Kim."

Seeing Kim being dragged back from the cottage, screaming. She could barely make out the shimmering outline, and the darkness had her!

Penny moved on instinct.

Chapter 14: Fallen Angels

The Tribes divided up the caves. They created borders and guarded them. They still sent their Elders to the council. Although they were disagreeing and fighting, there was still fragile peace. The Council of the Elders had fallen into philosophical arguments rather than governing.

Angel was watching and learning from them. He had his plan in place and was being patient. After all his years of imprisonment, he at least learned that. The more he studied the black book, the more he understood his past. He saw his own creation, the callous nature of the Seraph, who was sending him

He remembered the pain of his incarceration, the torment. He also understood that his interaction with the Spark of Light was unexpected. He had heard a voice in his head telling him to take it and to take the Dark Spark. He looked to his book for answers, but it revealed nothing. He slowly came to the realization that the book was thinking and planning, or at least someone behind the book was. It felt the same as when he took them, the same feeling to the voice. He knew from the Eternals bewilderment that it was neither faction. He wondered if the sparks were aware of themselves. "Are they conscious?" Or is this someone else pulling even their strings?

Again the book refused to answer him, and it seemed the book was discerning at what it revealed.

The Elders knew that he could read from the book, but they wanted his technology. He had become the architect of the future. However, what they didn't know was that he was communicating with each Elder of all the tribes privately. He was passing his inventions and designs to everyone. He knew exactly what he was doing.

The Elders were where he wanted them, bringing them closer and closer to conflict. All it took was conversations with each of the Elders one on one; they talked theology; they spoke about Olivia and the Eternals. He would make sure they leave with a firm belief in what he wanted them to believe. It didn't matter what, as longs as they had differences, he could exploit.

No one suspected him since his discovery of what they could do with the crystals he developed from hermit into a respected member of the society. They valued his opinion, which is why he was so dangerous. He had the trust of the

Elders. He also sent his inventions to the fishing tribe behind the Elder's backs.

A tired Angel laid down to rest, usually avoiding sleep due to the nightmares. However, sometimes, there was no choice. Closing his eyes, he almost instantly went back. He was in his cage again, the Shaitan close by. He saw the Seraph laughing at him.

This was the nightmare; he would remember things through his dreams. His memories came with the Shaitan's knowledge. They showed him the laughter. The relief that they had a fall guy, he thought they decided this was better watching their enemies in torment. Did that include him? It does now.

#

While Penny was still safe in her flat dreaming of Pandora early on the morning of the day, her life changed forever. Alex stood outside Pleasureland in Arbroath and was leaning against the wall of the building. He could hear excited screaming and the banging from the dodgems. He was watching a dad put his boy onto a trampoline outside of the main door. The boy was laughing as he jumped. The dad was watching on with a massive smile across his face.

Alex wanted to cut his smile off right in front of the brat. All he felt while watching the father-son bonding was hatred. Luckily for them, his instructions were to wait, and he obediently waited for the Operator to call.

Alex was the Operator's prime Agent, who he used to do the wet work, the killing, torture, and making people disappear. He could smell the sea salt in the air. Standing outside, he noticed the waves were high today; it might come in handy later, depending on his orders. He also noticed a man in a white suit. He was wearing a jacket, even though it was a summery day. 'He must be roasting,' Alex made a mental note of the anomaly. He always kept track of things that didn't fit; they usually meant trouble.

Watching all the surrounding families, he just wanted to leave. This facade of content families was all fake. He could see the shadow of darkness around everyone. This darkness spoke to Alex; it told him people's wicked secrets.

The Operator particularly liked this ability. It was a gift from the dark gods, the Shaitan. They freed him of his pain, delivered him to a purpose. The operator was eternal, and he would mentor him and teach him how to cultivate the darkness and his power.

Alex was sceptical, but then the Operator took a gun, put it to his head, and swiftly pulled the trigger. Alex thought it was a trick when the horror of what just happened passed, and he went to check. The Operator was just lying on the floor laughing. He stood up and spat out the bullet.

Alex watched as a couple walked along the path holding hands and eating ice creams. The woman didn't know that her husband was having an affair with their son's girlfriend; she was only fifteen.

When you had seen everyone's darkness, you had seen the world for what it was and people for who they were.

He remembered most of his previous life, the pain, and misery, being left alone with his drunk dad. He beat the living shit out of him. He often wished he had somebody else too, but he was alone with his dad—an only child.

He remembered being in a room, except it wasn't a room, but just darkness. There were people who were moving around the darkness, and they tied him down as he felt nervous. They had him strapped down for his own good. Otherwise, he would have rejected their love. People in the shadows weren't walking and floating.

He remembered the terror filling him. It was like a horror movie. In front of him, the figures moved together, swirling and becoming something else. It was a fog made from shadow. It approached him, whispering in his ear, "Don't be afraid; we come with gifts."

The fog entered him through every opening in his head, including his eyes. It flowed into him and consumed his fear. He instantly felt gratitude, as they had removed his weaknesses, and he felt their love.

Everything from that point was hazy. They showed him his life, where he was powerless against his dad and against his pain. Now they would give him power and purpose, and The Operator would be the father he should have had. What Alex didn't know was that during the time, they were in his memories and altering things, changing what he remembered, and more importantly, who he remembered.

Alex got the call, and The Operator told him to stand down. "The job was off. Feel free to tick that special job off your list with your free time."

This happened every so often, but he never knew why. Alex never knew what the job was until the time was right.

All he was ever told was to be somewhere at a certain time and wait. Now that he had a few hours to spare, he went to the house in his nightmares. He needed to face his demons; he needed to face him.

He walked through town, remembering the Global Video store. He would spend hours there, avoiding going home. His feet would take him up past all of that into the housing estates. He walked towards the place where he grew up and where his dad tormented him.

He walked up to Beachwood Road in Kirton and found the house he grew up in. Walking up to the driveway, he wondered if he still lived here. The place looked abandoned. The garden around the back had a pond while he used to live there, but now, he couldn't see it through the long grass. Walking up to the door, he expected to feel fear; that door used to bring terror. It meant he was home. Now the memory just filled him with rage. He tried the door, and as it opened, he quietly made his way in and looked around. The stairs were right in front of him. as he walked into the kitchen to the left and to the living room to the right. He went to the kitchen first; it was full of bottles and takeaway tins. He couldn't believe the state the place was in. as he went into the living room, where he was passed out on the floor. His dad was in his underwear on the floor unconscious; Alex looked at him with disgust and walked out of the room, and headed upstairs. He went straight to his old bedroom. It was just as he left it. It looked like his dad hadn't even been in it, like ever. He looked out of the window; the view hadn't changed a bit. It was all the same as he left it, some houses behind him and the marine base in the distance.

As he went into the smaller rooms, he found a rather girly-looking room. It took him by surprise; it had only been him and his dad before. So, who this room belonged to? Did he take a lodger? If that is the case, it wouldn't surprise him. After all, he would need the money for a drink. He went downstairs and back into the living room and looked at his dad, who was looking into his face. He could see his darkness, his soul, and his secrets. He saw from his dad's viewpoint the beatings he gave him. His dad woke up and looked at him in shock as if he saw a ghost, and as he tried to get up, it was too late.

He hadn't felt the blade at first. He only realized someone had stabbed him when Alex took his blade back out. Alex was a professional and was fully aware of what to do. He had slipped the blades up from below his ribs, through the diaphragm. This would stop him from breathing instantly and wouldn't allow him to scream. Alex stepped back, watching. He stood there as he wanted to see what would kill him first, the bleeding or suffocation.

As he watched him dying, he saw his dad's darkness again. However, he saw a girl and then a woman this time. She must be the lodger. He probed deeper, wondering where she was. He saw her with him, but he didn't remember her. "Who is she?" Probing more, he saw through his dad's eyes. He walked into Alex's bedroom and caught them telling each other stories; this enraged him.

More memories of her and Alex flooded back to the time when Alex was just a kid. She was there too; he could tell it was her. 'Who is she?' He thought. Alex lost the visions and realized it was because of his dad's death. He kicked and cursed himself for not paying attention. He wanted to see his life leaving his eyes. as he looked over at the tv, there was a picture frame. It got his dad, mum, him, and the girl. He picked it up and looked at the back. On the back, it read 'Blackpool 1995, Isobel, James, Penny, and Elliot'.

Chapter 15:
What you leave
behind

Before Penny knew it, she was running towards Kim, unsure of what she was going to do when she got there. Kim was stationary now outside the cottage, and the Phantoms were converging on her screams. Kim stood there, all three and a half feet of her, shrieking in terror. There was nothing but darkness that was surrounding her; she couldn't do anything but wait there; wait for the shadows to take her. Their chittering noise increased with excitement at their pray.

#

Penny saw the cottage door swing open, and Shug ran out, thrashing something that glistened it glowed in the dark; or at least some part of it did. The Phantoms disintegrated as they were cut down. This distracted them, and they drew their attention to Uncle Shug. Penny took this opportunity and grab Kim. This was a mistake, though, because as soon as she grabbed her, the Phantoms turned their attention back to them. The chittering was deafening now. It was going right to the core of her. Her ribs vibrated with the noise making it hard to breathe. At that point, something streaked above and swooped down. It had something bigger than a dagger, and it slashed Uncle Shug across the chest, cutting through flesh and bone. Penny screamed helplessly as she watched her Uncle drop to his knees and then to the side. This was the first time she got her first proper look at this flying creature; like the Phantoms, it was also made of shadow. The attackers moved with a strange grace; they were savage but working as a swarm, coordinated and controlled.

#

Something inside her took her over. She planted her hands in the ground with a deafening scream of rage. As she felt the dirt crunch under her fingers, a burst of light came from her, and she sent out a shockwave of intense light. Every Phantom it touched, including the flying creature, disintegrated.

The fight was over. Penny looked over to her Uncle and saw some movement. She wanted to run to him but couldn't as she fell to the ground in exhaustion. What she had just done had taken every bit of strength she had; her body no longer responded. She didn't know what she had just done, but her heart was racing, and for the first time, she didn't feel helpless.

"What was that?" Trevor appeared and lifted her.

Looking down, he gave her a subtle nod; maybe he was warming to her after all.

#

Katy brought Kim back to the cottage, where Uncle Shug had been placed on the dining table, groaning, his eyes were somewhere else entirely, but he responded to Penny entering the room. Penny weakly walked over to the table. She took his hand and held it tightly, trying to comfort him. The Elder and Katy were working furiously to stop the bleeding. They were doing everything they could to keep him alive. The wounds pulsated as they refused to be treated.

That moment, Penny understood that to be struck by one of these creatures meant death. She was grateful for the stool that Trevor handed her, as her knees were not feeling strong. Knowing what was coming next made Penny glad for an empty stomach. After they had finished, Penny looked up, and even after knowing the answer already, she asked, "Will he live?"

The Elder just nodded her head and looked down, said, "He's been cut by a dark blade from a Wrath, it's a mortal wound, I'm sorry."

As she looked down, Penny could see branches of darkness flowing from the dark wound. It was like venom spreading through his body. She thought she had hallucinated everything in the cave, but it was all real. She sat silently by her Uncle's side right until the end, who never regained consciousness fully. The whole time, he mumbled things about her mother that she couldn't make out. He was her last connection to her past, and he was slipping away, consuming his last few breaths.

Suddenly, he looked into the distance and spoke to someone no one else could see. He was hallucinating, barely able to whisper, "Where have you been all of this time? I looked for you... But how? The spark of what? How can you just stand and watch? You are her..."

The occupants of the room looked at each other, half with confusion and half with concern. He was delirious but didn't seem to be in pain anymore. In fact, he seemed comforted. "Penny is here. Do you see? I found her and took her to our people."

With a smile just visible at the corner of his lips, he passed away. His last whisper caught everyone off guard, and Penny fell back off her chair, "Do you see her? I brought Penny; Isobel!"

Katy came over and sat next to Penny. She threw her arms around her and sobbed, "I was so scared."

She explained that Kim had gone outside, curious about wanting to see. "She thought she could hide and watch them. They sensed her straight away. Fear to them is like blood to a shark". Kim had never seen them up close before and wanted to see them. Penny didn't know what to say, and thus, she said nothing and let Katy sob. Kim was sleeping in the bedroom with Trevor sitting by her bed.

Katy spoke about her childhood in the caves and growing up with the tribes. Told her about her Nana leaving the caves; they believed that they needed to raise their children in the world and not to hide from it.

The tribes had lost sight of what they were trying to protect. It had become too much about the survival of the tribes and not the salvation of humankind. The lineage of the light bearer would explore the world and return with new fresh insight to lead into a new age.

At some point, Penny had fallen asleep.

#

Penny was in the woods. She remembered these woods very clearly; they were a short cycle north of

Arbroath. She spent hours there just exploring or doing anything really that kept her from going home.

Sometimes Elliot would come with her to spend time and give her some company. They pretended to fight ancient battles, the ones Nana told them about. She would be the Seraph's champion, of course, and he would be the Shaitan's. They would make swords from sticks they found on the forest floor. Penny was the best when it came to climbing, and she always used that to her advantage.

#

Looking around her old playing grounds, Penny saw her Uncle standing, smiling at her. She hadn't seen him smile over the past few days, but it suited him. He looked different, in a good way; he looked younger

as if the weight of the world had lifted from his shoulders. Penny wasn't surprised to see him; she had become used to strange dreams and now realises they are more than just dreams. He walked over to her, "Sorry, Penny. This isn't what I had planned, but it is all my fault. We part ways here."

Tears began to trickle down her cheeks, and this surprised her. She barely knew him, but her memories of him from her childhood are perfect in every way.

She had idolized him since her childhood. He and her mother both used to take Penny and Elliot for long walks in the woods. Each telling stories and building dens out of twigs and branches or anything else they could find lying on the ground. This was probably why she always went back there when she needed to think.

Is this why they're here now? A happy memory?

She thought she had finished grieving him years ago when he vanished, but she was so wrong. She suddenly wanted more time with him. She needed answers to so many questions, which only he could answer. She didn't really understand any of this yet.

He seemed to know her thoughts, "Trust these people, Penny. They are good, and they are kind. The Tribes folk are an ancient branch of man

that has existed to stand against the rising darkness. They have always been led by their Elders unless the darkness rises into a war. That is the moment when the light bearer leads. You lead."

Penny is concerned now. She led primary school classes, not Tribes.

In no world, these two are the same thing or are on the same scale.

"There is a battle coming. Our enemy has been patient, and he's one of the fallen. He is here on earth, leads the clan, but no one has seen him in centuries. He always works from the shadows." Her uncle warned her.

Penny was becoming even more confused, "What do you mean in centuries?"

Shug told her the story of Angel and how he became the Operator. By this time, Penny had learned not to dismiss things so casually these days. However, this sounded too far-fetched – no one could be immortal.

"Trust our friends; they will look after you."

All of a sudden, Penny felt alone. She felt herself being drawn back to the real world. She didn't want to say goodbye to him; she didn't want to be alone. As she was being pulled away, Shug had time for one last word, "Your mother, I'm not sure you can trust her!!"

#

By this time, the sun had come up. It was a small skirmish but had the feel of a great battle. There was a low, thick fog covering the surface of

the land. Everyone felt moist and cold in their lungs when they breathed. The smell of wet grass was tainted by a fear that felt as thick as the fog. This had changed everything.

Penny felt a little responsible for it; she wouldn't believe the women in the cave, maybe had sent the Phantoms as proof. "Your mother, I'm not sure you can trust her!!" what did he mean? He was talking to nothing when he died.

Now Penny was a believer; she could still feel the energy coursing through her veins. She had power, and now she had unlocked it. She walked over to the window; Trevor was outside building a funeral pyre; he was placing black boxes through it. It seemed a strange thing to do, but all this seemed unreal. She was angry at her uncle; he didn't have the right to die and make her feel this way, not after leaving the way he did. Penny became concerned, turning to the Elder who was in her usual spot in the corner. "We have to report this. He's dead. We can't just burn the body." The Elder looked unconcerned, simply said, "all will be clear," Penny opened her mouth to argue, but the look on the Elder's face told her there wasn't much point.

#

As they all stood outside by the pile of wood, they all looked on, remembering Shug. Kim was the only one who was not there; she was inside, away from the corpse. Everyone looked at Penny to say something.

She opened her mouth to object when Katy took her hand, "It's okay, it doesn't need to be much."

Penny took a deep breath. There was tension in the air, even more than usual funeral. Penny had so many questions, and they had dozens of questions for her. "Will she lead them into the coming war? Does she even know?" Smelling the fresh air, Penny could feel the cold moisture entering her lungs from the fog hanging over the lake.

"My Uncle was a mystery to me. There was so much of him I didn't know." She thought. "What I do know is when I was a little girl, he would take me on the dodgems and make sure we hit every car at least once. He and my mother were always together, whispering, and it used to drive my dad crazy."

At this, she giggled, prompting laughter from the others. The tension seemed to fall away as some sunlight started to shine through the fog, "We had only just found each other again. He saved me from someone I'm only just learning off. I still don't know what it meant, but he came to me in a dream last night."

As she said that, there were a few looks shot around. Elder Claire cleared her throat, and everyone settled.

"I'm still making sense of what he said and what I saw. I have seen so much over the past few days; I am still making sense of all of this. He had more to tell me, but his time was cut short. What he did say was I could trust you. I find that hard but don't have much choice right now. I'll come with you."

#

Elder Claire walked over to Penny and said, "Penny, by now, you can feel the power and energy that flows through you. This power is like a battery. It has limits and needs time to recharge, so use it sparingly. Look into yourself and feel the flow as it spreads into every part of your being. Let it flow and let it reach in with your mind and take a tiny piece of it and place it into the wood in front of you."

Penny closed her eyes and searched inside of herself. As she took a deep breath and searched for it, she felt something flowing in. as she focused on the flow, she realized it was like a sun inside her chest. It had flared like the sun, and they were flowing into every cell. However, the flow was uneven and not constant. After focusing the flow into every part of her body, she took a tiny piece of the flow and put it into the wood.

"Now what?" She whispered to the elder.

"Now, you shape it with your will. Imagine it bursting into a flame." As she got the response from the elder, she did exactly that and focused her imagination. Suddenly, the pile of wood burst into flames.

Everyone took a step backwards and started walking. Katy was still holding Penny's hand, and she pulled her back. She soon realized why and what those black boxes were. There was a huge explosion that had been carefully directed upwards. The flames rose to the sky, turning blue like in Penny's dream. A few minutes later, the flames died just as quickly, and nothing was left. Everything had been vaporized by the powdered crystal in the black boxes. The only thing left was a mound of black glass. Trevor had packed the boxes with sand. Now that was a permanent memorial to Uncle Shug.

Chapter 16: The Hunted

Trevor thought it would be best to take two separate cars, one in front in which Penny, Katy, and Kim would be driving, and the other one behind in which the elder and himself were following them. Katy was one of the few people Trevor trusted, and why shouldn't he? After all, she was a skilled fighter and time to time, proved herself undercover. It bothered him that Kim was always with her. He thought it was too dangerous, but there was no separating them, not since Kim's dad died. Maybe this is why Trevor trusts Katy, and they share a common pain.

Her husband hadn't been taken by violence, but he grew sick and died. They didn't have a cure for the disease, but the outsiders used to call it cancer, which couldn't be treated. Like always, there was a huge debate, but he was left to die instead of trusting the outsiders and risk exposure.

The crystal technology had given them some huge advances. However, it had its limits as well. These limits can be overcome by the outsider's resources. Living in caves most of the time set the limits as to how far they could advance as a society. Thus, to ensure their survival, they need to integrate. This is the reason why Trevor started his undercover program; to know when the time is right. He led his undercover program, took his family to live outside and learned about the rest of humanity in their own environments.

This was the moment when he lost his family to a home invasion when they stayed in London. At that point, he lost all love for them and their resources. In fact, he almost withdrew his agents altogether as well, but the elders stepped in after seeing the value of his program. Something had to change, and it had been decades since the light-bearers had left the caves.

He got into the car next to Elder Clair, who was frail-looking, but that was limited to her looks only. Her hairs were white as clouds, and the skin looked like it would rip if you touched it. Before tagging along with her, Trevor thought she would probably sleep most of the way; and why shouldn't he think that? After all, she liked to sleep more and more. He knew what that meant, and so did she, but it went unsaid.

The elder rescued Trevor from his own mind. He was tucking into his own homebrew for breakfast. He lost all the love for a living and withdrew into his quarters. Spending life like this, he was skin and bone when the elder found him skin yellow. When she looked around, she saw his bare walls covered with dents and holes where he had thrown empty bottles. The floor was covered in pieces of shattered glass, and he was curled up in a corner. She didn't give him a tender hand but grabbed him by the scruff of the neck, and with surprising force, brought him to his feet.

To this day, he didn't understand her strength but knew it had something to do with the light she could channel. She dragged him forcefully to the medics and detoxed him, brought him back to strength. Under orders from the elder, the medics wouldn't let Trevor leave, and he was out of the strength to fight them. They nursed him for over a month. The whole time, Trevor never saw Elder Claire.

When the time came for him to be discharged, she came to his bedside.

"Gather your things and come with me."

He did as he was told and followed the Elder to her quarters. As he looked around, the quarters were much larger than his, homely in their own way and warmed by the central Furness. They were in some kind of lobby, with a table in the middle of the circular room. It was a place to meet guests. He hadn't seen one before, these were an elder's quarters, and they matched her station.

"Through that door," Trevor looked up and saw the Elder beckoning with her stick.

He walked through the heavy wooden door and reached in a quarter, which was supposed to be his. The room was large, having its own pipe from the furnace, providing heat when the vents are opened. A table was placed against a wall, with some fruit placed in a basket for him to eat and a jar of water to drink, along with a pen and paper to write. There was a single book 'Alcoholics Anonymous' Trevor had been studying this during his time at the hospital.

At first, he was hesitant to be at that place, but after some time, it gave him comfort. He recognized his own pain within the book, and he hoped to overcome it. A second table was there next to the door, with a large bowl of water for washing in. This was their tradition and the way they host and care for people. The bowl of fruit will never be empty.

"While we are within these walls, you may address me as Claire," Elder Claire said, and without another word, she turned around and walked out.

Trevor was following the car in front of him. He was surprised to see Claire was still awake, looking thoughtfully out of the window.

"They came to her in the cave," the elder eventually said, "I could feel the power. That's what drew the Phantoms to us."

While the sun was out, they were safe from the shadows and the monsters it sent. However, little did they knew; they were being tracked by something just as evil but more human. Trevor grimaced at the memory, "We should have brought more people; it wouldn't take much to overpower us."

Trevor turned his head and looked at the elder, "Claire, we took the gamble that we would be under the radar, but you have to accept we've been found."

Elder Claire closed her eyes and nodded in agreement, said, "I fear we will lose more than just her uncle before we can reach our destination. When we reach Inverness, we will stop at the train station and split up. The girl will come with us, and Katy will travel with Kim."

Trevor looked shocked. He asked, "You want to reduce our numbers further?"

"No. Oh, God! No. That's not what I'm saying," the elder replied with a heaviness in her voice, "I'm removing a child from the front lines of a war."

Suddenly, Trevor realized the elder was preparing for battle.

#

This excursion had turned into convoy duty; the light bearer was royalty to them, even if she didn't know it yet. She needed to get to New Pandora alive. The elder turned once more to Trevor before she settled her head to sleep. "Her powers are growing already. The darkness in her heart will serve her well as a warrior. The only question is, how much love is in there? Will she come back from the darkness when the battle is won?"

By this time, the elder felt tired. Her tiredness was catching up more often than not these days. She hoped she could teach Penny what she needed to know before she went to sleep for the final time.

Katy could feel her leg being restless. The main reason was partly because of the previous night, but being in a car with Penny also played a role in her restlessness. She was not sure what to say or how to explain. Penny was silent throughout their journey and hadn't said a word since they left. The longer the silence went, the harder it seemed to start a conversation with anyone. From the back seat, Kim had a smirk on her face as she looked between the two women.

"That was cool," Kim commented.

"Huh?" Penny gave her a confused look.

"When you made the bad guys disappear, that was cool." Kim cheered.

Katy laughed, "Yeah, I guess it was."

Now, the tension was also joined by uncomfortable giggling. It wasn't funny, though the tension was unbearable.

"So tell me about where we're going?" Penny questioned.

Katy let out a heavy breath and said, "I'm not allowed to tell you yet. Elder Claire wants to show you, and I think she's actually pretty excited."

"Okay, what about you? who is Katy Digby?" Penny asked again.

Katy chuckled and said, "Well, I grew up in New Pandora. My parents were engineers. They looked after the tunnels and helped to design the buildings. We would sit at night, playing with blocks and sticks. That was where they challenged me to build different types of structures."

"Expecting you to follow in their footsteps?" Penny asked.

Katy didn't say anything. She just nodded with an awkward smile.

"Then why didn't you?" Katy thought for a moment. "I didn't want the responsibility, and it was too much. If I made a tiny mistake in a calculation, people could die in a cave." Katy looked disappointed in herself, and regret could easily be seen on her face, "My parents never fully supported my decision. I was dropping down a rank by becoming security."

Penny wanted to ask what she meant by rank, but Kim decided she wanted to play a game – eye spy. Penny cringed; she hated car games, but they humoured her. Katy watched Penny playing with her daughter and smiled; she liked this. The three of them were in the car. She caught herself and pulled back her thoughts. She was the Light Bearer, and she was her temporary guardian. These thoughts wouldn't end well, especially since Penny wore the white robes and as she earned the rank last night.

#

Alex was at the cottage. He was waiting inside for the phone call, looking relentlessly around it; it looked like someone left in a hurry. His phone rang, it was The Operator. He asked, "Alex, are you there?"

"Yes," Alex responded.

"Burn the cottage, go behind the waterfall and enter the cave. Destroy that as well." The Operator said and hung up."

He walked outside, and after a brief moment of concentration, the cottage burst into flames. He started walking around the lake, watching the frogs and tadpoles, admiring the balance and cycle of life. He felt a little giddy after the cottage, and he loved using his power to give him a rush like drinks used to. He started skipping and dancing around the little rivers that flow from the lake. Eventually, he got to the cave and took a look at the cave's mouth. He felt like something was pushing him as if warning him not to enter; he wasn't welcome.

This was one of the original caves of Pandora, and it still carried the power of the crystals. Alex walked in, and the place glowed in response as if they defied him. They sensed their end was coming, and that was why the cave was pushing him away. Alex kneeled in the centre and extended his hands, and he reached out to the crystals with his mind. He started feeling every single one of them that were in the walls. He suddenly closed his hands into fists, and with that motion, he choked every crystal to death.

All of them went black, turned to ash, and all of the energy that burst out of them were absorbed by Alex. He growled and roared in the exertion and breathing heavily. His pool of power felt like it had just gone nuked. Taking the life force of the crystals gave him power so potent, it left him with raw power. This is something the Light Bearer would never do. It was considered destructive magic, and it was forbidden. It interrupted the natural cycle, and it always came with some consequences.

Suddenly, something happened, and nature became unbalanced. Walking out of the cave, that's what happened. Every ounce of life within the area of the cave was now gone. The plants were turned into ash, the frogs were dead, and the lake had turned to some sort of mud pile. He remembered when he discovered he could do this, one of his subordinates made him angry; in fact, even angrier than he had ever been when he let the girl escaped from the car. He tried to make the excuse that someone drove into the side of them, but that's exactly what they were, just excuses. Alex choked him to death, but as he did, the man's energy became part of his energy., making him even more powerful. The Operator explained that it was dark magic from the black book, and this was the first instance anyone other than himself had this ability. He acted proudly, but Alex sensed the danger at this development. The Operator was suspicious by nature and would see Alex as a threat.

Alex walked down to the road and inspected the dirt track. He could see the tire marks – two sets. He took some pictures and sent them on to the forensic team. They might be able to figure what kind of car they were in.

#

Penny suddenly felt a dagger in her chest. As she clutched it and was gasping for breath, she thought she had a heart attack. Katy got panicked and pulled the car over. Penny caught her breath in moments, and by this time, Trevor pulled up behind and ran over, asking, "what's going on?"

Penny looked up with traces of terror on her face. "Someone's coming, and he's hunting us!"

Chapter 17
The Triangular Castle

They dropped Kim off to a trusted friend of The Tribe. They would board a plane and go to Wales via London. Meanwhile, Katy refused to leave her post, claiming, "You will need me if someone attacks you again."

It was just Penny and Katy now, and they had driven for hours.

Things had become more relaxed, but then, the subject of Mark came up.

"You know, there wasn't anything you could have done for Mark? He had touched the book." Katy exclaimed.

Penny looked down at her feet, "Part of me knows that, but I can't stop wondering what would have happened if I had just asked more questions." She shook her head, "I need to figure what they are and why they did it to him; maybe then I can have some peace. The whispers can't make someone do anything that wasn't already in their heart, and they only stoke the fires. They don't start them."

This made Penny feel even worse than she already was. She couldn't imagine that amount of hate in a child.

Before she could say anything else, Katy announced they were stopping for the night.

"What you saw, the skeletons and flying wraths are mindless drones. There is something that lives in the shadows. Our writings tell us about it. A primordial being, made of shadow that interacts through its manifestations. Before all it could do, it watched and influenced. It took time to learn to make the skeletal phantoms and wraths. It learned what we find most terrifying and moulds its projections around that. It can almost reach into your mind. That's what we are taught, but a part of me used to think it was just a story to scare children until last night."

Looking outside, they were driving past a white cottage with an ancient arch coming from it and reaching across the road. As they drove under the arch, Penny saw a massive castle ruin. Turning to the right from that point, she saw some shops and offices, then the car parking area. The two cars came to a stop, and everyone got out. Trevor walked over to them and said, "We will stay here tonight; they'll keep us safe."

Penny looked around. She thought Trevor was talking about the people living in the white cottage, which they just passed. The elder was already walking towards the ticket office. Trevor followed her as well. Katy just smiled and beckoned Penny to follow. The ticket office was small and looked like a retro-fitted ruin, maybe a gatehouse. The elder was speaking to someone, and they nodded and started walking towards the castle; everyone followed them. As they walked, penny looked down the single-track road they came from; it was in the middle of nowhere. They were somewhere in the south of Dumfries. Penny walked up to the Historic Scotland sign, which said "Caerlaverock Castle." She looked at the picture of the castle layout, and it was a surprise for her to know that it was in a triangle.

Penny followed the rest of them up to the white path that led towards the castle entrance. It had turrets on either side and the whole of the front. Looking at the front, it was in excellent condition. Apart from the growing moss and some stone turning white, it did well for its age. Walking through the entrance, it felt like going back in time; the stone felt cold and damp but something else.

As Penny walked in, she felt something that strengthened her, and she felt safer. That connection to their pursuer faded to nothing, and she couldn't feel them anymore. Penny walked down the wooden ramp that had been put in place for wheelchairs; something struck her. "Why aren't there any tourists around?" she thought. The place was empty. Trevor told them to wait with him while the elder went with the tour guide.

They stood in the courtyard while Penny looked around. She loved history, and this place was amazing. As she realized where she was, she excitedly told Katy the history of the castle.

"Katy, this place, it's the only castle of this shape. Clan Maxwell held it until 1700, when they abandoned it after the final siege. Although the Maxwell clan were lowlanders, they stayed Catholic, which allied them with the Jacobite's at one point." Penny said excitedly.

Trevor walked over and smiled, "Do you know what happened to the Fifth Earl of Nithsdale? They captured him during the Jacobite uprising, taking him to the Tower of London."

A cheeky smile crossed Trevor's face. It was the first time Penny had seen him smile.

"He was one of us, so we helped his wife smuggle him out of the tower." "While he was dressed as a woman," Penny responded.

At this, he burst out laughing. Penny and Katy laughed, but not nearly as hard as Trevor.

"Sometimes, our history mixes with outsiders' history. If the clan starts a war, we will help balance it."

Whatever this place is to Trevor, he was becoming a lot more relaxed, almost happy. He explained that one of the Norway tribe members founded the Clan Maxwell – Maccus Well. A lot of the clans were descended directly from the tribes; technically, everyone is, but over the millennia, people have spread, and their origins were forgotten. This was for the best; outsiders weren't ready yet.

"So why here?" Penny asked Trevor. She was feeling more confident in talking to him while he was in a good mood. He said, "You'll find out."

The elder was coming back. She beckoned everyone to come with her, and she led them into the keep to the left. The room was bare and had no roof; the windows were decorated with intricate patterns above each. There was a bricked-up fireplace, but apart from the rest, it was slowly being reclaimed by nature.

Moss and climbing plants were covering the walls. Katy turned to Penny and said, "Okay, the first time might make you sick, so just stay still and breathe; you'll be fine."

Before Penny could ask what she meant, Katy grabbed her hand, and everything around them flashed a blinding blue.

When Penny opened her eyes, she was still in the keep, but it definitely was not the same one she was in a second ago. The room had computer screens on the walls, some with a load of numbers and others with news channels. The flooring was of tiles. The fireplace was now operational, and it had a blue flame; Penny figured it must be the crystals. Then there was a group of three people who hadn't been there a moment ago. Among them, there was a man in white, and two behind him were in darker cream. He introduced himself as Elder John.

Elder John looked at the group, "Where's Shug?"

Penny suddenly realized they didn't know what had happened at the cottage. No one needed to say it. He found his answer in the visitor's faces.

Elder Claire stepped forward and said, "John, this is Penny, the descendant of Olivia, daughter of Isobel and the Light Bearer."

Penny blushed at the title from the elder, but based on what she had learned over the past few days, she figured it was right. She fought herself for liking it and instinctively resisted the feeling. She was enjoying the attention; she liked the thought of all that power; no one could ever hurt her again. She had never felt like she had any power before.

Katy let go of her hand and gave her a concerned look, almost as if she knew Penny's thoughts. Penny blushed again under Katy's gaze, "It's ok, your still human."

Penny suddenly felt panic as she thought Katy could hear her thoughts.

"Don't worry. I can feel your emotions when I hold your hand, but you'll learn to control that, and really it's okay. You'll learn to master your dark thoughts as well as your loving ones." Claire uttered.

Penny turned to the group, who were now talking feverishly, "Where am I? What is this place?"

Elder John turned to her and said, "You are exactly where you were a moment ago. The Hermit's blueprints gave us the technology to phase just slightly out of the normal dimension. We are still in our dimension. It would be catastrophic if we breached completely, but just enough to disappear and hide."

Penny thought for a moment, "You mean cloaked?" Everyone giggled. John said, "I guess that's a simpler way to put it. My assistants will take you to your quarters for the night."

The men in cream walked out without saying a word, and everyone hurried to catch up. Everyone had their own room, and it was amazing. Penny only just realized she hadn't ever been alone to work this out. Not even in the cave. That woman or thing appeared to her. She sat on the edge of the bed and let out a breath. She tried to calm her thoughts to contemplate the insanity of the previous days. When she exhaled, a scream came out with it, and she broke down into sobs. She couldn't get control of herself again. She was crying hysterically. Mark was dead – her uncle was dead. The person chasing them wanted to kill all of them. She was grieving, terrified, angry, and hatred was brewing; Katy ran into the room yelling, "Penny, Penny, it's okay, calm down. You need to calm down, or they'll sense your power and come."

Penny got hold of herself as Katy held her tight, soothing her. They sat like that for a while before anyone spoke.

"How can I use my power if I'm tracked by it?" Penny asked.

Katy sat up so she could see Penny's face. She said, "Elder Claire has taken you as her charge. She will train you to use it safely, keeping yourself hidden. There's still so much for you to learn; just give it time, and in the meantime, we all need to be careful."

Katy laid down on the bed and Penny laid next to her, and they fell asleep.

The two of them woke up several hours later, as they still held each other. There was an uncomfortable silence, both feeling instantly nervous. Penny wondered about Katy. She had stopped trusting men, but over the years, she craved something more from her female friends. She never explored it and focused on her work as a teacher. Now she was wondering how she felt about Katy, and she was wondering if Katy was having the same thoughts. Shaking her head, Penny stood up and walked away a few feet. She brushed herself down and decided this wasn't the right time for a relationship.

Katy smiled and walked over to Penny, took her hand, and smiled. Penny remembered when she touched someone, they could feel what she was feeling. Penny realized it went both ways, and she felt nervousness, excitement, and a fondness. They smiled at each other and moved closer, but before anything could progress, the building rumbled.

They both ran outside to the courtyard, and they could see back in the normal uncloaked world; someone in a dark robe and hood was standing there. Penny couldn't see the face, and he couldn't see them, but he had his hand outstretched, and the feeling in her gut told her he was the one chasing them.

"How did he find them?" Penny asked.

Elder John said that he was drawing power from the crystals that were being used to phase them. It was down to Penny now to do something. Everyone was watching her, seeing what she would do. Penny just stood there looking confused. They thought she was some kind of saviour. She was not; she was just a primary school teacher who couldn't even protect her pupils. Penny ran into the keep and to her quarters. She didn't know how any of this would work but knew she couldn't fight him. She felt his power as she hid.

#

Outside, everyone worked on keeping the cloak up. The two elders were using all of their strength and knowledge to stay hidden. If he found them, then it would be a slaughter, and they would have failed to bring the Light Bearer to New Pandora.

#

Penny sat breathing heavily, afraid and ashamed. She could feel the struggle outside; she could feel the two elders flowing their own life force into the cloak to keep it in place. She realized they were getting weaker the longer it went on. She became scared that they would lose the battle and be too weak to fight. Standing up, she concentrated on what she was feeling from outside and replicated it. She reinforced the cloak. Feeling the darkness outside, she hesitated but heard a voice in her head, it was her mother, saying, "Stay strong little light."

Penny screamed, and through a massive burst of energy, it threw the attacker backward against the wall. He looked injured and unsteady when he got to his feet. Looking around with confusion, he staggered away, but Penny had a suspicion he was just going outside to gather himself.

He'll be back but with force this time. They would be leaving today, taking on the last stretch of their journey. The crystals in the walls were recharging and recovering from the attack; Penny could feel it.

Penny felt everything; when he was done absorbing the crystal energy, he became more powerful. She must ask the elder about that. For now, she needed to rest, and they needed to come up with an escape plan.

Chapter 18:
Prey

Alex felt powerful after absorbing the crystals. Now, as he turned his attention to the cottage and reached out with his charged senses, he could feel every atom in the small structure. His senses were this way for some time now after the crystals.

Suddenly, Alex realized he could smell them! Five separate people. He went through the rooms looking for clues. There was a familiar smell, but he couldn't place it. It frustrated him.

Every part of this place gave him déjà vu. He decided there wasn't anything left to gain from it. He went outside, sent a pinch of his energy over to the building and watched it burn.

Elliot had spent years studying his energy; everyone had it, but 99% of people couldn't access it. The Operator unlocked his potential; the Shaitan was all-powerful and had his complete devotion. In return, they have unlocked his full potential.

He remembered when he first woke up; he felt every inch of his being, every sense, heightened. They spent years training him, except it wasn't years. To him, it was decades, but they had returned him to the point they took him. Existing outside of time, their reach was endless. Locked away, they needed their followers to enact their will.

181

Over those years with the Shaitan, he learned what it was to be a god. He learned how the Seraph had feared the power of the Shaitan and tricked them into their prison. How their jailor Angel saw the injustice of what they did and turned. Now he understood the callous nature of the Seraph and what they had planned for Angel, now the Shaitan's Operator on Earth.

Now he was their assassin. He spent his earlier life being afraid; his dad used to drink, beating the shit out of him. His mum left, abandoning him. He wasn't close with her, anyway. Throughout his life, the only truths he knew were pain and fear. Taking himself through life until he got into a car crash, his mentor, The Operator, saved him. Humanity was just lies and filth; everyone had their darkness and secrets. Seeing everyone for who they are is a curse and an edge in most situations. The Operator took him under his wing; Alex wanted his approval and wanted to please him.

Alex felt something in the cottage. It was the same power he took from the cave. He would do the same with them as he did with the cave. Suck it dry until ash was all that was left. He waited for his instructions. It came as a text "follow and capture, only kill her protectors, I want the girl alive."

Alex smiled. He found out his target was a woman and that she had power if she was the one from the cottage. He put on his hooded cloak. He liked his cloak. He had a flair for the dramatic, and it fitted the part. The fear of others; so much more intense when they couldn't see the face of their killer.

182

Alex used the connection to the cave crystals to track the girl. She absorbed their energy when she interacted with the cave. Then, he took what she left, and now there was a connection that would act as a GPS. It surprised him to make a connection so quickly. There was no resistance from the person's subconscious. Almost as if her subconscious trusted him. She might have power, but she was weak. Alex climbed onto a motorbike and followed the trail.

He followed his prey to Inverness, driving over the Kessock Bridge until he could almost smell her again. And again, déjà vu!

He couldn't shake the feeling, but concentrating on his hatred as the Shaitan had taught him, he pushed it out.

They were still here. He stopped a little further north. They had left the main road at one point but carried on. Now he was driving towards the town centre. Something caught his attention, and he went around the roundabout and into a B&Q car park.

Alex looked through the parked cars. He couldn't tell if they were still here. There were too many people.

He saw a burger van and went over to it. A child told its mummy to look at the monk, pointing at Alex. He was in the cue, and in front of him, there was a woman speaking to a little girl, "We'll jump on a plane. Have you ever been on a plane before Kim?"

The girl never replied; she wasn't happy about something. "It's okay, Kim. We'll get you home to your mum soon."

Alex sniffed the air and recognized the scent from the cottage. He couldn't tell if it was the girl and the woman; his senses were going back to normal. The high from the crystals was fading.

Anyway, he knew neither of these people was who he was hunting for, neither they had power, although the girl had something about her. She didn't have power, but perhaps potential.

Alex left them alone and reported back to his master, informing them of what he had learned. There was a girl called Kim, who was being escorted by an unknown woman, and they were getting on a plane today.

Another team would pick them up. He uploaded pictures of them, which he took and got back onto his bike. A few people were pointing at him. Well, it must be an odd sight for people to see someone dressed as a monk on a bike.

He went south, hit the road to Perth, and opened up his throttle. The connection wasn't fading as it should. It should have had the same lifespan as his extra senses, but he could still feel her. His hatred of her was building that was directly proportional to the longer the connection stayed. Maybe that was what was powering it.

They were at an impressive distance in front of him now. It was more like echoes than a solid connection now. It looked as if distance affected it. He must remember that. He thought back to his early weeks with The Clan. His mentor wouldn't let him off the leash for some time. He didn't trust him, and Alex didn't trust his mentor. It took time before they bonded.

Now, he was the father that Alex deserved. They went on a mission together, where they had to assassinate a militia leader in the Congo Jungle; things needed to heat up over there.

The world had forgotten the civil wars. His mentor got hurt, took five bullets to the chest; he was immortal but could be incapacitated. His body was constructed of the same stuff as everyone else. If it was damaged, it needed to heal, and that would take time. This happened once before as well. A few centuries ago, the Shaitan showed him as part of his history lessons.

The Tribe had him cornered. They used arrows and swords that were made from crystal resin. They hurt him enough to drop him to the floor, took one of their swords and cut his arms and legs off and over his head. It took The Clan nearly a century to found him.

It took one of them to rise and unlock their own potential. Had risen in power and found where the body parts were hidden. He put them back together, and The Operator healed when his arms attached themselves and his head. He could move but was weak after all this time. His saviour went to him and offered his life up. The Operator choked the life out of him, absorbed his energy, and used it to finish healing. He took the lives of three more operatives before he was back to full power.

Back in the Congo, Alex pulled him to safety, removed the bullets, and guarded his body. While he was recovering, they had time to talk. They talked about Angel and about The Operative. They discussed Alex's life and his family. During this period, Alex would bring local villagers that he had kidnapped to feed his mentor. When he was back to strength, they finished the mission, and from that point on, they had a bond that no one could break.

Alex was the only person on this planet The Operative would refuse energy from. It even surprised him to develop a fondness for him. He was to be a means to an end and was the secret weapon against The Tribe, the only person who the Light Bearer would never strike down. Her own brother, Alex, was closing in now. He had passed Dumfries and headed south still.

He realized they were heading for an old castle that was built by their ancestors. When their precious tunnels collapsed over time, it forced them to the surface. They mined the collapsed cave rock to build their castles and cottages. They put the crystal throughout the building, these wards of the darkness and its minions, but it would be a power source for him.

He walked up the narrow path towards the door and was amused to see a cannon sitting outside the gate. He wondered if the Tribe remembered why it was a rectangle. They discovered that certain wards and shapes increased the defensive properties of the crystals. He walked into the courtyard and looked around. He couldn't see anyone but could sense many people.

He stretched out his arms and went to his knees. Alex sucked the life out of all the crystal in the walls. He sensed something else. There were people here, but how? They were invisible in front of him but out of his reach. He increased his pull on the crystals.

They were resisting him all this time. The crystals were defending themselves, or someone was defending them. It was a battle of wills, and he would win. The more they struggled, the more information he gained. Some ancient minds were pitting themselves against him.

Then there was a power that caught him off guard, something that took him by surprise.

The next thing he knew, he was flying into the wall, and picking himself up and walking out of the courtyard. He reported this to his mentor. They weren't going anywhere; he had them cornered. He decided to come back with numbers. He got the food from his carry-on from the bike and called The Operator.

"I've found them, and you won't believe what I've found out!" He said.

Chapter 19:
An Ancient War

There was a flurry of activity as everyone was running to prepare. The Clan had never detected them before. Penny just felt like she wanted to sleep, she felt the exhaustion was catching up to her, and her exertion against the hooded man left her drained. She could feel the energy coursing through her, but only faintly now.

Katy joined her with a look of concern on her face. Penny was white, and her eyes looked withdrawn.

"You need to rest. We're packing up. I'll come to get you when it's time." Elder Claire came in behind her and sat next to Penny on the bed. Katy made her excuses and left.

The Elder turned to Penny with a weak smile on her face. "You look tired dear, you used up almost all of your energy fighting him," she said.

The elder didn't look much better herself. She looked exhausted too. Penny responded, "Don't worry about me; you lay down, elder."

Penny was beckoning Elder Claire to lie down on the bed. Laying down, the elder replied, "This conversation would be easier if you call me Claire."

Penny felt like a stone had hit the bottom of her stomach. She suddenly had a horrible feeling about this. "Lay down next to me, Penny; we will wonder the dream realm together," Claire said.

Penny did as she was told, and before too long, both women were fast asleep.

Outside the room, there was panic in the air. No one could remember the last time The Clan had discovered any of the cells. Not since they had created the phasing technology, the one they used to cloak.

Katy found Trevor in the courtyard. "Who was that?" She asked.

Trevor looked thoughtful, sniffing at the air as if the smell of dung from the fields could give him a clue.

"I'm not sure, but he wielded the power of the ancient ones," he responded.

Katy was looking confused. She asked, "what do you mean?"

Trevor began telling Katy about some of the earliest histories of The Tribe. He told her, "All myth and legend have a basis. We used to use the crystals for our daily life routine work or in a way that would be described as closest to magic. Our ancestors found out that if they train with it in a different manner, the use of crystals could be much more than just to cater to daily household chores. After some training, they realized they could use some abilities that were similar to the Light Bearers. After some time, I started doing simple things, like create fire and tricks for kids. During the original war with The Clan, our ancestors discovered that they could take energy from crystals as well, and this amplified their abilities and senses

for a short time. They then took bags on their backs into battle filled with crystals. These magical battles turned the tide of

the war. The clan was shocked, unable to comprehend what just happened, and thus couldn't combat it. Then Angel appeared. This was the first time when the man who was leading The Clan showed his face. He was being called The Operator at that point."

#

Penny was now in dreamland. She was in the past again. However, she wasn't alone this time; Claire was with her. They were standing between two vast armies.

"This was the last battle of the original war," Claire pointed to one side, "The operator and his Clan are over there; our ancestors knew him as Angel." She continued.

The opposing army was much, much smaller, but Penny could sense an immense power coming from them. Suddenly, both women were standing on a cliff overlooking—the battle.

Claire was silent, whereas Penny didn't know what to ask or say, so they just watched. A lot of discussions were going on among The Tribe ranks, along with pointing shouts of "the traitor" and "the hermit."

Penny recognized the latter name and understood Angel was the hermit.

The Clan sent a part of their force forward, marching as they banged their swords on shields. They looked as organized as Romans and as fierce as the warriors of Sparta. They edge closer and closer; Penny could see them better now – big muscular men and women. Their bodies were painted with what looked like blood; it was easier to hear them, whereas scarier to look at them.

The Tribe forces were unflinching, standing their ground, and no opposing force being sent out to meet them. Then the Clan forces broke into a run, instantly changing into an arrowhead formation. The arrows had put away their swords, and now, they were just holding their shields, charging at the line like a battering ram. The first person of each row in the arrowhead did the same. They would charge and break the line in the middle. Suddenly, they started bursting into blue flame starting from the front of the arrowhead. Penny could feel the power flowing from The Tribe. It wasn't just one of them, but they were all using the same power like hers.

Turning to Claire, Penny commented, "I'm not the only one who can do this?" The arrowhead had now destroyed everyone, and a few survivors who were left were now running back.

As they reached their line, a man walked forward, the ground rumbled, and the frontline of The Tribe came flying forward, bursting into clouds of ash. Penny was watching all the scenes carefully and was flabbergasted by all of it.

Penny felt the energy from the ash flood over to the man. It felt like he suddenly became ten times more powerful. He then clapped his hands together, and a sound similar to a clap of thunder emerged. It echoed through the valley, and the entire Tribe army flew backwards except for a Woman, who stepped forward and looked into that man's eyes, locked into a battle of wills.

Then The Operator threw energy across the battlefield, and she reciprocated their energy attacks, cancelling his out. They were locked together, and it looked as if they were in a tug of war but pushing with their energy instead of pulling the rope.

Claire told Penny, "The girl's name was Olivia, the very first Light Bearer, who led us; she was a daughter of Eve." There were lightning strikes that were sparking off the energy between the two.

Penny could feel the hatred between them, and it caught her by surprise.
she never expected that she would feel such hate from Olivia.

Something started happening behind Olivia, and the army was back on its feet. They all were holding crystals in their hands, absorbing the energy releasing from them. It perplexed penny; she remembered that she took energy from the surrounding crystals as well to fight the hooded man, but this was on a much larger scale.

She felt a sudden coldness from the army and the crystals became ash, just like the frontline that had just died at the hands of The Operator. This tipped the balance of the battle in their favour.

They all put their hands on the shoulders of the people who were in front of them. This kept on going, and Olivia was the last person who was at the receiving end, absorbing all of that energy. Her power spiked beyond anything that Penny could comprehend. It was as if she was a giant.

The Operator faltered as he suddenly started looking afraid. The lightning strikes were now monstrous and seemed to arch off deep into the ground.

Then the earthquake came, splitting the ground into two, separating the two enemies by a massive land movement. The battle stopped as both armies got swallowed by the ground.

Pandora was angry as well. It felt like the end of the world was here. Claire shouted over the noise, "This was the moment when Pandora was split into many continents, making the planet Earth what we know today. It was the moment that became knows as the end of the world. Both sides took heavy losses this day and not from each other."

Penny watched all of it as both armies became swallowed up by the ground. They were just gone, along with Olivia and The Operator.

"Unfortunately, The Operator survived, just like he survived all the time. It seemed like he can't even die."

"We learned a painful lesson on this day. The crystals were living beings of the purest form, and that's why they've got such potent energy. When we absorbed their energy into ourselves, we committed a crime against nature and the gifts that had been given. Pandora took its revenge on us. This disaster was ours. We took our enemy with us, though, and at least we had that; we were satisfied because of that at least. The war was over, but both factions survived through time. The Operator is still out there, and he wants another war. His tactics have changed and have become more insidious. He's infiltrated most governments throughout the centuries. We stopped him once and had peace for one hundred years before they found him again." Claire told Penny Everything.

Suddenly, Penny and Claire found themselves at the bottom of the green valley again. Time had frozen up, and everything stopped. "Penny, what's in front of you is a marathon, not a sprint. There will be many battles on many fronts. He is calculating and callous." Claire mentioned.

"We are not as innocent either as the history books tell. This secret was only known by the elders of the tribes. It is forbidden to use crystals in this way, and this is why they can never find out what you did here, and no matter what, you must not do it again. There are no shortcuts to success, the power you gather this way is not yours to use. And this is why you need to build your power naturally to defeat your enemies." Claire said to Penny.

Penny became confused again. She said, "I felt so much hatred coming from Olivia."

Claire was looking directly at Penny. She said, "This is a very important thing. In fact, this is something the others will never tell you, so let me have the honour to tell you this; your power comes from both the dark and the light. You see, your heart is human, and thus, it is capable of wielding both powers. You just have to be aware of both powers. Remember, it is our actions that tell us whether we are good, not the power behind our actions."

"You're an unknown element because you grew up away from us, and because of that, most will not trust your intentions; they will find it hard to accept your actions and will doubt your intentions the moment they find something that is not according to their expectations or ways. To fight, you will have to kill; and to kill, you must be capable of hate things that despise you. You're not a part of some mythical fairy-tale. There is no oath to do no harm. And to keep the darkness where it belongs, you will need to decide first who you are. They will try to recruit you, and for that, they will confuse you with what's real. Remember, the enemy is cunning." Claire explained to Penny.

"I need to rest now, and it's time for you to wake up, dear. I regret I won't be able to join you on the rest of this journey. It seems like I spent too much energy fighting the hooded man. I suspect he's someone you've encountered before. I don't know if you have noticed this or not, but there was a unity in your energies when they converged." Claire said his final words before leaving the dream.

This confused penny, who only remembered a hooded man, stood out, asked, "What do you mean? You're coming with us, aren't you?"

Claire just smiled and said, "In some form or other, but for now, it's time for me to rest."

Everything all around just swooped into the darkness, and Penny quickly woke up, right next to Claire. She was still breathing, but as Penny tried to wake her up, she wouldn't wake up. She worriedly ran outside to get some help. On her way to the main hall, she found Trevor and Katy talking in the courtyard. "Come quickly; it's Claire!".

Penny was out of breath.

Chapter 20:
The Escape

Katy and Trevor come running into the keep haphazardly. Trevor ran to the Elder's side. He screamed, "Claire, CLAIRE!"

The Elder didn't wake up, "She's still alive." Katy said, "She's just unconscious."

Trevor ordered Katy, "Go, get a stretcher."

As she came up with a stretcher, they carried her to the tunnels. They both carried the Elder out, and Penny followed them. She was not sure what to say. The air suddenly shimmered, and it became difficult to breathe. Something was in the air that Penny's body wanted to reject; it was something heavy and unnatural.

At that time, Someone else has arrived, someone much more powerful than the hooded man and her.

\#

Elder John was in the courtyard already and was uncovering a trapdoor, "These are smuggling tunnels that run to the coast. When we reach the coast, boats will be there, prepared and ready, waiting to take us to Wales. For now, we need to hold on.

Trevor smiled, "I've rigged a surprise for him; he won't be following us."

Elder John told Penny to take over from Trevor. "Take Claire through the tunnels first."

Before Penny could even object or understand why he asked her this, Trevor had handed his half of the stretcher off to her. Under the hatch, there were stairs, and taking the weight of the stretcher, descended Penny. There were torches in the walls as well. It was an excellent opportunity to practice. She concentrated on each one, and they all alighted. She noticed explosives rigged to the entrance and stairs. This must be Trevor's surprise; it made sense to cave in the entrance. She just hoped he knew what he was doing. Or else, they might find themselves buried under a ton of rock.

The people from the Tribe's cell followed them behind and got into the cave. They made their way through the

Tunnels, and as they progressed forward, Penny ignited each torch to light the way forward.

"Good thing you're here," Katy said to Penny.

"I'm starting to get the hang of it now, but not sure what we were doing," Penny responded.

They moved further forward, and they ran out of torches; it was just blackness ahead.

"Can you make a ball of light in front of you? I've read about the Light Bearers and what they can do; I'm certain I've read

that somewhere." Katy asked Penny.

Penny concentrated on his energy and tried to channel it, but nothing was happening. She regretted getting cocky now.

"Just take energy and imagine a ball of light in front of you. Don't forget it needs to be fed; so image it has a power cord like a lamp, which's energy is leading through you." Ketty suggested.

Penny concentrated again, but rather than just concentrating his energy to channel through her hand, she thought about a small ball of light floating just ahead of them. As she exhaled a deep calm breath, a small ball of light just appeared in front of them, illuminating the surrounding area. It started as a small marble and gradually grew, swirling like a blown flame contained within a bubble. Penny said excitedly, "I can do magic."

They carried on walking forward. "Katy, how did you know to do that?" Penny asked.

Katy was quiet for a moment, then after deep thought, she said, "Growing up in New Pandora, where we're headed. It fascinated me; the tales of the Light Bearer are bedtime stories for most children they used to tell us. Well, I took it one step further. I read everything I could find, questioned Elder Claire repeatedly. So you could say meeting you was a lifelong dream."

Penny felt she was under pressure again. They thought she was this saviour, which she believed she was not. She hadn't even decided yet if she was going to stay with them or not. However, there hadn't been time to think; it had been one disaster after another. Suddenly, there was an explosion behind them. The tunnel shook under their feet. Penny felt the rocks hitting her head and heard a few screams from behind her. For a moment, she thought the tunnels were collapsing, but they stood intact. Penny cursed Trevor under her breath, but it wasn't like he did it on purpose.

It felt as if hours had passed since they started walking. They finally reached the shoreline and came out of the tunnels. Penny and Katy put down the stretcher to rest. Hours had been passed, and it was nighttime now. They looked around for the boats, but there wasn't any waiting. Penny watched as people came out. There were more people than she remembered, but not all of them made out safely.

#

After some time, Elder John and Trevor came out as well. Trevor gave Penny and Katy a nod before flashing a light into the Darkness. After a few minutes, four speedboats came to shore. They placed Elder Claire onto the boat first. They carried the supplies they brought to the ship, and then the people hopped onto the ships as well.

Penny sat next to Katy. They hadn't got the opportunity to talk about their moment in the keep. Something happened there, which they wanted

to share with each other, but both were too nervous about discussing it. At one point, their pinkies brushed, and Katy took Penny's hand. They held hands and watched the stars as the boat sped across the water, heading towards Wales. This time, though Penny kept her feelings to herself, she found that her abilities were coming intuitively now as she used her powers more and more.

She was learning to trust Katy but just wasn't ready. As she was got used to her energy, she grew a sense of how to guard herself. She looked at Katy. She had no-nonsense hair tied in a knot and sharp features. There was a smile on her face, and she looked happy. Worries and distant, but there was happiness in it as well.

"Kim will already be in London, won't be long now." Penny didn't really know, but she felt like she needed to say something.

The boats made landfall on a beach in north Wales near Flint. There, they found more smuggler tunnels that led to Flint's castle. Penny was drained out of energy, but she still pushed on. All she could think of was just to go home to fall on her bed.

She could still feel the hatred from whoever was pursuing her, but she had told no one that Uncle Shug had said that Elliot was alive or what he told her about her mother. She had no idea what he meant but believed that she would only find him if she stuck around. Also, she was enjoying being around Katy; she wasn't looking for a relationship, but maybe they could be close.

They all entered the tunnels, and Trevor took the stretcher back from Penny. Penny lit the way.

She confusingly asked Trevor, "How come the Phantoms haven't come while I've been doing this?"

Trevor, who has limited knowledge about this, and was unsure of what to respond, thought for a moment and said, "Two reasons, one because we are underground and there are crystals here surrounding us, it keeps things well hidden. The second reason is, they aren't sentient, not in the way you think. They are puppets of something bigger, and it can only focus its attention for a limited time."

They finally reached the ruined castle. This one was in a much worse state than the one in Scotland. In that massive darkness, Penny could see some headlights flashing in the distance. Trevor came out of the hatch, saying, "Good, our ride is here as well."

Someone walked towards them, and Trevor walked ahead and got into a conversation with him; Katy followed and joined them. Katy suddenly dropped to her knees, screaming. Penny ran over to her and asked what the matter was?

"They have Kim!" Katy sobbed.

Penny stepped back in shock as well. Kim was supposed to be safe.

"What? How did this happen?" She asked shockingly.

The stranger explained, "When we went to meet them at the airport, we couldn't find them. We then found her escort, Jean, on the toilet floor, strangled. Realizing what had happened, we left before someone else discovered her body."

"Not Kim; she's only a child!" Trevor expressed; his voice was low and dangerous, and he was clenching his fists.

Penny felt it too, not just her own feelings, but she felt everything, everything everyone was feeling. Her guard had dropped as she was overwhelmed by the flood of emotion. It was like she was under some psychic attack.

She couldn't beat it anymore and ran off into the distance; not knowing what to do or how to shut it off, she just reacted. She stopped when she felt the emotion fade. Then she realized that the guilt was hers. It was because of her they were in this mess. It was because of her they were in danger. She felt like she was stabbed in her chest with a dull blade. She hit the ground sobbing. The stranger walked over to Penny and put her hand on Penny's shoulder. "I'm Anna…" she started; Penny let out a breath that sounded more like a sob.

At that moment, the idea popped into her mind – If she just stayed here, stayed like this, and didn't move at all, she would be okay. I just stayed here and didn't go any further. Her body was shaking; it was ready to break. Suddenly, it went dark.

Penny woke up in the back with Katy; she hadn't stopped crying. When she saw Penny awake again, she leaned over and put her head on Penny's shoulder. Penny just took her in her arms and held her tight. Trevor was in the passenger seat in the front.

He started explaining about New Pandora, "We find it in the old cave network. Wales has one of the biggest concentrations of the original tunnels in the world. It was where the original chamber of the Council of Elders sat and still sits today. It's hidden by the same technology as the castle was, and not many know about it still today. This allows us to coexist with the residents. Where they see a bricked-up entrance, we have a doorway. Where they see an empty tunnel, we are using it. And where there they see rock and dirt, we've excavated of the centuries and millennia to create the city of New Pandora."

As Trevor was done explaining the network of tunnels and Tribe cells around the world, she realized there was a world hidden from view. It had always been here, watching us.

Chapter 21:
New Pandora

After a while, they arrived somewhere called Poachers Cave in Cilcave. Trevor explained it was almost as old as the planet. In fact, the locals even thought that it was haunted.

"That's kinda our fault; they sensed us there even if they can't see it.
They think it's cursed." Trevor continued explaining.

Anna was smirking as she listened. Penny saw a hint of mischief, memories from a miss spent youth.

When they finally reached their destination, they got out of the cars and grabbed their stuff. Trevor was carrying Elder Claire now. As they got out of the car, the cars left, leaving them in total darkness that surrounded them. It was so dark. They couldn't even see each other or even their own hands. The only way to know the presence was each other's voices.

The caves were dark and wet. Water was dripping from the roof. Penny was carefully walking and had to watch her footing, and the entrance was very narrow, so she had to make sure she didn't get herself bumped into the cave walls.

Anna explained that fossils from the seabed had made up the ground. Looking through a small passage to the right, she could see a small stream of water, and it was trickling into the cave.

When they got out, they reached an enormous cavern. It had a spiky thing up top. Anna carried on explaining this ahead, "That's called a chandelier for obvious reasons. It slowly dripped water rich in calcium and other minerals. That was what created the formations, you see."

Penny walked over to a large mound that had developed under the chandelier. As the water dripped, the minerals formed a structure reaching up. It looked like two fingers trying to pinch together.

She saw it was hollow. Anna smiled and said, "Go for it. I'll meet you on the other side." Penny grabbed a torch. Trevor warned her not to use any powers here since they'll be sticking around, and those people could detect her power if used. Going into the entrance, Penny slowly made her way through. She felt the same bright blue flash from before at the castle, and then a lot of noise came from nowhere. Penny realized that she was no longer inside the rock formations, and the whole cavern had disappeared.

They were on a platform. Anna giggled hard and said, "Sorry, I couldn't resist."

"You must be careful of that one. She likes to play tricks," a voice warned her. Then a group of men and women had appeared. They all were in white. The one that warned her walked towards them, and Anna made a run for him.

"Sorry, dad, you know me," Anna said as she threw her arms around the Elder.

Penny realized she was still bent over like she was going through a cave. She immediately straightened herself up, looking around, making sure nobody had seen her in that stupid position.

The men in white moved to greet her, "My name is Jacob, and this is Margaret, Ishabel, Francis, Jim, and Grant."

The others nodded as he called their name; some smiled while others gave nothing away.

"Trevor will take you to your quarters, and we will summon you when we are ready," Jacob said, and they walked away and left the new arrivals on the platform. Anna left the group and followed her dad, talking excitedly, almost skipping.

Penny looked around at her new home. It was bigger than anyone could have imagined. She was speechless. It was like an underground city, something straight out of a sci-fi movie. There were massive structures built into the walls. As far as her eyes could see, the long tubes were connecting them with lights flowing through. She couldn't see them, but she wondered if it was a train network.

"It's one piece of technology we gave the outsiders, underground trains," Trevor said as he walked up behind her.

She looked over to Katy, who was talking urgently with someone.

"I think we should leave her for now; she'll find her, don't worry," Trevor commented. "She's better than me at tracking."

Trevor picked up some luggage and asked Penny to follow.

As they followed. Penny turned around to look at Katy, who was still talking, and gestured her to move ahead and that she would catch them up. They went into the nearest structure. Taking Penny into an elevator, he informed her that they had assigned her elder quarters; she was their most honoured guest.

"You're going to be very comfortable, and these are the biggest quarters we have." Penny grimaced, "You keep referring to them as quarters; sounds so military." Trevor chuckled and shrugged.

Trevor kept silent for a long time. They walked out of the elevator and moved to another platform. Every single person who they passed stopped and looked at her. Some people even turned and gave her a half bow.

"It's the whites. They're confused because you are so young, whereas they are used to see old goats in those," Trevor said.

"What colour do you wear?" Penny asked.

"I don't, never liked rules," Trevor commented.

They reached the platform. Penny kept sensing there was something wrong with Trevor; she asked, "Trevor, you're not saying much, I mean even less than usual."

"This thing with Kim being missing, it reminds me of something," He told Penny.

Penny remembered Katy explaining about Trevor's family being killed.

Standing on a platform of a train station, she looked down to the tracks, but they weren't there. In their place, two lines indented slightly from the ground.

"Magnets," an unfamiliar voice said.

Penny and Trevor turned around and saw Elder Margaret standing there. The train arrived before they could say anything else. It was so quiet; Penny didn't even notice it. A magnetic rail track, no friction reduced the resistance, and this increased the speed and fuel efficiency. Penny remembered the concept from a science article on one being attempted in Japan.

They all boarded the train.

The Elder sat next to Penny. She was uneasy at how close she sat. However, she just knew she had no choice, and there was nowhere else to go. She couldn't help but think of the warning that Claire gave her in the dream, that there would be a fraction of elders who wouldn't trust or support her straight away because she was not raised among them.

#

"So you are the one?" Margaret's voice was low and calculating.

Penny just nodded and said, "They seem to think so."

"Arrogant to boot."

Penny suddenly realized that this elder was in the opposing camp.

"We'll see what you are made off. When you have rested and fed, come to the elder council chambers. You will receive a seat as our equal. Unfortunately, it's your birth right." Margaret said.

Penny coughed. She was choked at the surprise.

"Yes, I felt like choking, but we voted at our last full session, and, well, you already seem to have some supporters."

Margaret said and turned her face to Trevor, "Trevor, you will take Elder Claire's seat to represent her until she is well again."

With that, the elder got up. By this time, the train had reached a stop, and she left the train at that stop.

Penny also stood up to get out of it, but Trevor stopped her and said, "Our stop is the next one."

Looking at Trevor, Penny figured he was just as shocked as her.

"I'm no politician, Penny," Trevor commented.

"Well, neither am I, so I believe we will make a good pair. Also, what is the council? I mean, I know what it is in principle, but I know nothing about life down here." Penny expressed her fear.

Trevor smiled awkwardly, "I guess it's the same as it is anywhere, arguments and politics, you know."

They reached their stop and got out of the train. The platform was bustling with people as they tried to make their way through. Penny smelt a fragrance; she could tell it was Lilies, but surely not down here.

They moved ahead, and she almost bumped into a group of gossiping teenage girls.

"Sorry," she excused and moved forward.

Things aren't really all that different down here. The surrounding people looked normal, wearing normal clothes, and seemed to have normal lives.

Feeling butterflies in her stomach, she followed Trevor over to some structures built into the rock. It reminded her of Petra in Jordon.

"These quarts.. eh homes," Trevor smiled; "have been here since the beginning." He continued.

Penny put her hand to the wall. It felt rough and cold. She almost thought it would talk to her if she stayed long enough.

Walking through the entrance, she saw a large circular room with three other doorways.

"This is where you'll be staying," Trevor said.

Looking around, Penny's eyes went wide. Overcome with excitement, she ran forward and went straight ahead through the door. Instantly, her senses were in a state of amazement.

The room smelled of cinnamon, and it reminded Penny of Christmas. The fireplace was already alight, warming the air. The glow felt so good against her skin after the past few days. The chairs felt soft and filled the room. Too many for her, but they must be for guests. She carried on into the next room, which was the kitchen.

She found a strange-looking man with a mix of surprise and nerves on his face. Penny instantly thought they had made a terrible mistake and walked into the wrong home.

"Miss?" The man said.

He got onto his unsteady feet, almost falling over himself. Trevor came in the running behind Penny and said, "So you met Leon?" Trevor asked.

The awkwardness between them wasn't going away.

"He's your helper. He will keep the place clean and will cook for you." Trevor said.

Penny was uncomfortable, "No, I don't want a servant."

Leon cleared his throat, "Miss, I'm one of the best-compensated workers; serving you is the highest honour of my life". Blushing, penny apologized, "I'm honoured by you," she did not understand why she said that and immediately regretted it.

Trevor offered to show her to her room. They walked back through the round room and through another door.

"I'll come back for you in an hour and take you to the council; then the actual battle begins," he grinned and left.

Her room was enormous, with large crystals all over the room, producing lights, and with her own fireplace. This one wasn't lit, and the air felt cold.

There was a bowl of water on a table. Penny suddenly felt afraid after she realized that she hadn't been alone since the cave; Katy had always been with her in all the situations. All her thoughts were with Katy, and it was her she missed and longed for.

Chapter 22:
The Siege

Alex was pacing as he talked to himself, "How can you be so stupid?" He started hitting himself in the head.

The castle looked untouched. The call with The Operator didn't go well. "So you failed? She was in the castle, and you couldn't stop her. She doesn't even know her own power yet, and she bested you!"

Alex was getting his reinforcements, and his mentor was coming as well. Alex was listing the questions in his head so he could respond to them later. The field of energy was like nothing he had seen before. Before today, his power was only matched by his mentor. How could he be beaten? That energy spike entered him without resistance, like when he connected to the girl. There wasn't any defence. He'll need to make a note of that for next time.

Three large Land Rovers appeared from nowhere and came to a halt behind him; The Operator got out of the first one before it headed back up to block the road.

"Alex, why do you keep failing me? Was it a hard mission? This was simple, extract the girl and bring her to me. What could go wrong that you failed to do" Alex lowered his head with no answer; he was speechless and felt like a teenager being scolded by his father.

"Tell me what happened?" The Operator asked.

Alex, still speechless, looked up again and said, "I'm not sure; I felt her power but couldn't see her. I started to try and sense where she was hiding when I felt that power field. Then I could feel all of them up; there was a whole-cell up there, just out of reach."

The Operator had become aware that The Tribe had come up with a way to hide themselves up from the darkness. This was one successful way to blind him, and it kept working for all this time, and he wasn't even aware of it. He had never come across it before, though and was intrigued, which is why he came personally. He wasn't really angry with Alex, but he needed to be kept on his toes.

The hair on his arms felt on edge. He could feel the mini-battle between Alex and Penny still settling. It always reminded him of old train sets when the electrics get too hot. Looking up at the battlements, he remembered the great battle he was at was fought here too.

In 1640, the Maxwells, who were descended from the bloodline of Eve, were guarding their most valuable secret. They had taken refuge in their stronghold, this rectangular castle; it was the most ambitious building of the time, typical of The Tribe showcasing their technology.

The siege lasted about thirteen weeks. Eventually, they surrendered. The Operator oversaw forty Maxwells put to the sword. The history books stated that according to Sir Henry Vane, the Earl and Countess of Nithsdale and their page were allowed to escape. This is what really happened.

It was the final day of the siege. The explosions were running out over the field, and the mote around the castle was red with blood. The sky had been black for the last few days; it seemed like the darkness was drawing in, attracted to the blood.

The Operator smiled, enjoying his ally's assistance. He could feel the fear building within the castle walls as people were terrorized and hunted by Trisks.

The Trisks were the darknesses muscle. When enough blood is spilt, and there is enough suffering, the darkness becomes strong, strong enough to manifest these creatures.

The blood, along with the dirt in the ground creating mud. The Trisks take form out of this blood-soaked mud and wield a heavy sword; nothing can withstand them. The

Wraths swoop down from the sky, tails of scorpions and sharp short swords. Stinging a slashing their victims, or just lifting them into the sky with their large wings and letting go of them to make them fall on the ground.

After a few days of this, the occupant's signalled that they had had enough, and they couldn't take it anymore. They wanted to come out. They even considered death; this would be better than the terrors that came through this eternal night.

The armies moved forward and were ready to take possession of the castle.

To this day, no one knew how, but the earl, his wife, and his daughter escaped. The daughter was the one who they were interested in, and because of whom, the whole battle happened.

The Operator slowly walked behind the Soldiers of the clan. There was a rumble and some small bangs; the Operator fell through the ground. He was in a cavern, surrounded by crystals, and before he could understand or react, a long thin sword made from our crystal sliced clean through his neck. His head had hit the ground before he realized it was a trap.

He watched helplessly as they cut off each limb and boxed him up like luggage. Then for the next hundred years, all there was, was darkness until his loyal Clan found him.

A young man he had never met, but one who followed his teaching gathered enough power to track him.

It took time and the life force of his many followers to fully regain his strength, and since then, he kept himself away from the frontline.

Too much of a target unless something needs his personal attention. His immortality had become a curse, being trapped in that box, but his loyal followers who willingly let him drain their energy to heal were a true gift. He had started with the gifted boy that found him, that was also tactical. He might have been a competition.

A big hairy man, who looked like Hagrid from Harry Potter, came across, holding a rifle in hand.

"The offices are clear, commander," he said. In response, all he got was a nod.

The Operator was consumed in thought.

"Something felt familiar about this." He said to himself.

The large castle from the front was almost identical to how he remembers it; the platforms at the top were partially guarded for archers— the large arch over the centre with the

Maxwell crest above. The two turrets were on either side of the entrance and felt like that old trap all over again.

He cautiously walked towards this medieval marvel; he was always impressed with the architecture of The Tribe. He'd heard descriptions of their ancient city underground, New Pandora, but had never seen it; he wasn't even sure if that place did exist or were just rumours. He also heard that it was a marvel of technology and engineering, and over the centuries, it was just getting larger and larger.

He still hadn't narrowed down exactly where it was yet, but he had a few educated guesses. "With the age of this city, it must be within one of the original channels of the tunnel," he assumed.

However, there was a problem with that as well, as they were scattered around the planet, just like the Clan and the Tribe.

Penny must be safe behind its gates by now and was probably out of his reach. He suddenly found himself in the courtyard; he had been walking but so lost in thought, his legs had taken over.

The air was almost crackling from the efforts of earlier, but it had a stillness that made him suspicious. He couldn't feel this energy or field that Alex talked about. However, Alex had his left hand in front of him as though he had come across something. Putting his hand on Alex's shoulder, he instantly felt it as well. His mind was puzzled. "Why can Alex feel this and not me? Had my student surpassed me? Something to do with his bloodline?" His mind was clustered with various thoughts.

He guarded his thought while in contact.

"He couldn't have," The Operator said to himself.

Alex realized The Operator was planning on killing him. The Operator couldn't afford someone to surpass him; he must lead the Clan. With all his power and knowledge, the book wasn't in his possession anymore; it had just disappeared when he was trapped.

The Operator drew from the book, and without it, he had no real power in himself. Just the knowledge of the Eternals, enough to still convince his followers he was all-powerful.

For the first time since being called Angel, he found that he was not omnipotent anymore; he had limitations. He was simply an energy user, like everyone else. Feeling vulnerable for a moment, he wondered about the Shaitan, who called him their Prophet.

"Why have they left him now?" He asked himself.

He felt a sudden shift in the energy field and heard a familiar sound of crystal dust crackling. He immediately grabbed Alex, and with all his strength, he pulled him out of the Castle. The men never stood a chance; his movement to them would have been in the blink of an eye.

There was a loud explosion that rocked the ground, then a loud rumble as the castle fell in on itself. This old fortress, which had stood proud for over seven hundred years now, was nothing but a pile of rubble and dust.

The dust blotted out the sun, casting a grey shadow over the area. Gathering into the vehicles, they made a quick exit before the authorities arrived. Alex was sat next to his mentor and said, "I failed you."

His mentor stayed silent for a long time and did not even look at him. He was lost in his own thoughts. After some moments of silence, he said, "I have a job for you. Here's a list of locations they might have cells at. Destroy all of them!"

Alex took the piece of paper and smiled, looking at it. He was getting another chance to prove himself to his master. The Operator had a plan, and he wasn't bothered about destroying the cells. They were of little consequence. The government believed them to be terrorists thanks to his planted MP's in parliament.

The idea was simple. He had lost track of the Tribe after he came back to the world; they had somehow disappeared.

Frustratingly, it was the first time he had lost them since they were forced above ground; nothing like this ever happened earlier. With white skin, no freckles, apart from their hair and eyes, there wasn't any colour in them at all. The lack of sun made them evolve to look differently, just like people from different parts of the world had evolved according to their environment. The best resource he had was nothing more than heavily financed political parties.

Little by little, he outed the Tribe to the world. Made them into a terrorist organization. In fact, he even facilitated some attacks that were apparently claimed by the Tribe. Now, he had the most efficient intelligence agency, which was working for him to find them as well.

Cyber Intelligence, one of Clant's many company fronts, became a contractor. Now, The Operator had his eyes and ears all over the country. This did nothing good; with frustration, he realized they must have developed technology to hide. Now, he knew that they had, even if he

didn't completely understand it yet. Now, he would sit back and see what would happen; if you kick the bucket, the insects scurry.

Chapter 23:
The Council

The cool air burst and hit Penny's lungs as she opened the door to Trevor. A stark contrast to the warm air from the fire.

"You ready for this?" Trevor asked, smiling, half with mischief and half nerves.

He turned and started walking; Penny quickly caught up.

"This helper, I understand it might be normal here, but I'm not a helper kinda girl," Penny complained.

Trevor looked at her with a straight face and said, "Then you must fire him, but know that he won't be able to find a job that pays the same."

They hit a crowded tunnel, which was so jampacked that people were bumping into each other constantly, giving away the vibes like they were at the Glasgow subway.

"Okay, okay, I'll keep him. But he will have to accept a few changes. I do my own laundry, and no one serves me food," Penny exclaimed.

"Unless I'm in a restaurant," She continued after a pause with a smirk on her face.

Trevor burst out laughing. The noise of those people was nearly drowned out by Trevor's belly laugh. She didn't think him capable of it.

There was a lull in the foot traffic, and penny could see posters on the wall advertising restaurants and bars. New Pandora was becoming more and more a mirror-like the outside. world

Spotting a sign asking for witnesses to a mugging, Penny stopped and said, "I guess I thought things might be different here."

Trevor walked a few steps backwards, over to Penny, and responded, "Where there are human beings, there will be a crime. We have the same problems as the outside, just without the sun."

By this time, they had left the tunnels as well. Leaving the tunnel, Penny faced a view that made her gasp. Looking over the city, there were large commercial buildings with neon signs. The city was full of bars and restaurants and was filled with the fragrance of a mixture of flowers. She spun around and saw a massive garden full of flowerbeds; she saw children playing on the large patches of grass and adults sat on the benches. The smell from the Lilies reminded her of her mum. Penny couldn't believe what she was seeing. She looked at Trevor with a look of awww.

"The crystal dust, it can be safe using a chemical process, then added to the soil. It allows for the plant to grow, even without the sun. They get their energy from the crystal fertilizer. You see, we had to adapt when the outsiders became a threat." Trevor explained.

That last sentence made Penny break eye contact. A feeling of unease filled her. They walked further and approached a grand building, which

was arching over the entrances and windows. Intricate designs along a border, running to the length of the wall. Each pillar holding up a balcony was depicting a figure. She could hear raised voices out of one of the windows.

"She's an outsider. I will never let her lead us. She will dishonour these halls."

Turning to Penny with a look of disappointment, Trevor extended his hands and offered her the path, "after you."

A security guard quickly walked towards them as they entered. It might have rushed to stop the stranger from entering in but then caught Trevor's eye and went back to his seat.

"It seemed like Trevor carried clout, even without those white clothes he's changed into," Penny thought.

The hall was even grander than the building exterior. It looked ancient but was well maintained. Portraits were covering the walls, each one of a different person wearing the same jewel around their neck, making them look like the mayor or something.

Penny noticed the same jewel around Margaret's neck now. Trevor walked forward and greeted the elders, "I would like to formally introduce you to The Light Bearer, Penny Whyte, a descendant of eve."

Silence filled the room, but Penny never noticed that. She was too busy looking at the mural on the roof, a depiction of some sort of war of the gods.

There were clouds, one side was filled with wise-looking men and women sitting in meditation, and the other was shadow-like creatures snarling.

"Close your mouth, girl." Elder Margaret's voice fell upon her ears. Penny looked down instinctively. Elder Margaret was looking right at her, almost looking like she wanted her dead.

"So we know who was shouting when they came in," whispered Trevor.

"Let's take out seats, shall we?" This voice she heard was soft and familiar; Penny turned around to find Elder John, who was offering her a seat next to him. Trevor took the seat on the other side of her; she felt like she had her bodyguards in place.

Margaret banged a gavel and began the meeting, "I bring sad news to the council. I'm sure though everyone is already aware that Elder Claire had taken ill mysteriously."

That boulder was at the bottom of Penny's stomach again. She continued, "With the only person present, our newly appointed Light Bearer. Penny, can I ask, why didn't you heal her?"

Penny was confused. She was unaware that she could."

Horror struck Penny, she suddenly felt like she was in a court hearing, and she was about to be prosecuted and cross-examined. She had no answer to this question.

"How was she expected to do it without training?" Trevor answered loudly; he was standing now, fist clenched.

"Elder Trevor, please take a seat. I wasn't aware she hadn't received the basics yet." She responded.

There was a tone to the way she said it that brought the boulder up to penny's throat. Then all the mixed feelings came rushing at her, like before. Panting for breath, Penny quickly stood up. The room was spinning, and she couldn't breathe. Trevor grabbed her arms, "breath, Penny, just Breath. These aren't your emotions. You let your guard down. Just breath." Trevor worriedly told her.

As she breathed in, trying to regain control, suddenly she was hit with the smell of lilies, just like by the train. She calmed down and apologized awkwardly.

They were all on their feet at that point. Some were smiling warmly at her with sympathy in their eyes, and some were arms cross, looking like they were chewing on bees.

"I think we should do this tomorrow. Penny needs time to rest after the journey." Margaret went to complain when John got in there first, "I think that's a good idea."

A few others rapped their knuckles on the table.

"Fine. Tomorrow's first thing then." They got up, and Penny headed straight for the door. Trevor was hot on her heels. She instantly felt better outside, like some kind of weight had been lifted from her.

"She was testing you, pushing boundaries. She knows if the people accept you, you will lead us." Trevor caught up to her and said.

Realizing this is just like the outside world, Penny assumed this women's power was being threatened.

Penny reached her room and found a book sat on the table. It was similar to the black book, but this one was white. She had seen it in her dreams but never in the flesh.

It was so white. Even light was almost beaming from it.

"That's the Book of Light, our most sacred object. As your helper, I am a custodian of the book; now that you have arrived, it's all yours." Leon said, raising his hand to offer Penny the book.

Penny walks over to it and puts her hand on the cover. The feeling was becoming familiar now. She had travelled somewhere in her mind. The smell of Lilies filled her nose again; looking around, she realized she was in the underground garden, but no one else was here other than her.

She could hear humming, which reminded her of her Nana. It was the same tune. Turning, expecting to see her grandmother, she bumped into someone and fell over. As she looked up, she saw it was Elder Claire.

Claire sat on the grass, fallen from the bump. Her laughter was like sunshine, so full of joy. Penny began to laugh as well.

"So you made it, and I'm here and not there, so I made it too," Claire exclaimed.

Penny tried to ask what she meant by there, but she was ignored.

"So you met the council? They aren't a bad bunch; just, unfortunately, they are human." She had said almost as though she wasn't.

"Are you my Claire or the other Claire from the cave?" Penny asked unsurely.

Claire sniffed a flower and shrugged her shoulders, "You tell me. This is your construct."

Penny took Claire's hand, "What do you mean construct? You must be here, so you can teach me to heal, and I can bring you back." Penny asked her.

Claire started to walk backwards, complaining, "I'm afraid you don't understand."

Claire started to change shape, her features, her height, and her size.

The voice had changed as well, "You see? I'm not a person." It said.

Penny looked confused. "I'm a book! I'm older than all of this, all of you. I've seen species rise and fall, the world being birthed and then destroyed. I've seen other things that are out of my reach; those things are contained by my sisters. The one that ran away." It expressed.

Penny assumed she was too tired for this and that was she couldn't comprehend what the book was saying. Firstly, she couldn't believe she was talking to the book. Also, she was confused about how it could be as old as it was saying; it was in pristine condition.

"Why? Thank you." The Book explained. Penny looked confused.

"So it can read my mi..." penny thought but was interrupted in the middle.

"Yes," it simply replied, interrupting Penny's thoughts.

"You may get your rest, human; you're dismissed." The book commented.

With that, Penny was back in the lobby. Leon was still standing next to her.

"Go ahead; it's all yours." Leon looked as though it had just been a few seconds. He was carrying on the conversation as though she hadn't just been standing there for ten minutes like a statue.

"What can you tell me about this book?" Penny anxiously questioned.

Leon nodded his head in denial, "Nothing, I'm afraid. Apart from one thing that it is older than anyone really knows, its sister for the first time is in my care as well."

At that, penny became interested, "What do you mean by its sister?"

"The dark book; the Book of Darkness. It is the sister book to this; it's the complete opposite. A dark book that only brings bad things, I don't even like having it in my residence." Leon continued his explanation.

Penny looked Leon in the eyes, "I'm asking you as the Light Bearer.
Bring me that book tomorrow." She ordered.

She didn't know why but some part of her craved to see the book again.
She needed to see if it could communicate in the same way this one could.
She wanted to know what it did to Mark and how he died.

She would commune with the Book of Darkness and will learn its secrets.

Chapter 24:
The Black book

The footsteps told Penny that Leon had returned with the Dark Book; he had a very disgruntled look on his face, which could easily be recognized by anyone from far away. He put the black in front of her. Noticing the gloves he was wearing, she figured he really didn't want to make skin contact with that book. Determined to find out what happened to Mark that day/night, Penny rested her hands on the book and listened; the familiar feeling of coldness travelled up her arms and into her chest.

As the heat from her body became sucked into the book, she didn't smell the lilies. Also, there were no whispers this time. She was sitting there, for what felt like an hour, shivering from cold, although the heat from the fireplace was firmly in the air. The Coldness that came from within when all the heat had been taken, she was aware of the heat against her skin from the fire, but it seemed like it never penetrated. As she took her hands back, she instantly began to get warm; she wondered why the smell of lilies never came. She did not imagine the smell; it was happening too often. She couldn't figure out why it kept appearing again and again; there wasn't any common denominator.

As she was enraged with the feelings of frustration, there was a knock on the door just in time to stop Penny from kicking the book into the fire.

She thought destroying it might be for the best; the thing was cursed.

"Penny, there you are!" It was Katy; Leon had let her in, and she was running across, throwing her arms around her.

"I've been looking for you; I need your help!" Katy asked.

Penny suddenly couldn't speak, just the sight of her again, and she felt a rush. "Kim is being kept in a house in South London. With everything going on in Scotland, they haven't had time to move her."

Penny suddenly sat up straight, "So when do we go for her?"

It came out of her mouth spontaneously, even before she could realize that she had said it.

"That's the thing. I'm trying to convince the council to mount a rescue, but with Scotland, they are diverting all resources to evacuate the whole country."

Penny didn't understand what she said. She shook her head, "What do you mean? What's happening in Scotland?"

Katy explained, "A man called Alex was ransacking cells. He had discovered three bothies in the highlands and one castle in Duffus. He wiped them out, tortured them, and killed them all."

"Is that the hooded man?" Penny nodded.

"The council meets in half an hour to decide what to do next. I was asked to summon you. But before that, I need to clear my head, so walk with me through the park?" Katy asked.

Penny found herself blushing again at the thought, but the presence of Kim brought her back to her senses. Penny still couldn't get over this underground park. The smells and insects, it was prospering better than the ones above ground.

"You're not saying anything," Katy said as they walked.

Penny thought for a moment, "Shug when he was diving, he whispered something to me. He said my brother, Elliot, was alive but died before telling me more."

Kim stopped dead in her tracks, something had dropped in her head, and she went to say something when

Trevor appeared, commanding, "You two are going to be late, come with me".

Walking into the chambers, Penny found herself feeling annoyed and frustrated. She was not a politician and had no interest in becoming one.

"Can I refuse this?" She thought.

They all sat around the large round table in the chambers. Elder Margaret began, "I would like to start by apologizing to Penny. My remarks and questions were uncalled for in our previous meeting. Sometimes I get a bit ahead of myself. I hope you understand this, and I hope there will be no harsh feeling between us."

Looking into the women's dark green eyes, Penny didn't believe a word of it.

"We all know about the evacuation of Scotland, and also one of our little ones is being held in London. This is a hard time, and we need to choose between the life of one girl and the lives of countless cell members, including children. There is no right answer, but we do need to vote on where we put our resources." Elder Margaret asked for votes.

Katy was standing in the background. She wasn't a part of the council but was allowed to attend on account of the decision of her daughter's fate. There was a hole in front of each council member. In front of them, they also had a white and a black ball.

"Elders, if your vote is to evacuate Scotland, then place your white ball in the hole. If your decision is to abandon our brothers and sisters, then place the black ball in. Remember, the decision in these chambers today will decide the fate of countless lives." Elder Margaret spoke.

"Not a very unbiased speech," Penny thought.

They each reached out and anonymously placed their votes. Nine people were voting, including Penny, and in the end, only two balls were white. Others favoured allocating the resources to evacuate Scotland.

Katy ran from the room, sobbing, and Penny ran after her. "Elder Penny," she heard Jacob shout, but she decided to ignore him.

Catching up with Katy, she took her in her arms and held her; she was still sobbing uncontrollably. Trevor came out and walked over, putting his hand on Katy's shoulder, "Fuck em, we'll go ourselves."

"Get ready. We'll be heading out in a few hours." He continued.

They had discussed the plan. Each person knew their role. Firstly, they would go home and rest, prepare a bag with food and water. Trevor will bring weapons and explosives; Katy went to get medical supplies just in case. Penny's gaze went straight to the dark book when she walked into her room; Leon had left it. Falling into the chair next to it, she gazed into the fire, watching how blue it is, and how it danced around like a little bally. There was a crackle which Penny enjoyed, and then slowly, she realized the crackling wasn't coming from the room. It was the black book.

She quickly switched all her attention to the book. The whispers started knocking her head, echoing. Before realizing, what she was doing, she reached out a picked it up.

"Open me, open me." It echoed through her until she felt it in every cell.

Opening the book, she discovered she could read from it. "I think it's trying to tell me something," Penny thought. Its pages turned on their own and stopped at a piece of history.

It was entitled the Eternal War. Quickly with a mix of emotions, Penny realized this was telling her about a time before Adam and Eve and before there was any concept of humans' existence.

In the beginning, there were the Eternals, a race of beings made from pure energy and thought. They were made from the energy of three sparks.

These sparks led to the creation of the world we know today as Pandora, and life blossomed.

It was full of majestic animals and huge lizards that once ruled the planet. Quickly, the Eternals began to disagree on how to interact with the world; some wanted to help and guide life, while others wanted to step back and just observe. They broke into factions and decided to respect each other's differences and coexist.

The ones who would guide and encourage became known as Shaitan and the others Seraph. The Shaitan loved the creatures; they played with them, loved them, and protected their favourites. The Seraph, on the other hand, sat and watched, growing ever impatient with the interference of the Shaitan.

The Seraph blamed the Shaitan for different species dying out due to their interference and favouring one species over the other. This gave unfair evolutionary advances, giving one species intelligence well above the rest.

To keep the balance and reshift the things to the way they were earlier, the Seraph decided that they would teach the Shaitan a lesson and would fix everything by wiping out all life on the planet and starting again.

The distraught Shaitan mourned their pets and shut all communication off with the Seraph. Out of the ashes, life began anew the great cycle of life and death began, the Spark of Light fed life, the Spark of Darkness brought death, the third spark made sure that these opposing forces stayed in balance.

Again, the Shaitan fell in love with Pandora's creatures and nurtured them into pets. Feeling like it imbalanced the world again, the Seraph destroyed them again.

The Shaitan began feeling hate in their hearts for the first time, enraged they fought the Seraph. Life cycled as it always does, and new creatures began to populate and flourish while god-like beings were locked in a heavenly battle. The sky was full of thunderclouds for hundreds of years, causing floods and devastation.

Life prospered and died from flash flooding, fires caused by lightning, and volcanoes full of ash and lava destroyed everything below. Eventually, one of these volcanoes created an ash cloud that blotted out the sun.

Again, everything died while Pandora's creators fought their eternal war. The hatred between them grew stronger and stronger with each passing moment. Neither side could best the other; the Spark of Balance always kept everything, including the Eternals, equal in power.

The Seraph created a being, like them, but the energy was different. Angel was created to destroy the Shaitan, his energy born from the Seraph's hatred; they had unburdened themselves into this poor creature who was born to die for their sins. The Shaitan saw what was coming retreated into another dimension; they stopped Angel at the cost of their own freedom. Trapped in their dimension, their hatred for Seraph grew, they absorbed all of Angel's hatred.

Managing to grab the Spark of Darkness and bring it with them, they became darker and darker, eventually filling their hearts with hatred. This once-loving race of Eternals became monstrous; it became demons.

Now they destroy, driven by one thing. They want to bring enough darkness into the world for them to cross over from their dimension. Then from the world, they can use man's darkness to destroy the Seraph, destroying the world along with them.

Suddenly, there was a large bang as the book dropped and brought Penny back from her thoughts. She refused to believe it; this book was their weapon; it was all lies.

It was trying to distort the truth; the Seraph is kind and loving; she had felt it herself. She threw the book into the fire, but it would burn; the fire just moved around it.

"You can't destroy me," the book whispered to her.

Confused at the change in tone, before in her flat, it sounded sinister and evil. This whisper was neutral, not threatening but not comfortable either. She didn't know what any of it meant, but she had a mission to get to. She pushed the book from the flames with poker and left to find the others disturbed by what she had just learned – a history before history.

Chapter 25:
Kicking The Bucket

The winds were high in this part of the country, which was made worse by the height of the hill Duffus Castle rested. Surveying what was left of the stronghold, Alex wondered about its appeal. Observing the crumbling walls with amusement, he ran his hands along its rough surface, smelling the dampness. It gave no shelter, but with the technology, they recovered. He understood how they were doing it. Three bothies had already fallen, but the occupants had escaped destroying everything of value. The disgruntled grunts from his men were being drowned out by the wind howling through the ruins.

His commander was always up straight and alert. Alex realized that the field was energy, and he could absorb it into himself to reinforce himself. Reflecting on his orders, "Go, kick the bucket and watch the insects scramble."

Well, these insects didn't get a chance to scramble, turning to several prisoners on their knees and hands bound with cable ties.

He was in a playful mood as he managed to defeat the field quick enough to stop them from escaping.

No, he would have his fun. The thought popped in his mind, and he walked over to a bucket of water to wash the blood off his hands. He had just spent the last two hours torturing the first of his new toys. One of the women lost her cool and broke into hysterical crying, "You didn't even ask us any questions!"

It was true, however. He had no information which he needed from them, and thus, he was just perfecting his craft on some insects. That was what he had done, pulled the arms and legs of an insect, just as kids do. There were two things he had learned, though; it was better to keep them alive. He would take the nails, then the fingertips, working his way up each finger.

Slowly, taking piece by piece, the whole arm, and then the legs. The second thing he would do was hook them up to blood bags. His aim there was to practice until he learned to keep them alive as long as possible. He had some time to kill before moving on.

Turning back to his prisoners again, he was getting ready to pick the next one when an old man asked, "Why are you doing this, Elliot?"

That threw Alex a bit. That was the name on the back of the picture.

He turned around again and walked away, thrown by the man.

"Did he recognize me? Who was he?" He thought and questioned himself.

He was pulled out of his thoughts by his phone ringing.

"Alex, I want you to go to London. I have a task for you; I'll send the details." The Operator said and hung up without anything else.

This intrigued Elliot. He knew his purpose wasn't to capture but to rattle. They wanted the remaining cells to try and run.

MI5 had the information. The Tribe terrorist organization was mobilizing and heading to London from Scotland. They were getting picked up at the border, lambs to the slaughter. With the terrorist threat being as high as it is and the unprecedented numbers of prisoners the government had, there was no choice but to outsource the holding of these prisoners. The Clan had a company that easily won the contract, thanks to the influence they had over parliament. Alex turned and nodded to the commander, then walked away to screams being silenced by gunfire.

The operator stood in the guard tower and was listening to the sound of buzz cutters and tattoo buzzers. The smell of disinfectant was overpowering as he watched them spray naked prisoners walking by, reminding him of a conveyor belt; efficient!

They had their clothing taken off them, sent forward in a line to be disinfected. With them living in the ground like insects, you couldn't be too careful. They were shaved from head to toe, hosed down, and tattooed with a QR code to identify them. The Operator picked up the microphone.

"You are no longer people; you are no longer citizens. Being born in New Pandora, you never registered your births; this means you don't exist, and now you exist as I see fit! You will remain here until I make the decision of how and when your pathetic life will end. Serve your purpose and do what you are told, and you will live a little longer."

While he was talking to his prisoners, there were men walking around with large needles attached to some sort of gun. They were injecting something into the necks of the prisoners.

"My men have just finished the last part of your processing. You now have a small explosive in your neck pushed against your carotid artery. Piss me off, and you die, don't do what you are told and you die, try and escape, and you die, leave the fence perimeter, and you die, if I get bored, and you are in front of my eyesight, you die, if you ever forget that you are nothing but insects... then you die!"

The Operator took a lot of lessons from his mistakes, even more so than his victories. Over time, he had learned how to take away someone's humanity; this ability turned out to be something vital to make a prisoner complaint. From Egyptians with the Jews or Whites with the Blacks, people always wanted to take away someone else's humanity to make them subservient.

The Operator observed and learned. He pushed certain minds down paths that would lead to more experimenting with this. The most efficient in history was his Nazi venture. When Germany surrendered in the First World War, The Clan had the long game in mind. Starting rumours of a stab in the back rather than a defeat on the battlefield and then insinuating it was the Jews and Communists to blame. They installed officials loyal to the Clan who would spread the message.

During the war, an art student who took part in the war came to light. One day, the Operator was in Vienna, at the theatre, and after he had drinks, he began talking with two young men. It was quite intriguing because usually, The Operator never spoke to anyone he didn't know, but this was an exceptional case; one of the young men caught his attention. He was flamboyant and drunk and talking about the music score of the production with such passion. He described the musical notes as strings attached to his heart, a masterpiece of the soul. After buying the man a drink, the Operator discovered his name was Gusti. He was a student of music and would later become a composer and have a footnote in history.

The other man, standing next to him, stood a shorter serious character; when he spoke, it was for a purpose, not ever wasting words. He had dark hair and serious deep eyes; his soul was strong but full of pain. He had fought in the war as well, running communications along the front and being awarded more than one medal. His pain was in losing the war; from running up and down the line with communications, he believed he had a good grasp of the war effort. He believed it was going well, so when he got word that they had surrendered, he was floored. Now he was angry and resentful, almost psychotic with rage; he was perfect!

The camps they created helped the Operator to learn a lot; they were efficient and soul-destroying. These were modelled after them, given black site status by the government, meaning the public won't ever know of its existence; they were autonomous.

The noise of a fight brought him back from his memories; a couple of the male insects had realized they had hope and decided to fight back. The Operator pushed a few buttons, and BOOM, with a small blast, they were gone. The explosive was enough to burst the side of their neck open, but they couldn't take their heads off. They rolled around the ground with streams of blood pulsing out of their necks as the life drained from them.

"In place," a message from Alex appeared on his phone; the trap was all set; it's time now to see who comes. He was becoming worried and jealous of Alex's abilities. Obviously, because his own abilities were limited to that of a normal human. With the book in his hands, he was their Prophet, but without the book in his possession, they have forsaken him. While in possession of the book, he was able to absorb its power, making himself unstoppable.

While the Operator could absorb the power from willing believers and followers, who surrendered their life force, Alex should take it by force, and he was also more sensitive to the light side, able to feel it in a way the Operator couldn't.

The Operator realized it wouldn't be long before Alex would be too strong to control, and this was concerning him. The Operator knew that Alex had gone to his dad's house and killed him. He was sloppy, and there is an investigation now; it was Alex's pure luck that no one saw him; he would have been recognized. The police took fingerprints, which they found to be his, but he was legally dead.

The fingerprints they found were his dad's and his, but they both were dead. Other than these two fingerprints, they also found Penny's as well, after which Penny got disappeared without a trace. She was now wanted for questioning for the murder of her own father. Without realizing what he was doing, Alex created the perfect situation. She couldn't hide anymore; the second she'd picked up by facial recognition, it was his.

Chapter 26:
The Rescue

Penny still didn't understand how the air was available down here, which seemed to be impossible without the wind. She followed the scent of flowers and the flying insects to the park, where she met Katy and Trevor. Her nostrils were filled with a sweet smell; it was her favourite smell as she loved the smell of flowers, and in this garden, the smells were so much stronger than the outside world, even with the wind.

As they made their way out of the park, Penny turned to Katy and asked if she was okay doing this.

"You have to be kidding; I've thought of nothing else since," Katy responded.

Nodding, she looked behind her, taking in the size of the place; she couldn't see the end of the cavern. All she could see were a few short towers with the tubes running between them. She was still in awe of the place. People were giving them odd looks.

"They aren't used to seeing elders down here," Trevor commented.

Looking around now, Penny realized they were entering a different part of New Pandora. They were going towards the lower part into the ground. Penny started to feel beads of sweat on her forehead. The air here was hot and sticky, and the place was filled with a familiar odour, but Penny couldn't put her finger on what was causing it.

"I had hoped to break you into the depths of New Pandora gradually, as I told you before. New Pandora has the same problem as up there, but only without the sun. We need heat and energy, and that comes from the central furnace." Trevor explained as they walked further deep.

Walking into a large cavern, there was a blue glow illuminating from the deep down, and Penny could see hundreds of people mining and tending to equipment. They all were wearing trousers only, probably because of the heat. They carried on further into some more tunnels until they reached a point where there were doors to either side all the way along.

One of the doors was open, and Penny could see a single bed, a table, and a chair. There was bread and cheese on the table with some water. Penny could hear the noise getting louder and louder with every inch they got closer and closer to the exit of the tunnel.

When they made out of it, they were in the middle of a marketplace.

People were shouting to attract customers over.

"Fresh fish, some still alive."

"Hand-made toys, perfect for the little ones."

Dialogues were never-ending. Each shopkeeper was doing his best to attract the most customers. They were all dressed in rags; the air there had a stench of a sewer.

"Is this how people live down here?" Penny asked through her hand, pinching her nose.

"I'm afraid it is. We don't have all the answers here, and we definitely aren't perfect either, but we are trying." Trevor responded.

"Not hard enough!" Penny quickly shot back.

Trevor and Katy left it there. Penny was furious, and it wasn't going to do anyone any good.

"Let's not forget what we are doing," Katy said.

Trevor and Penny nodded, and at that, they left.

"There's a supply run up ahead, where we can find a train that will take us to the surface, and we can phase back," Trevor exclaimed.

Running a little forward, they find the train. It was an old rickety thing, reminding Penny of a tram in Blackpool.

It was attached to ropes and seemed to work on a Pulley system rather than power. They hopped on the train, and Penny was instantly disgusted. The pulley system was operated by two very strong men, who were yanked at the cables and heaved the train upwards.

The look of concern on Katy's face overcame Penny's objection, and she turned her face to look outside of a window. There was nothing but rock, but she could bear to witness it rather than watching what was happening. She understood they weren't slaves, and it was their occupation, but the class system in place here was worse than that of Victorian Britain. Yet, she felt no anger or resentment from these people towards them in their white clothes, but only a warm smile.

Penny got off the train into a small cavern with a short narrow passage up ahead like the one she used to get to New Pandora. The cavern was bare apart from some graffiti and beer cans on the ground. Trevor took out a square device, double-checked the cavern for intruders, and pressed the button. Penny was getting used to the blinding blue light by now, and she had learned to close her eyes.

As they made their way through the narrow passage, they found themselves in the night sky. Instantly, they all took a huge deep breath and then laughed, watching each other. It seemed like Penny wasn't the only one who missed the fresh air that actually moves.

They walk into flint, a small town close to the entrance to New Pandora. It was dark, probably because it was midnight; no one was around. Trevor said, "I'll get some transport," and disappeared.

"We'll get her, you know; I can't explain it, but I feel a connection to her, and that connection tells me she's not been harmed," Penny consoled Katy, who seemed like she was going to burst into tears. Penny quickly hugged her tight, trying her best to make her stop crying.

"Thank you; I'm terrified that they've done something terrible to her; you don't know them yet, Penny, you don't understand the evil they are capable of, even to a little girl,"

Penny had many questions in mind regarding what they were going to face, but before Penny could ask more, Trevor pulled up in a car, and they got in. Katy went to ask where he got the car from but was cut short when she noticed the wires hanging from the steering column.

"Ah, okay! it is going to be one of those nights." Katy commented with a deep exhale of breath.

They had a good time in London. At that time, during nights, the roads were calm, and they used to sneak into cars for a ride. This reminded Katy of those nights. The night sky was clear, the stars were out, and before they could reach the lights of London, they were clear to see.

Penny found Katy, deep in thought, on the back seat.

"Penny, for your thoughts," she said with a smile. She always thought she was funny with that one.

"When Kim was born, she nearly died, or did die; I never found out which. It is why she was rarely out of my sight; I constantly fear that she will be snapped away. This was when Elder Claire came in as they were working on her tiny little body, doing her first to get that first cry. I felt a terror that can't ever be described, a shiver of coldness went from my head to my toes. My heart felt as if it was doing 200 beats a minute but also completely still. A feeling of complete and utter helplessness and vulnerability took me over. Claire took out the Book of Light that was in her possession back then, placed it down, and laid Kim on top of it. She then placed a cloth over the top. At that point, I thought she was dead and became distraught. I remember I cried the loudest that moment and felt as if my heart was ripped out. But Claire told me everything was okay and just signalled me to watch. Then the Seraph granted me a miracle. What I saw at that moment was nothing less than a wonder. The cloth glowed bright like the sun, and I heard the best sound in the world; Kim was crying, she was breathing, my little miracle baby was alive. After that, she would do strange things like set fires and move things without touching them. It was unheard of, the elders were all energy users, but they were trained over a period of years. There hasn't been a natural-born energy user in generations. And this is why we kept it secret, so we would appreciate it if you did not say anything." Katy went on and on with her story, and Penny let her. she wanted her to let all out so she could feel light and better. She only nodded, amazed at the story and surprised that she could still be surprised at this stage.

They arrived at a secluded park close to Kim. Trevor set the car on fire so that blame could fall on the youths. They then moved towards the house; their plan was already discussed in the car and was already on the motion, and everyone was clear on what to do. Trevor, with soft steps, made his way around the back of the house. There was a guard at the back door. Trevor fired a dart into his neck, and he fell flat on his face, but there was a second guard that Trevor failed to notice. He sounded the alarm.

Radioing guards inside that they were under attack, he took up a defensive position. The men in the house did the same and reinforced their line towards the back more than the front. It happened exactly like they planned.

At that point, the front door and a good chunk of the wall came flying forward, knocking out two of the men. Now only one of them left, and he quickly ran to Kim, picked her up, and pointed the gun at her head.

"You're too late. He's here for you," the man expressed.

Penny looked confused. As Katy ran into the room, she had to hold Katy back from the front as she saw the danger Kim was in.

There was a thud outside, and then Trevor walked through the back door as well. He moved towards the man's back, hoping he would be unnoticed, but he was wrong. The man turned and fired a shot at Trevor, but the bullet was stopped in mid-air. She didn't know how but Penny stopped the bullet and was now controlling it. She didn't know what to do next; she couldn't send it back to him as well; after all, she was not a killer, so she dropped it.

"So you are weak," a familiar voice fell on her ears. She couldn't believe it; it was impossible. A man walked in, lowered his hood, and showed his face.

"Elliot!" Penny mouthed, no sound came out of her mouth.

He stopped suddenly, looking uncertain. Penny rushed forward to hug her brother. All this time, she thought he was dead. However, he flicked his hand at her, and she found herself hitting the wall. She was still awake but barely. She was taken a massive hit to the head, faintly heard Elliot telling the man, "We only need the two girls. The other two can die here."

Suddenly, a high-pitched loud screamed. Penny thought the building was collapsing around her. Then a wave of something hit her, and she the darkness took over; there was nothing but just blackness.

#

Alex had been told to get to a South London address. They had the little girl he spotted in Inverness, and she was going to be the bait in a trap. He took one of the Jeeps and headed to the airport, where a private helicopter was on standby.

He was still trapped in the thought of the man calling him Elliot; that was the name on the back of the picture at his dad's. It was his face but not his name, and he had no idea who that girl was. He boarded the helicopter, and they took off almost straight away. It wouldn't take much time before he would be landing in London.

Arriving in London, he found that he felt the connection again to the girl he was hunting. It seemed like she was on her way to spring the trap. Without wasting any time, he made his way to the address. With each passing distance, he felt as if the connection was getting stronger and stronger; she was definitely here.

As he reached the address, everything seemed calm. He walked in and greeted the men before heading his way upstairs. He wanted to be out of the way and surprised them when they came in. The men were expendable; they would distract them so he could trap them. He heard a fuss outside, and the men swiftly moved into positions.

The front door was blown off from its hinges; he felt the power from her. He needed to be careful. There was some commotion and chatting going on downstairs; it was not time for Alex's entrance.

It was the first time he saw the powerful girl. He hesitated for a second before she realized she was the girl from the pictures.

Then he was brought back to the room by a gunshot. He watched as she stopped it in the air.

"She's fast but indecisive; why doesn't she just kill him?" he thought.

The bullet dropped, and he sighed, "So you're weak."

He moved forward and lowered his hood to show his face. He was intrigued by how she reacted to him.

"Elliot!" She half shouted. It startled him; "Why is she calling him this name as well. I'm not Elliot!" he thought.

She rushed towards him, and he sent her flying off a wall. She ordered the other two to die; she heard a scream. It was the little girl; she screamed, and the wave of power that came from her sent Alex flying through the walls out of the house. He was landed on a patch of grass across the road, unconscious.

Chapter 27:
Hard Truths

The vibrations went through her back. Penny felt slight pulls in the change of direction, and then a bump brought her fully back. As she opened her eyes, Katy was the first person she saw; her head was on her lap. It took her a moment to regain her memory, "wh… What happened?"

Katy nodded at Kim in the front seat. Kim was beaming her back with a massive smile. Her eyes told a different story, however. Massive black circles were sinking into her head. Penny quickly felt awkward and sat up, "Sorry, Kim, you should be here with your mum."

At that, Katy threw her arms around Penny's neck and said, "Thank you, we wouldn't have been able to without you."

Katy pulled back but kept her hands around Penny's neck. Her heart was racing, and Penny couldn't help but look into her eyes. She felt caught by them, unable to look anywhere else. Katy leaned in, and they shared a soft kiss, full of promises of more and a conversation later.

Kim in the front instantly began mocking, whereas Trevor just laughed his belly out. This was the second time Penny heard it. "Maybe he's softening up a bit," Penny thought. They sat awkwardly in the back now. Katy still hadn't let go of Penny's hand.

"When you were knocked against the wall, and the hooded man ordered us to kill, Kim screamed, and something happened. When she screamed, she somehow tapped into her own energy and floored everyone. The house was destroyed in the process, and we barely escaped before being crushed." Katy explained to her what happened.

Penny remembered the events and suddenly became concerned. She asked, "Elliot, did you see if he…"

Trevor interrupted her sharply, "You know that man?"

Penny was suddenly unsure of what had happened. She simply said, "He's my brother."

With a look of shock on his face, Trevor suddenly pulled the car to the side of the road. He denyingly said, "Penny, your brother died in a car crash. We would have extracted him as well if he was still alive. It's just not possible."

Not sure what to think, Penny stayed quiet. With no answer in her mind, the only thing she knew just now was that her head was hurting and that Katy's touch somehow made everything okay.

Penny wanted to push the issues just now. She knew that she had been told that her brother was alive, but she didn't expect it to be like this? It was unthinkable that he could be the one who was systematically clearing out cells in Scotland.

They had reached the cave. Trevor dropped them off and drove away to ditch the car. By this time, the sun was coming up. They watched as the darkness became shadows, and the shadows grew longer with the first beams of light. All of a sudden, the sun cracked through and announced the beginning of the new day, a bright declaration banishing the darkness and bringing in the light.

Katy felt all of it; the moment in the car was a declaration; it was a banishing of old shadows. Penny still had a bit of light in her life. For the first time in a while, Penny felt happy, standing there with Katy and Kim. Then they made their way through the narrow passage into the large cavern; it was just as Penny remembered. The chandelier-looking formation above, dripping onto a mountain of rock below. She didn't want to go through the tunnel this time, so she was waiting for Katy to take the device out, and everything happened smoothly then – the blue flash and the platform.

Suddenly, there were three angry-looking elders in view – Margaret, Jacob, and Francis – who were waiting there for them with Anna in tow.

"Kim, we are so relieved that you are safe. Please go with Anna, she'll take you home, and your mother will meet you there." Margaret suggested.

Kim did as she was told, looking back with a cheeky look on her face.

Penny hadn't noticed the walk of the platform the last time. She was too amazed at the sight of the place. It had mini gardens all around it.

How could she have missed the smell? The flowers were as intoxicating here as they were in the main gardens.

Jacob started, "Katy, I know you were concerned for your daughter and what you have done was natural. I would have done the same for my son, but I wouldn't have brought the Light Bearer with me and risked a trap. From our intel, it sounds like the hooded man was there waiting for you."

Penny suddenly felt a flash of anger, "I make my own decisions, and I'm no prisoner."

She decided to keep the identity of the hooded figure to herself and hoped Katy did the same. John spoke this time with his hands up, "Well, this will have to wait; elder Claire is awake and wants to see you, Penny. But don't think this means there won't be....."

His voice was drowned by the sound of clapping. They had reached the main promenade, just before the train station. On the big screens above the station, a news report was being broadcasted, Penny couldn't hear it, but she could see it was a live video of them returning with the caption "Hero Light Bearer returns after rescuing Kim from the clutches of the Clan."

The clapping was thunderous now. The suspicious looks seemed to have turned into admiration. Katy began clapping behind her as well. Penny tried to stop her; after all, she was with her as well on this mission and played an equal part, but Katy just shook, mouthing, "Take it."

Margaret looked like she was chewing on bees while the other two just looked thoughtful. The crowd stepped back as they created a path to the station for them, constantly clapping as they walked through. Penny felt uncomfortable; she preferred life when she wasn't in the limelight, but now, everyone was watching her. Walking down to the train, on the train, and everywhere, in fact, it was the same.

Penny went straight to the hospital to find elder Claire. She was desperate to speak with her. She found her sitting up, whereas the medical staff was trying to reason with her over something. "You should stay here for a few more days; we don't understand what happened."

The elder just looked at Penny and beamed. She waved away the medical stuff and beckoned her to come to sit with her next to the bed.

Penny got into the large room, which was filled with flowers, lots of colours, and warmth; a large part of the room was taken over by the furniture. She thought about the workers below, who were working hard on the furnace, and wondered what care do they receive.

"How are you? You seem much better than the last time I saw you." Penny began but was ignored by Elder Claire off course.

Claire has no intention of talking about her health. She was interested in something else.

"Tell me about your adventure. How did rescuing Kim went?" Claire asked.

She started talking, and bit by bit, told the elder everything, including the kiss with Katy, which she regretted, and kept on rambling. Claire had a straight face the whole time; the only emotion was a slight smile and the twinkle she always had in her eyes.

Well, dear, it sounds like you are getting to know your own power. It bends to your own will, the peace of energy your pinch-off; it's like a piece of putty. It hasn't been moulded into anything yet, but with your thoughts and willpower, you can turn it into whatever you want. You are limited by two things only, experience and energy reserves. The more you increase, the more they both increase." Claire explained Penny.

Penny somehow understood what Claire was telling her. It felt like instinct; Claire wasn't telling her anything she didn't seem to know on some level.

"It's not as simple as pinching a bit of energy of and using it. It needs to be the correct amount; too little and nothing will happen, or something unexpected will happen; too much and the effects are much larger than you anticipate. Both of these facts are crucial in the heat of battle." Claire continued.

Penny suddenly felt like there was a mountain to climb, but Claire just smiled like her usual self and measured her.

"The book will keep you right; it's a wise council," Caire said.

Penny saw this as a good opportunity as any, and she started talking, "I've spoken to the books; like, I mean... they formed personalities and spoke to me as though they were conscious."

Claire looked both impressed and worried at the same time. She confirmed, "Both books are conscious and have their own distinct personalities. They are, in fact, the oldest known entities in the universe."

"What do you mean?" Penny asked. She thought it strange that they would be so old.

"Who made them?" She asked.

The elder looked at her cautiously. She started, "When the celestial being, known as Angel, came to earth, he stole the two sparks of the Eternals. When he reached this plane of existence, they had to become something physical that could exist here. The sparks became books - One light and one dark. From the way you are wording your questions, something tells me you have spoken with both?"

The question came with a look of concern. Penny considered the women carefully and answered, "Yes, but the dark book tried to tell lies, twist history, twist the truth."

Penny looked down on the floor when she answered; it seemed like she was uncertain of the last part herself.

Claire shook her head in disagreement and explained, "I wish that was true, but the books can't lie. Remember, Penny; there always are three sides of the truth; their's, your's, and the actual truth. They only show the truth that is known to them. It doesn't mean it's complete truth; people's version's of events rarely are; it's just history from another point of view."

Penny was flabbergasted. She didn't know what to think; this was all getting too much for her to absorb all this. She just needed some space. Looking around the room, she suddenly realized how and where she would be best put to use.

"Claire, can I ask you a favour when you're fit enough to return to the council?" she asked Elder Claire.

Later that day, Penny was back in her large rooms. She's looking around the room, wondering why she needs so much space. She was lost in her thoughts when she heard a knock on the door. She walked across the bare wood floor and opened the door; Katy was standing outside with a bottle of wine and some food.

"I assumed you must be hungry, and Leon also told me that you sent him home early," Katy told Penny as she opened the door.

Penny suddenly felt self-conscious; she wished she hadn't done that; the place was nothing less than a mess. She had left her whites all over the floor when she changed into jogging bottoms and a top.

"Oh shit," she suddenly thought, looking at them awkwardly, dressed like this; she seemed like a frumpy middle-aged woman. Katy sensed the sudden panic; she stepped forward and took Penny's cheek in her free hand and gave her a long gentle kiss.

"Would you like to come in?" The words left her mouth before her brain had started again, but she was okay with it. Katy was wearing a black top with a neckline that showed a bit of her short cleavage. Her plump breasts pushed up with a bra, leaving a pleasing effect that gave Penny trouble concentrating. She was trying her best not to look in that direction and make this moment uncomfortable.

Katy walked into the kitchen and started dishing out the food. "Why don't you make a nice spot in front of the fire for us," she shouts through.

Penny wasn't there, though. She was running through to the bedroom to change into something a bit more sexy. She came back after failing; she forgot that she hadn't brought much luggage and she hadn't done any clothes shopping. Katy looked up, "Where'd you get to?"

Penny just shrugged, "Needed to freshen up a bit."

Katy was carrying the food and sitting there, waiting for her. Penny walked in and sat next to Katy in front of the fire. They spend the night talking about their childhoods — both the good and the bad.

Penny didn't go into deep details but gave Katy the gist, and Katy just took her hand, making her feel instantly safe: safer than she's felt in years.

"Shall we go to bed?" She asked, to which Katy just smiled and nodded her head.

Chapter 28:
The Camps

Alex woke up across the road from the house. He looked at the remaining rubble and cried out with rage. The pavement around him cracked as he shouted. Walking up the dark street, he could feel the connection fading.

"She's running back to whatever rock she came from," he thought.

His phone rang. Looking at the screen, squinting at the brightness, in the dark, he decided to ignore the call. He had no interest in being shouted at for another failure.

The girl from the pictures called him Elliot as well. He had no memory of her, and no matter how hard he pushed himself to concentrate, he couldn't remember her.

He put his hands on his head and screamed, "How is that possible? "

He needed answers, but his instincts told him he couldn't trust his mentor to provide them. His phone rang again, but this time he answered it, "So tell me, Alex, what happened this time?"

Alex groaned as he began to recount what had happened. Humouring the man on the other end, he was fed up with the treatment he got when he did all the work.

The Operator hung up the phone after chastising Alex for yet another failure. He sat back in his large leather chair. There was not much on his desk, no trinkets or family photos; even after spending an eternity on this planet, he had never taken a wife. If he did, she would be very disappointed since he made an unic. Some cosmic joke, maybe. This didn't matter because he was okay with this setting, maybe because it added focus to his work. He was a man who didn't entangle himself in love or any of that sort of weakness. Tall and strong, his heart was the same, strong and solid, as if it was made from stone.

It was time for him to take a tour of his new camp and inspect the new inhabitants. He did this regularly now. There was for completing the work. There were targets to meet, and it wasn't going to happen on half measures. Since discovering how the Tribe had been hiding themselves and their technology, he had now got access to the crystals.

He always had the knowledge of how to make advanced weapons and defensive systems. He learned it from the dark book long ago, but he did not have the crucial ingredient that was needed to make them. The crystals were hoarded by the Tribe.

Now, as he finally has his hands on a supply. Oddly enough, after vacating the area, the crystals didn't grow back like they normally would after a harvest.

This meant that someone cultivated them as well. This also meant that he had a limited supply. The prisoners were hard at work, creating blades, explosives, and bullets. The blades and bullets would penetrate any armour, and the explosives could range from hand grenades to napalm-type devastation. There was also a line of workers who sued to create armour; although the armour won't protect against the new crystal weapons, it was against conventional weaponry.

He was building his plan all this time; he used the insects had and had scattered the ones that got through the border are being tracked.

They would be followed to the location of New Pandora. They have now developed the device that could help them that phase, allowing him to invade. With his weapons and overwhelming numbers of pawns, it would be quite clear that his victory would be inevitable.

He was planning it as a siege; it would take time, as they had been embedded for thousands of years, and their stronghold was so secret and advanced that it had never been discovered before. He needed to strike before the Light Bearer gained experience and confidence in her abilities. So far, the highest concentration of insects had scarpered to Wales, but they were still widespread. He needed an entry point; a location to attack; he needed his beachhead.

The courtyard was empty and quiet; all the prisoners and security were working in the factories, kicking the dry dirt as he walked. he was disgusted at the sight of sick on the ground; he knew they would bring nothing but a disease.

"Disgusting roaches," He thought.

As he furiously walked into the first factory, he ordered one of his men to clean the mess outside. Watching them work, he was impressed. Every prisoner was working without complaint—a sea of black men scurrying arms in building, creating the destruction of their own home.

They were so without identity now that they just went along with it; on some level, they must know but were not very much bothered by it that they were indirectly helping in the world's destruction and digging their own grave.

He was always amazed at how weak the human mind can be; it was not at all hard to manipulate them.

There was one worker at the side; one of his men was giving him water; the Operator marched across the wooden floor, barely noticing the smell of rot coming from his slaves.

"What are you doing?" he asked loudly.

The guard explained that the man had fainted and needed rest and water before he could work again.

"So he can't work?" The Operator asked as he gazed his eyes upon him.

"No", the guard replied.

At that, The Operator took the guard's gun and shot the prisoner point-blank between the eyes. For a second, there was utter silence, and all the slaves looked over. However, they quickly got back to work, unmoved by what had just happened like unemotional beings, reminiscent of drones.

"If you can't work, you will die." The Operator shouted over the heads of the slaves.

Then quickly turned to the guard, pointed the gunpoint black, and shot him in the head.

"No one will treat an insect as if they are a human being!" after that, The Operator stormed out.

#

The council chambers seemed much larger than Penny remembered, or she felt smaller; she wasn't sure which. Trevor was sat in a chair outside as the elder Claire was back, and he had to stand down from his position in favour of her.

Margaret called the council into the session; she went straight on to condemn Penny's reckless actions that could have drawn unwanted attention.

Then with a smirk, she started, "You should have known better than this spring school an obvious trap."

"Ehem, ehem!" Elder Claire cleared her throat. She got the attention of everyone. She then declared, "I would like to put forward a motion. The workers down below have long been forgotten by this council; we should be ashamed of ourselves. I believe it would be the right course of action to create a school and medical station. The medical stations will only treat minor illnesses and injury with our main hospital taking the brunt of the worst. The education standards down there are abysmal."

It seemed like John was standing up to say something, but Claire raised her hand to stop John from objecting to that point.

"I understand that our education system is free to anyone who chooses to use it, but down below, it is often too expensive to transport their children to the main city each day. It will be far better to install an educational facility down there."

Margaret stood up and, while pointing why it can't be done, explained, "I applaud elder Claire's caring nature and concern for the workers down below. We simply do not have a teacher spare to open such a facility, nor do we have medical staff to run a medical station."

Elder Claire gave Penny a kick under the table; it was her turn to speak up and put her thoughts in front of everyone. she said, "I would like to second the motion, I believe it is in the best interest to include the entire community within the educational and medical establishment. There just aren't the opportunities down below as there are up here. I am a teacher to trade and will move my lodging down below and run the school myself; Elder Claire is teaching me how to heal. After learning that, I can use it for a medical station outside school hours on every other day, with a Sunday for rest from both."

It seemed like she was confident in her skills and knew what she was saying. These were not just words, but she was determined.

Jacob stood this time. He seemed to tower over the table; he looked like Penny's dad, which gave her a fear of him. "You… are an elder of this council, you can not live down below, we couldn't guarantee your safety, and you can't perform your duties here as well as there."

Penny shakily got up again and tried to remember what Claire had told her to say, "I invoke the right resign from this council, in doing so naming my successor." There was a murmur, but a very happy looking Margaret stood up, asking, "and who would you name as your successor?"

"Trevor…." She suddenly panicked and shouted over to Trevor, "You never told me your last name" Trevor laughed and shouted back, responding, "Longbeard!"

Penny bursts out laughing and almost doesn't get the words out, "Tre…vor… Long…..beard!"

She then burst into uncontrolled laughter. It was a mixture of the silly name and the tension being broken by it. Also, she didn't realize the release she would feel at letting go of being an elder.

"Very well, it is done, Trevor Longbeard will ascend to the elder in place of the Light Bearer; maybe this will bring honour to his name and this council." Claire nudged

Penny to leave her chair and walk away as Trevor walked over and replaced her in the seat.

Penny walked out of the chambers smiling and went to find Katy. She decided to look for her in the park first and made her way straight to the park.

She could never have enough of this place — so much colour, so much smell. Then, there is the smell of Jupe again! She turned around and saw a man who turned and pretended to walk somewhere else; she grabbed him and asked, "Talk! I've smelt your cheap aftershave the moment I arrived in New Pandora."

He turned white because of fear but tried to keep his calm. He explained that he was a member of an atheist group, and they don't believe in the ancient eternal beings. He rambled on further that her abilities can be explained by science, and that's why he was following her, just to observe her. he also told her that they were growing in numbers with each passing moment. At this point, he was up straight, chest out and proud. He had short dark hair and wore a brown tunic. Without hesitation or putting in any effort, he answered Penny's every question.

He continued, "I'm one of the cooks down below. I heard what happened in the chambers; I can't believe that you would do this for us. They said that they couldn't guarantee your safety down below. You'll find that we run things down there. Prove yourself good to your word, and we'll guarantee your safety."

At that, he turned a ran away. Things were a lot more complicated than Penny initially thought. The man openly talked about a group of atheists being in charge down below. Do the elders know about this?

Moments later, she found Katy and asked her. Upon her enquiry,

Katy answered her, "Yes! They do know. This is why they refuse to help.

They are nonbelievers and are considered less than us."

Penny couldn't believe what she was hearing.

"What do you think?" Penny questioned Katy.

Katy considered for a moment, then responded, "People reap what they sow."

The words were nothing less than daggers to Penny's heart. How could Katy think that? Katy was full of love and compassion; how could she be so cruel to people because of their beliefs.

"I think I need some space," Penny said, turned, and walked away. She didn't even give Katy a chance to respond and went back to her room.

She couldn't be distracted by Katy just now. She had a school and hospital to set up. Her mind was already trying to process a dozen things that needed more of her attention, on top of which was Elliot. She still didn't know what's happened to Elliot.

The books were right in front of her, and as she saw them, they caught her attention. She walked over, and for a reason, she picked up the black book. Even she didn't understand why she did that.

"Well, hello Penny, I've been expecting you back."

Chapter 29: The Choosing

Penny was not in her rooms anymore but in a dark space. There was nothing around that she could see apart from the shadows. She then noticed there was something moving within the shadows.

"No," she thought; it was the shadows themselves that moved.

"You have always been taught to fear the dark child, always told to watch the shadows. I created the darkness, but I didn't make it the monster that it is. Angel opened me up, and I showed him the truth. He saw both; he was shown the light path that he could take and the dark one that showed him his past. He couldn't see past his own truth and pain. He loved his creators, but they didn't care about him. They cast him to the side and were going to destroy him. Your pain runs deep."

The dark surroundings changed, and she's found herself back at Arbroath Abbey. She panicked; it was the first time she was seeing this after that night. She hadn't even thought of getting back here after that night.

"Please not here; I don't want to be here." She begged.

She was feeling everything at a more profound level – the ground beneath her feet, the grass, and even the little stones that covered the area. The familiar walls with missing stone; the locals had stolen stones from the abbey to build their own houses. She heard the book in her head, but it was a voice now, and she saw someone standing next to her. he was wearing a dark suit, black shirt, and tie, no colour at all. Sharp thin features that reminded her of an old CBBC program, 'The Demon Headmaster.'

"I remember this place," he said.

His voice was dead. Peny was not sensing any kind of emotion or conviction from it.

"You took us here. I'm just an observer, a guide if you will."

They heard a commotion coming from the other side of the ruined wall. Penny couldn't help herself; she had to find what it was all about. So she went around the corner and saw a man thrusting himself upon a girl. This froze her feet on the ground, and she couldn't move forward. The victim was no one else but her; she saw her own rape. She saw her lying there, dead behind their eyes, begging silently for it to end. She pushed gathered herself up and rushed to attack him, but everything went dark again, and then they were in her house at Beachwood Road.

Her dad was on the couch, drinking, when the front door opened. Noticing the sound, he said, "Penny, about time."

Penny walked through. She was younger now — about 12 or 13 — not long after her mother had died.

"I'm sorry! the chip shop was closed." She responded.

Now she remembered. He used to send her to the chip shop. It took her around half an hour to walk to it, and he would blame her for it being cold.

Today must be a Monday, and it was always closed on a Monday. Then Penny realized what happened next. Elliot walked into the room as Penny hit the floor, the handprint fresh on her cheek. He launched himself at their dad, but dad was far too big for him to handle; without putting her any effort, he easily threw him off. By the looks of it, it seemed like he broke his nose.

"Why would you take me here?" She was filled with rage, and one could easily tell she was getting furious with each passing second.

"I want nothing to do with this man. I don't want to see his face ever again." She furiously declined to see her father. After that, she was brought back to darkness and then to the same room but looking slightly different. It was far more run-down, wallpaper was starting to peel off, and the place was filthy, her dad unconscious on the floor.

"I don't remember this," Penny said.

The guide said, "No, you don't because they aren't yours. this one is a part of Elliot's memory."

Penny turned around and saw Elliot walking into the room. He looked different, older, and far more like the person she saw in London.

"This must be after the car crash," she thought.

He was wearing a long hooded jacket/cloak. He has a look on his face she had never seen before. He walked off to his dad and pulled out a knife. Penny screamed, but it was effortless; it was nothing but a memory.

"This is an echo of time, a memory! Nothing can be changed here." The emotionless voice made the situation so much worse.

The darkness came again, and Penny braced herself for what he was about to see next. She could feel the hatred building, the rage rising.

Now she was in her classroom. The pictures on the walls were from the victorian projects. Her heart started to warm.

"You were a teacher and educator; that's interesting. You have compassion; even though you were always in pain, you want to give." It said.

Penny gave him a strange look, unsure of what he was getting at.

"Apart from the truths that I need you to know, know that this journey is guided by your own subconscious. When Angel went through this journey, he saw nothing but his pain and became consumed by it, whereas you are different. Your heart is showing your compassion with your pain. Your heart refuses to be consumed by darkness but also refuses to give it up. You still cling to your dark thoughts and your pain. You are right too, the elders will preach kindness and light only, but the truth is that darkness offers true power. Let your heart free as your heart will decide your path." Penny was listening carefully to its every word.

With that, the darkness came back, and the dark book and the light book were in front of her with the shadows dancing around.

"Now choose." The voice was a raspy whisper again. "This is the choice your brother hasn't been given. He was bent and moulded to Angel's will."

Penny suddenly thought for a second and asked, "So, if I take you to him, you can show him his journey? He can be Elliot again?"

After some more silence, it responded, "Yes! If he chooses light, then we shall restore him and give him back to you. But if he chooses dark, then he'll be lost forever. Now it is time for you to make your choice, child."

Penny thought for a long time, then asked again, "Why do I have to choose? why can't I have both?"

Penny was unsure after this question about how it ill react and how things would turn out to be.

There was again silence for a short time. Penny knew she screwed things up with this question, but then, a new voice spoke, "She could be the one." This voice was loud but not overpowering; it was both warm and cold.

She woke up in front of the fireplace, sitting crossed-legged. Both books had somehow made their way in front of her. The decision in her head had already been made; her brother was in need to have the book; he needed to remember who he was. Sensing the decision, the black book simply disappeared.

\#

Alex had been going from bothie to bothie, ruin to ruin, but there was nothing there. Everyone was either capture, killed, or escaped. The Operator was just keeping him busy and out of the way, and Alex had realized that. He began sensing a coldness from his mentor. Alex was immediately surrounded by feelings of resentment and paranoia. The Operator was like a father to him, but now, he was pushing him away. Alex failed to understand what caused this change. Whether it was some mistake, he made or did something terrible that he wouldn't even telling him the cause. All he knew was that secrets were being left from him. The crunching under Alex's boots was telling him that he was being distracted. He was trained to walk through woods silently, but this was clumsy of him. He was proving his presence to the enemies or whoever was around.

As he realized, he quickly slowed down his Pace. Obviously, he couldn't go further if there was a risk of getting caught or being hurt. He surveyed what was in front of him. The trees were branchless; someone had been harvesting the branches for arrows or greenstick for cooking. The tops of the trees were black; someone got a cheeky wee distillery on the go. At that, his heart sunk, and he realized he would smell it by now. The dwelling in front of him was probably evacuated like the rest. Then to his surprise, he heard something – a chittering of teeth. His ally had turned its attention to this location for some reason. The Phantoms were close by, and right on cue, he saw them attacking the bothie. There were two doors, windows built into the roof, and all around the build. Someone was in there, and he suddenly felt a connection. Someone or something was here, but who? Alex couldn't predict who the person was and what would be his or her motive, whether he would be a friend or foe. Walking towards the stone-built bothie, the Phantoms moved to the side to clear a path.

The darkness is an ally of the Clan, and they have an understanding that only The Operator truly understands. Walking into the bothie, Alex heard movement in the main sitting room. The hall was long and uneven, and the floor had rotted through in places. There was nothing that could be considered as a part of a roof at this part.

Alex reached the sitting room, but no one was there.

"Why was the darkness here?" He thought. He then remembered when he first encountered it. The Operator explained to him; he explained, "When Angel escaped from the Seraph, he created a hole, and some of the darkness escaped. Once on this plane, it became sentient. The shadows gave their eyes and ears everywhere; it was a powerful ally. When it needed to interact with the world, it manifested as different creatures depending on the need. Tonight, it was Phantoms. They came when the darkness senses energy being used. Then his question was answered;

there was the book of darkness on the floor, the black book. He quickly rushed over to it. He had been told tales of it and seen it in his visions, but it had been lost.

The boy that burned his family found it, and it drove him to madness. He took off his cloak and wrapped the book carefully. He made sure not to make any skin contact. He wasn't ready yet. Leaving the bothie, he found that the darkness had assembled its full army. Alex stood to regard them; it was an impressive sight. He often wondered how they were all controlled by a single mind. Was it a hive mind? Is each of them constituting a single part of it as a school of fish? The Phantoms had moved into perfect formations; the wraths were circling in the sky, and the Tusks were hanging back.

Their muscly form was easy to spot in the distance. Their overbearing swords made out of shadow itself made them more than formidable. He made for walking away, and the army reacted to intercept him.

"What the hell are you doing?! Stand back!" The army moved forward towards Alex.

He stumbled backwards, afraid he couldn't fight them all. With horror, he realized what this meant. Only one man could give orders to the darkness; only one man can turn them on him and no one else. That man would be no one else but his mentor, The Operator.

In all this commotion, the cloak slipped from the book, and his skin made contact with the smooth leather of the book's bindings. There was a flurry of shadow that engulfed him. Being convinced he was about to die, he closed his eyes, cursing his old mentor.

That was when he felt a sharp cold wind against his face. He opened his eyes and found himself on top of a large hit. In the distance, there was a castle, but he had no idea where he was.

Realizing that the shadow that engulfed him wasn't the darkness but the book, he realized it transported him to safety. I truly had chosen him for a purpose, and the book belongs to him now. Covering up the book again, he started walking.

First, he needed to find out where he was, and then he had to find New Pandora. Then, maybe then he can seek forgiveness from his mentor. Now the anger was fading; he confessed that it was his fault. He made him angry when he failed, and he failed a lot lately. He needed to find the New Pandora, and all would be forgiven.

Chapter 30: Reunited

It was a moving day, and Penny was terrified. She had fallen out with Katy, and her heart was hanging low. She was still a bit confused about the book, considering it just disappeared in thin air. This isn't possible, both technically and logically.

"Maybe it went to Elliot, maybe it was fixing what was done to him," she hoped.

She badly wanted her brother back. Looking around the rooms now, she realized they never felt like home; she always felt like a guest in someone else's house. Picking up her bag, she turned to Leon and said, "Thank you for looking after me."

Leon shrugged and said, "To be honest, you wouldn't let me do much. At least you let me handle the luggage; I also took the liberty of sending appropriate clothing to your new dwelling. You wouldn't fit in wearing whites all the time. Also, white is not a colour you can wear at that place all day long and still keep it tidy."

Leon was one of those people Penny actually liked for what he was; no fake, no hypocrisy, and no double standards.

Penny gave him a peck on the cheek and made her way across the walkway to the park. She was going to miss smelling this every day. The park was still her most favourite spot down here; walking through it today felt like goodbye for some reason. It was silly since she could come and sit in it anytime, but she felt like she was going to miss a significant part of her here.

Walking into the tunnels at the far side, following the path that Trevor showed her the night they sneaked out, she found her way to the lower levels. Trevor was waiting for her, "I thought I would walk with you a bit."

Penny was glad to see him. It felt like forever since she had seen him.

"Trevor, where have you been hiding?" She asked him as she ran over and threw her arms around his neck, squeezing him a bit too tight for his liking.

They turned towards the overcrowded walkways and started walking.

The stench hits her; this was going to be the hardest bit to get used to.

"The sanitation needs to be fixed down here," Penny commented.

Trevor nodded in agreement, responded, "There's a lot that needs fixing down here, these people are the forgotten, and no wonder they have no faith in the gods."

Someone overheard the talk of the gods and gave them a wide birth; Penny realized it was not a topic for down here. As they made their way to the barracks where Penny would be staying, she began wondering what they would think of her and her Book of Light.

"Will they reject me? Burn me as a witch?" She asked.

"No!" The man in the park responded, interrupting their conversation in the middle. "They would try and explain it with science."

This answer was supposed to make her relieve, but instead, it gave her a creepy thought of being kidnapped for experimentation.

They had reached penny's room. They walked in, and that is exactly what it is — a room. The first thing that hit her was the heat; everything was so hot down here near the central furnace. Then she was flabbergasted when she was hit by the smell of the flowers. Her room was full of all the flowers from the park. It looked beautiful; the colours and the smell made her feel instantly like she was at home. She was overcome with a feeling of wellness.

"This will do; I'm going to be fine here," She thought. "Would you like to see your classroom?" Trevor asked Penny as he held her hand. They were crossing the busy walkway again and reached the administrative offices. People immediately stopped doing what they were doing and watched as they walked in. The place was bare, they had desks and chairs, but none of the technology Penny had seen above. The situation was totally opposite in contrast to the situation above. While still holding her hand, Trevor took Penny through to the back. It opened up into a large room, which was filled with chairs and desks. There were jotters and pens on every desk ready for the student. There was a teacher's desk as well at the far end of the classroom. Penny could see it had all the stationery and equipment she had in her previous classrooms. The walls had boards installed on them and were ready for work to be stuck up. Penny couldn't believe that Trevor had done so much work in such little time. She said, "I couldn't believe you did all this in this little time,"

"I had help," Trevor nodded to the corner behind them. Her words hinted Penny who he would be referring to, but she turned around anyway and saw Katy standing sheepishly.

"I thought these non-believers don't deserve our help?" Penny said coldly.

She couldn't help herself, her perfect image of Katy had been destroyed now, and it couldn't be repaired.

"I'm sorry for what I said, I was orphaned when I was ten, and my parents wanted to help down here. They brought them food and blankets. Some people down here even sleep out on the walkways. One day they were robbed and murdered over some bread. I've hated them ever since, but maybe I'm wrong. My parents would be as ashamed of me as you are if they heard me say those things. I'm sorry. If you have me here, things will be easier for you. After all, I just want to help you down here?" Katy said. Embarrassingly, looking down on the floor.

The defence around Penny's heart instantly crumbles. Katy was standing there, looking so vulnerable, and all Penny wanted to do was cuddle her up. Trevor gave her a heavy push forward, and she slipped forward and fell into Katy's arms.

When they detached from each other, Penny looked at Katy and Trevor and began to explain everything that happened with the books.

Penny wanted to go find her brother after he was restored by the book. He would need help after getting his memories back, and she wanted to be there to help him out. Obviously, they would have to extract him, and he was in danger.

She suddenly realized she was here playing teacher while he was out there, probably freaking out. Trevor said that if there was a way, then he would find it, and Penny kinda believed him as well. She knew Trevor would not let her go alone anyway and would do whatever he could in his power to help her out. He is one of those people in her life she could trust this with and firmly believed that he would not let her down. After that, they were gone advising her not to get anxious and not to plan anything on her own alone.

However, being his sister, Penny couldn't get the thought out of her head; the only thing that was roaming in her mind was Elliot needed help. At the same time, some other thoughts were making room in her mind as well. These thoughts consist of, "He was out there alone, but he murdered their dad. He's done so much evil. Will he make the right choice?"

It was just the previous day that Trevor said he would look into it, but the anxiety was getting the best of her with each passing second. Her thoughts were interrupted by a group of nervous-looking children walking in. They took chairs at the back of the room, slowly filling up towards the front. It was clear to her that nobody was interested in being at the front. Penny stood up and addressed, "I'm Miss Whyte."

The class just looked at her blankly.

"This was going to be a long day," Penny thought. This thought was nothing less than just a distraction.

She was back in the classroom.

All the students in the class were working through some numbers and letters while Penny was trying to gauge their level of education. They were all very different from each other. It seemed to be dependant on the parents and how much time they've spent with the child, which could be predicted a little by Penny.

Penny found herself shivering. It was odd since it was always so hot down here; she shouldn't be cold. Then suddenly, she could feel it; her connection to Elliot. It was like an invisible string on her heart. The cold was overpowering, where ever he was; Penny could tell that he was cold and scared. She could feel his fear.

Closing her eyes, Penny tried to settle her head, but she started to get flashes of Elliot. He was running, scared, and alone, just like she feared. Leaning against an old stone wall, he was trying to hide from something.

The expression on his face told Penny there was no hiding from what he was running from. The book was in his hands, and he was clutching it for dear life, occasionally reaching out into the air trying to find something trying to focus on what was around him. She wanted to get a feel for where he was but filed to do so. Suddenly, it clicked to her that he must be somewhere close, close enough for her to feel him. She needed to get closer to him, but she couldn't make anything out.

The darkness was grabbing him, as he was being hunted by Phantoms and worse. Penny stood up and said, "That's enough for today. leave your work on the table, and we can come back to it tomorrow and start from where we are leaving it."

She heard a familiar sound of chairs screeching against the floor, and the room got filled with all the talking, but it didn't settle her. She thought about going to get Katy and Trevor, but there wasn't time; Elliot was in trouble, and she couldn't risk not taking any immediate steps. She made her way to the supply train that went to the surface and got on board. She still couldn't get over the fact that men have to hall it upwards. This time though, she was more advanced in her abilities. She had learnt lessons from Claire. Using some of her energy, she propelled the train at a speed the occupants clearly weren't used to. Reaching the top, there had been more than one casualty to the train's accelerated motion. Penny almost ran out of the train and into the cavern when she realised that she didn't have a device that could phase her back into the normal dimensional space.

She looked around and reached in, unsure how much energy this would take or even if it was possible. After a deep exhale, she took what she estimated it would require, focused on the moving air, the feeling of being back. She was finally able to focus on feeling the blue flash, which always gave her a queazy motion sickness kind of feeling.

Suddenly, she felt a massive shift. There was no blue light this time, but there was a burst of energy that hit everything in the cavern. She phased back but also briefly phased anyone that was too close to her as well. She briefly saw the glimpse of panic on their faces before they returned and were out of sight.

Running out of the cavern through the narrow tunnel, Penny hit the cold night air. She could hear a chittering sound, which was coming from the distance; she knew what that meant. She closed her eyes and focused on the fear and panic she was feeling in her gut. She knew very well that it wasn't her's; it belonged to Elliot. She used this fear and panic to connect with him and saw ruins that were around him. Looking around, she now knew exactly where he was. He must be looking for a sanctuary from the darkness; he had made his choice.

Penny was running towards Flint Castle when she felt a thrill of triumph in her gut. Her brother had come back and was looking for her.

The darkness, on the other hand, was trying to capture him now that he had turned his back on them.

Upon reaching the castle, the chittering was almost deafening. There was a whole army of them and others. The wrath was in the sky, with their scorpion tails swishing. The venom was strong enough to give you unstoppable hallucinations, which will trap your mind in the dark dimension. The whole scene around the castle was frightening enough to make even the strongest men flinch.

However, according to Claire, they were also very fragile creatures and tended to stay back and make calculated attacks from stealth. The Tisks were the muscles, big and strong, and they carried heavy dark swords. They were all here, and Elliot was getting more and more cornered with each passing second. The chances of slipping out from them were getting eliminated one by one.

Penny watched as they closed in on him, encircling. With speed she was running now, Penny felt like she was flying. She concentrated and raised a shield around her, reinforcing it, using it as a battering ram, and making a path through the horde.

She reached Elliot, who was standing there just panting at her in surprise.

"What the hell are you doing?" Elliot questioned.

Penny turned around to face the darkness, but they started to walk backwards and retreated into the shadows. They hadn't given up; they were just regrouping.

"Elliot! I heard you; I saw you searching for me for help!" Penny turned around again to face him this time, and stepped forward, and held his hand.

Alex gave her a wicked smile and said, "I was looking for you, but with you as the prize, I can return to my mentor, and maybe then he will forgive me for my failures."

Penny realised with a thud in her stomach that he hadn't made his choice yet; he couldn't have; he was still dark.

With a jerk, Penny let go of his hands and ran forward. He moved his hand to throw her, but she was ready for him this time. She shielded it and grabbed the dark book that was shoving in his hands, and kept a hold of it.

She found the book happy to oblige, and they were both taken to a dark place. Only she and her brother were there with the shadows. Alex spun around and saw her in confusion.

"What the hell have you done?" He shouted at her.

"I'm taking my brother back, and it is time for Elliot to come back to me!" She yelled, looking into his eyes.

Chapter 31:
Family ties

The shadows were moving all around Penny. She had been here before as well; this was the first time she was with someone else. Now it was up to her to make sure that he made the right decision. She would take her brother back, and she was insisted on it.

Elliot, unsure of what to do, seemed to be frightened of the shadows. In fact, Penny realised this was as far as she had planned. Her stomach was full of butterflies as she spoke to Elliot, "What happened to you?"

Alex just looked at her with rage. He couldn't understand who she was and why was she taking such a big risk by being here with him. Did she not know what he had done to the tribe?

"Who the hell are you?" He asked directly.

Penny was totally speechless. How could he not know who she was? She knew that they had brainwashed him and conditioned him, but how could they just remove her from his mind; it seemed like she had never existed for him.

"I'm your sister!" Penny almost shouted back.

He took a step back and slowly started to walk backwards, away from her. Alex was shaking his head; he was having a hard time taking this information in. The girl in the pictures. and the girl in front of him; the long black hair; the eyes; the voice.

He was getting angrier and angrier when he thought about it; something was stirring; it had been stirring since he saw the picture.

"Why do you call me Elliot? I'm Alex!" He countered as he took a couple of steps forward.

Penny shook her head, "No, you are Elliot, my brother, and I love you!"

Alex took a few more steps back.

The whispers started, "The girl who has made her choice knows who she is and the boy who doesn't even know his own name."

Penny could hear a low gurgle echoing from the shadows. It sounded like some sort of twisted laughter.

The whispers continued, "The boy who is so headstrong with his path and the girl who doesn't yet know hers."

The gurgling continued to echo louder and louder until it was bouncing around their heads. Now the shadows swirled around them, and they were outside a house. Penny felt the warm summer's sun on her skin and could smell the pollen in the air.

"It must be the height of summer, but where?" she thought. "Where are we, Elliot?" She questioned to confirm the location.

Alex just stayed quiet. He refused to answer to that name. Besides, he didn't want her to see this, and he knew exactly where they were.

The house stood on its own, at the top of a field. It was well maintained with a lovely garden. The flowers were in full bloom, and there were sheds and greenhouses in the distance. There was even a swing set out front. It was a family home. There was a figure in the distance who was in a dark hood.

Crossing the well-cut grass, they could see it was Alex. Penny suddenly felt queazy, unsure of what was about to happen. She turned her face to see her brother, and by the look on Elliot's face, it seemed like he didn't want to see it either.

"So there is still a hope yet," Penny thought.

He was still in there somewhere. Suddenly, they were transported into the house; they were in the Landing. There were screams in one of the bedrooms and then a horrible sudden silence. A little girl ran into the room shouting, "mummy."

Suddenly, a high pitched scream. Just like that, that scream came to a sudden end as well.

"I was given orders," he uttered.

It was a tone she had never heard from his mouth; there was no emotion behind it. She looked at him in horror. Then they were transported back to their home in Beachwood road, where she had to witness the reported beating that her brother took and the eventual murder. Penny was becoming concerned she was losing him, and there was nothing but pain here and murder. She started having the second thought as she wasn't sure if she wanted him back or not, especially after what she had seen. That wasn't the only thing. In fact, he had spent the past year killing people and their families that threatened the Clan.

She suddenly had an idea; she started to tell him about her memories of her brother, Elliot. The time he beat up a boy in primary school because he pulled up Penny's dress; the stories they used to tell each other; the fun they used to have with their mother before she died; and how much they all loved each other.

The memories disappeared as quickly as they came. However, Elliot wasn't concentrating on them. The more he saw, the more pain there was on his face. He started getting uneasy; frustration was clearly on his face. The darkness came back, and they were surrounded by shadows again.

"We can only restore the willing; this one is too weak for the truth," the whispers reacted.

Alex yelled, "NO! Show me the truth, and I'll decide!"

This sent the shadows into a frenzy, "So it is time for the boy to choose; is he Alex or is he, Elliot?"

Penny found herself in the ruins of Flint Castle, and Elliot was nowhere to be seen. She was worried for Elliot that he could choose the wrong path, but he needed to do this himself. However, she had an internal feeling that he would come back to her.

She could hear the chittering in the distance. She had an idea, and immediately, she used a little less energy and phased herself again. The Phantoms appeared, but they couldn't see her. Her technique worked! She started to walk and found that with each step, she used a little bit of energy. As useful as this was; it had limitations; it was bound by time.

She needed to get away before she phased back. Also, she needed the energy to phase, either way, so she was worried as well about what would happen if she let herself went dry and didn't phase back.

"Will she just automatically phase back, or what happens?" She thought.

Something told her it would be better not to find out. Making a mental note, she made her way down the shortest route. Halfway back, there was a group of people running towards her. She got scared; she assumed it was a group of enemies who came for them after regrouping. However, she kept on moving forward, cuz, the phantom was on following her in the back. Moving ahead, she recognised the group; there were Trevor and Katy, who were running to her, with a bunch of armed men behind them.

She sped up her running and phased back. She greeted them.

"What the hell were you doing out here alone?" Katy scolded Penny, while Penny just kept looking at the ground.

"My brother needed me," Penny spoke. She was defiant now.

Her brother was the only stability she had in her life. No matter how messed up he got, he was her rock. If he needed her, she would go to him.

"It was a trap; he isn't your Elliot anymore! From what our intel is telling us, he is called Alex now, and he is as evil as they come. He had wiped out cells or just simply killed families for being too close."

Penny shot her gaze to the ground again; she did not know what to say about it. This point is something she couldn't defend. After all, this was all true. She remembered the memory she witnessed a while ago, the memory of that little girl.

"Maybe he had gone too far," she thought. Then she also remembered that she saw regret in his face; there was shame in his eyes, indicating to her that he was still in there.

There was a thumping sound behind them. Penny turned around and saw a massive creature who appeared out of nowhere; the Tusk looked like something from Greek mythology. It charged through them like they were nothing, the Phantoms, following him, charged as well. The men had gathered themselves and opened fire in counter. The Tusk disintegrated easily as the bright blue bullets cut through it. It was not the time to celebrate victory. Phantoms were charging just behind him. They immediately turned their weapons to the Phantoms and Wraths overhead; they were going to be overwhelmed. They were too much in numbers; it wasn't possible for them to overcome the charging phantoms in that limited time.

Penny quickly grabbed a massive amount of energy and created a ball of pure light in front of her, then allowed it to become unstable. It quickly got unstable, so much that it couldn't be controlled by Penny, and exploded. The results were the same as she intended. It left them all untouched but disintegrated anything made from shadows and darkness.

Penny thought she heard the darkness cry out. Maybe she could hurt this creature. Then suddenly, she felt a shiver; she got weaken and fell to the ground. Trevor picked her up into his arms and carried her back to the cavern and onto the train. That was the last thing she could remember.

When Penny woke up, she was in bed. Elder Claire was sitting next to her, and she had a smile on her face that said, 'you're getting a lecture'.

"So you need to learn how to fight without getting yourself killed," Elder Claire commented.

Penny smiled and said, "yes, please."

The elder told Penny to come to the city park later when she got fully recovered from her weakness and got released from here. Penny sat up and asked Claire what happened to Elliot and what would happen to him about the things he had done and about the intel they had on Alex.

Claire looked upset, "We don't know all the details, but for the last ten months, we have been tracking an assassin. He's been assassinating cell members or sympathizers. We don't understand yet how they are being identified. We suspect there is someone senior that's passing information to the Clan. It isn't for sure yet, but there is a hinch that we have a mole inside our ranks. It's the first time in history that this has happened. Trevor is looking into it for me, but for now, our priority is to get you in shape; we need to get you battle-ready."

Penny just laid there emotionlessly. Nothing appeared on her face, but thousands of thoughts were running into her mind.

Elder Claire continued, "We are going to attack them at their new camps. We need to rescue our brothers and sisters."

"How?" Penny asked.

Elder Claire responded, "Normally, we wouldn't stand a chance. But with you, as a fully trained to face them and to lead us into battle, we might just do it.

Penny nodded her head like she understood everything.

"You rest now. Later we talk about war and what side your brother is on." Elder Claire said and left the room.

Chapter 32: A Call To Arms

Sitting in the shadows, The Operator was communing with an old friend; the darkness can't talk exactly; it's primordial. He was a creature of pure dark energy and pure thought. It existed in the darkness, hid from the light, and worked with shadows, turning the shadows into creatures to manifest its intentions, up to the point where their partnership had been fruitful. The Darkness's very nature made it impossible to hide from, although the part of it, the thought, could only exist in one place at a time. Every piece of shadow and every piece of darkness on the planet is like a sensor to it, making an escape from it impossible. Even in the sunlight, the escape is impossible; because you have your own shadow, you can't just escape it, and this is why it is so perfect. Undeniably, it was the ultimate predator. After all, one couldn't run from their own shadow.

In the past, it would lead to mass slaughters, but then, the Tribe disappeared, and even the Darkness couldn't find them. Before that, the light from the people of the crystal worn as jewellery kept people safe from its sight. This is where The Operator came in, and everything changed. He was the eye when it couldn't see. If he spotted a cell that was obscured from sight, he called on the darkness if his own men weren't available.

Now the Darkness felt different; it felt like a wounded animal who would ruin any or everyone who would come in its way. However, as The Operator reached for his thoughts, he felt fear. This was the first time in history when his old friend had been wounded. He was unable to comprehend how was this possible? He then saw the battle and its memories. He saw the horde attack; then the Operator saw a blinding light exploding, destroying the shadow manifestations. However, that's not what wounded it; the manifestations have always been destroyed by weapons made from crystal. The shockwave from the blast had hit its consciousness. It's non-corporeal, so no weapon had ever touched it, whereas energy attacks were never powerful enough to be more than a little inconvenient. In fact, The Operator, who was as ancient as his, couldn't hurt it.

This shockwave that the girl produced was something different, something new, something that they had never seen before, and it had the ability to hurt it, and that made him terrified.

The Operator immediately realized she was more powerful than she knew, and she wasn't a normal light-bearer; she was something else.

"Could she be the one that had been prophesized a long time ago?" The Operator thought.

The prophecy was made by him himself when he was Angel.

'They will come off both light and dark, the destroyer of the gods.'

He was never sure what it meant when he did it; he only translated it from the book. He always considered it to be a group of people. His understanding made him believe that the Tribe was the one that would destroy the gods; maybe he was wrong, maybe he made a mistake, maybe it never meant a group of people, and it meant a single person, maybe it meant her.

"You get it?" Claire asked Penny as she looked reassuringly at Penny.

However, she didn't manage to strike a single target successfully.

Claire had set up several targets around the park. Penny's task was to run in a circuit and hit those targets as they appeared. Round-crafted ornaments made from crystals of different depths, which looked like crystal dream catchers, were hanging in the trees. They were supposed to light up as she hit them but instead, they just kinda fizzled.

Breathless and realizing how unfit she was, Penny walked over to where Claire, Kim, and Katy were sitting. As Katy watched her walking to them, she invited her to sit down. Penny slowly walked to them and sat with a failure's face. Katy instantly jumped up on her knee and threw her arms around her.

"Okay, so take a rest and then back to it in a while," Katy ordered Penny.

Penny started to tickle Kim as Katy watched on warmly. Then Kim ran off to play, pretending to show Penny how to run the course, throwing her hands out, imitating as if she was throwing energy blasts. Claire started to explain, "Your energy works alongside your intuition. When you run and jump over a gap, how much energy do you put into your legs? Do you stop and think? Do you make a calculation? Or do you just jump and trust that your legs know what they're doing?"

Penny, listening to her carefully and understanding what she was trying to say, exhaustedly put her hands to her head.

"I understand what you are telling me. But it's like I'm trying to make that jump before I've learned to run!" Penny metaphorically spoke her mind out.

They were distracted by a sudden glow in the park. They turned to see what caused this glow. Everyone was staring at the crystals as well. Somehow, they've all been activated.

"But I've been sat here, then who is...?" Penny complained but stopped when Kim appeared. It was Kim who caused this glow.

"See? It's easy," Elder Claire commented.

"How did she do that?" Penny asked.

"She shouldn't have been able to," replied Claire.

#

Alex was trapped in this dark place, and shadows all around him, keeping a guard on him. Maybe this was his punishment. He remembered her now, growing up together, playing at Nana's and their mother.

He was criticizing himself, "How could I have forgotten her?

His thoughts were chaotic now, lost in memories he had long forgotten. From a distance, he could smell the fish at Arbroath harbour, the smokies at M&M Spink next to the harbour.

Then, he was at the Commercial Inn. His target was at the bar, and from memories, Alex remembered he killed him in the toilets. Then, he was standing over the body, still not feeling remorse. However, there was something he didn't like about killing him. Something was scratching at the back of his head. However, because he didn't have a conscience, he didn't give it a thought. He felt out to the Shaitan, hoping they could hear him, and they did. They spoke to him earlier; it was his first memories as Alex.

Now he felt like there were two people inside him, one was Alex, and the other one was Elliot. He was back in the darkness, but this was different. He could see himself strapped to a chair and fighting to get free. Shadowy figures were dancing around him, taunting him. Every time they made contact with his head, he watched himself contort with agony. They were also pulling thread-like stuff from his head, which was his memories, so technically, they were pulling his memories little by little. They were feeding off his screams and were getting stronger and stronger. This was the Shaitan; they were torturing him.

The book whispered to him, "Time stands still here, you fought them for ten years; for ten years, they had you and did this, ten years they fed on you until you were no longer you. After that, they sent you back to the place in time you came from. They had altered your memory, changed who you are. And their Angel gave you a new name, just as he did to himself."

The shadows swirled, and he found himself at the harbour in Arbroath. He was still holding the book but was back in the real world. His head was spinning, and it was getting harder for him to absorb and concentrate. The only thing that was constant with him was his anger. They tortured him for years, and now he remembered every minute of it. They drove him mad to the point where he has killed so many people, including numerous children.

He felt a pain in his chest that he hadn't felt before. The scratching he was feeling in the back of his head had spread around his head and gripped his neck and chin. He couldn't move his arm. He felt as if his body was seizing; he fell to the ground and lost consciousness.

#

The council of Elders was in full session now. They were discussing the camps and what they needed to do about them.

"We can't rely on the girl," Margaret expressed. She was dead against Penny being involved. "If she sees her brother, then she might fail to attack him, leaving us open."

Elder Claire listened to her calmly and spoke, "With respect, you are wrong. She has already faced her brother and seen inside his head. She walked a memory path together. She has seen his evil."

Listening to Claire, the hall was filled with chitters as the council burst into private conversations.

Margaret banged on the table and said, "We need to take a vote. First of all, will we attack? And if so, will Penny be with us?"

Elder Claire spoke up again, "No Margaret, and she will lead us!"

There were murmurs of both persuasions. Then the voting began. First, they all voted in favour of attacking the camps and freeing their brothers and sisters. Then, they voted against Penny joining them in the attack. This is not the way it should happen. But they were against Penny from the start anyway." Elder Claire thought.

Jacob spoke on behalf of the black ballers, "We believe she hasn't received enough training. This is as much for her safety and well-being as it is for ours. We believe she has great things to do in her proper place."

Elder Claire got up and walked out, closely followed by Trevor. There were murmurs of surprise around the room at the breach in protocol.

Penny got furious when she found out about the news, "I'm ready, and I don't care what they say I'm going. They can't stop me from being there."

Claire nodded, "I agree. But going along and attacking separately could disrupt their tactics and cause their mission to fail, which already has higher chances of happening. It's dangerous".

"Then use us. You have your own private army who is loyal to you down below," a voice occurred. Penny knew exactly who this voice was. She smelt the Jupe. So, she looked up at him.

Chapter 33:
The Attack

Trevor didn't miss the cold of Scotland. The wind was hitting the face, and the ground was always hard. Even though Katy was trembling, but he didn't think it was because of the cold; he tapped his hand on Katy's shoulder and said, "Kim will be fine. She is safe at home, and we are exactly where we are supposed to be."

The wind was howling through the bothie walls. They weren't very useful when it came to providing much protection, but they wouldn't be there long, so it was okay for them. Their target camp was close by; they were downwind, and they could smell it.

They had heard reports of the conditions, and it smelt worse than they had thought. The plan was simple, but not everyone knew about the whole plan. Trevor knew they had a traitor among them, and that's why everyone was unaware of the whole plan. They only knew their own parts, and nobody apart from Trevor and Claire knew the full plan.

"Get some rest; we don't know when we can rest again," Trevor suggested.

Katy was missing her daughter. There was no way she was going to be able to rest until this was done. There were other cells doted about, but their cell had the most important role, and they couldn't afford to get fail. Failing to play their part could jeopardize the whole plan and could affect the mission. The pressure was almost too much. She wished Penny was there.

"Why did Margaret block this?" Katy thought.

Katy had a feeling that Margaret wanted Penny to fail. She also had a feeling that she wanted this plan to fail as well, maybe because she was furious that she was not being given the whole plan. She thought the council should have been fully briefed, at least.

According to the by-laws, "In times of war, the head of security is also the war chief and is the final word on all tactics and decisions."

There was nothing but darkness outside; they were safe with the crystals until dawn. Their plan was to attack during the day. At night time, there was too much danger in an attack; there were not many places to hide when the darkness covered most of the field. The darkness was something they still didn't entirely understand. The creatures of darkness moved like a flock of birds as if they were one mind and if they weren't protected by crystals. The creatures came running out of the darkness.

There had been stories of people being dragged down by their own shadows, and these incidents had been increasing at a rapid pace.

There was some movement in the distance, Katy suddenly became fully alert. She could feel the blood pumping through her head, and she was bursting with adrenaline. As she focused on the place, she saw much more movement there. She realized there was a whole army out there, an army of Humans, not Phantoms.

"Here we go!" Katy alerted the rest.

They quickly grabbed their weapons. Katy started firing out of the window. The bullets were just normal ammo; they were saving the crystal for something worse. Normal ammo worked for humans, but not on the creatures. Crystals would come in handy if and when the creatures would come.

They fired a barrage of bullets at them and saw a lot of them going down and hitting the ground hard. The enemy line stopped. They had to stop to consider their next move. After a while, the movement started again, the soldiers got back up and started walking towards the bothie. There was a panic among them; the coming army wore the armour; Katy and everyone did not know what kind of armour, but they were not prepared for this; they did not have any plan for this.

"Try hitting them with the crystal. See if that works," Trevor said.

Trevor told them to switch to crystal rounds; they would go through anything. By the time they switched from normal ammo to crystal, the enemy was already inside. Katy got a few rounds off and took down one of the soldiers before a butt of a gun knocked her out. As Trevor saw Katy go down, he lost his temper and ran to pick up a large crystal plated blade and marched in the running, putting down three soldiers before being knocked to the ground.

When Trevor woke up, he saw himself confined in a concrete cell. He was in the cell alone by himself, but there was a camera watching him. As Trevor felt the cold concrete underneath him, he realized that it was even colder here than it was in the bothy.

Casually scratching his back, he checked if the package was still there; it was there.

Before leaving Pandora, they all had a package put on their back slightly out of phase. It contained a sidearm, an explosive, and a small EMP. He smiled as he realized that the spy had taken the bait, and so had the clan.

In the council, he gave very little away about the plan, but he did say that he was going to take a cell overlooking the camp. From his position, he would be coordinating the attack. The real plan was to be captured. He still didn't know who it was, but now he knew the traitor was an elder.

The Operator knew there was an attack coming, but now they would be blind. If things went well, they might have to cancel the attack with their commander captured before they even launch. Feeling pretty pleased with himself, he walked back over to his desk, where Katy was sitting tied to a chair.

"You know, after all this time, I've discovered that darkness isn't something that needs a lot of work on, not in the modern age. When you have lived as long as I have, you see the big picture. The world as a whole has more light and love in it than ever, more freedom than anyone has ever had, less poverty than any time in history. The difference is modern technology; people focus on the bad, they focus on the paedophile from the BBC and the rest that got discovered. It seems like an epidemic because it's being reported far and wide. The reality looking throughout history, people morals are the highest they have ever been. People are held accountable on much higher levels than ever before. The only difference between now and a hundred years ago is the internet. The world isn't getting darker, but the perception is that it is. This is doing more damage to your cause than anything I can do." The Operator kept speaking on his own, regardless of the matter if Katy paid any attention to it or not.

Katy just looked at him with disgust. She had no interest in a conversation, and she didn't have information about the other cells that were attacking.

"Kim? That's your daughter, right?" The Operator asked.

Katy gathered the courage and tried to break free and jumped at him but failed to do so. All she managed to do was fall over in the chair.

"Now, now, you don't want to hurt yourself. Or else, you'll miss the show." The operator suggested Katy as he walked towards Katy and lifted her up.

He walked over to the window and observed the camp. The operator was kind of a perfectionist and took pride in his work.

"None of these insects would want to be released anyway. There is nothing of them left." He said.

As he turned his face back to Katy, Katy hit him with a stick and knocked him out.

Katy must have broken the arm of the chair when she fell to the side; The operator failed to notice it earlier when he was getting herself up, and thus, turned his back to her. He made his mistake and, as a result, got knocked out. At the same time, Katy made a mistake as well by making too much noise. The guards outside heard the noise and broke into the room. She pulled the sidearm from the hiding place on her back and charged them with all of her might, managing to take them down by surprise; they thought she was unarmed.

She slowly made her way into a long hallway. The bare hall had a number of doors, but she was looking for the one that would lead her to the control room. They have an assumption that it would be close to The Operator's office. However, every door in the hallway looked exactly the same. There were no signs or indication of which door leads to what.

Spotting a double-doored entrance or exit at the end, Katy made a dash for it. She kept her ears focused on her surroundings and listened at the door for any movement inside. She heard two people talking at the other side of the door. She burst through the gun first.

"Don't shoot. It's us," Trevor yelled.

She found Trevor and a few of the cells.

"The rest didn't make it," Trevor told Katy.

They gathered themselves together, and with proper precautions, they moved ahead. After checking into a few rooms, they found the control room.

"When the guard came for me, they assumed I was unarmed, so it was easy to surprise him, then I got these guys and headed here," Katy told Trevor about his escape. Trevor wanted to know this to make sure it was not a scheme or a trap set by The Operator.

"Let get the explosives planted; we need the distraction if we want to make this work. The rest of the attack force was hidden outside and waiting for a signal to attack. They hadn't been told what it'd be. but they were told to continue regardless, no matter the cost, these camps need to be answered." Trevor explained.

The commander of the attacking cells was John, and Anna, his daughter, was his second. They kept looking to the hill they thought the Trevor would be on. They were waiting for a signal from his side to move forward.

They knew he had been captured but were assured that he would figure out a way to escape somehow, and thus, they stuck to the plan. They would start when they got the signal, and when they engaged from the front, more cells would come in from behind to join them.

"I have a surprise for them as well," Trevor said.

Daytime had come, and they were expecting the signal at any moment. The tensions were rising, and the troops were getting restless. All the wait was killing them.

Katy was working on one of the consoles. The reason she was here was to do one of the most important jobs, to deactivate the bombs in the prisoners' necks. They could remove them safely when they would get back to New Pandora.

For now, they had to do what was needed. Trevor had finished planting the explosives. According to his plan, when he would trigger the explosion, it should kill all their systems, and they wouldn't be able to reactivate in time and would be out of range.

The plan had been working finely so far. Everyone thought this was a full-on attack to take over the camp. Without Penny, there was no chance for them to take over the camp. All they could do was punch a hole in the wall and escape with the prisoners. Trevor looked over the courtyard as the prisoners were being led over to the factories. He couldn't believe how they looked; they were just skeletons with skin. Running upwards, a man fell over; the guard simply shot him and kicked him out of the way. The prisoners who were captured in the factories were out of harm's way. It was time now.

"Katy, is it done?" Trevor asked.

Katy gave him a nod, and it was the final key.

"Then let's get the hell out of this room; it's about to be rubble," Trevor yelled.

They ran into the hallway, bumping into The Operator and some guards. The Operator flicked his hands in the air, and their guns flew out of their hands and dropped to the ground. The timer was going unnoticed in the background. Trevor was slowly counting down in his head, 4… 3… 2… 1…

"Down!" Trevor shouted as he pulled everyone to the ground as the doors got blown off the hinges knocking. The Operator and his Guards were on the ground. Trevor sent his signal!

Chapter 34: One Last Trick

Jacob gave the command, the forces un-phased and charged as they kept firing their guns at the guards and the walls. Three rocks went flying past Jacob's head, bringing down a part of the front wall and the guards above it. Making a drive towards the broken part of the wall, Trevor noticed that the guards weren't putting up much of a fight. In fact, there wasn't any kind of counterattack at all. He felt something suspicious and immediately radioed to Anna, "Be cautious; something isn't right."

Anna gave the order and attacked from the rear. The explosion happened that could be seen by Jacob breaching the hind wall. Again, there was no major reaction from the force's side; something really didn't feel right.

Jacob ordered everyone to stand their ground but, at the same time, to keep moving further. He wanted to see how it would play out. Watching the field of battle, he could finally see them reacting and sending more people. They were trying to entice them in, but they did not understand why they were doing this.

He kept up with his tactic, why risking the lives of his men when he could take them one by one if needed. Anna was ordered to do the same at the rear.

#

Trevor and the rest were hiding in a closet.

"This doesn't seem very heroic," Katy thought.

"Trevor, why are we in a closet? Can't you hear the battle outside?" Katy asked Trevor.

Trevor just nodded but said nothing. Katy knew to trust her old friend. He was not a coward, but if they were in a closet, then that was exactly where they were supposed to be; it must have been a part of the plan.

Looking down, she saw she was right, they were in the cleaning closet, and there were chemicals all around the cleaning closet. Trevor was working with those chemicals, improvising some more explosives; he handed them out. Those explosives were crude but would work well for smoke grenades when smashed in the contents mix.

The smoke would actually be chlorine gas which was deadly, so that was also good. Going out into the hallway, they realized it was deserted; not even The Operator was there.

"He must be concerning himself with the attack," Trevor thought.

#

Jacob could see the enemy was reinforcing themselves on the inside now; this tactic wouldn't work anymore. He ordered his men to push forward and take control of the courtyard. He coordinated his attack with his daughter. They were winning. The enemy was falling back to the main building, leaving the courtyard free; it was a straight shot to the factories.

His men were moving onto the factories, and Anna's men were staying there, keeping the exit route secure. Suddenly, there was a white gas coming out the windows, and a few men jumped out, landing awkwardly and breaking arms and legs. They were easily picked off as they tried to raise their weapons.

Jacob was coming back with the prisoners. They just walked in the direction they were pointed and were certain that they weren't running, no matter how much they shouted or encouraged; it was like something from a zombie film; they looked dead. Nothing was behind their eyes. "Their brain isn't working. What did they do to them?" Anna thought.

That was when a figure came out with his arms up, holding no weapons.

"Dad, it's him!" Anna pointed at The Operator as he came out.

Anna aimed at his head and pressed the trigger. She put a bullet in him, and he went down. A moment later, he got back up and spat that bullet out.

#

He smiled and raised his hands in the air again. At that moment, storm clouds filled the sky, winds started to move at a greater speed, the rain and lighting came as well, but this all was still not the worse part of all was that it blotted out the sun and brought the darkness into the Warfield.

First, they heard the chittering of the Phantoms, "Crystal rounds!"

Jacob shouted, but it seemed like he was a bit panicked. The screeching of the wraths almost drowned out the thunder. The lightning struck, and that was when they saw them; the horde was ready to charge. There were too many, but they were trapped, at least for now. However, if they were unshackled and charged, they would just cut straight through them within a couple of minutes.

As they watched them, they immediately started to look hesitant. They turned around, and the wraths flew away from them in the opposite direction. That was when they heard it, shouts of an army larger than the one that the council could muster. The horde split down into two from the middle as their line was crumbled by the charge. From the clothes, it seemed like the army was made up of people from down below. They all were being led by a woman in white.

"Penny!" Jacob thought, "She ignored our orders."

Thank god, he thought straight away.

Penny destroyed them in their droves with energy blasts while the army flanked. They were moving at a great speed and shooting the wraths out of the sky; the Tusks were too slow to catch anyone. They started to take casualties when the darkness had regained itself. Penny felt its presence; she could feel it as a brain controlling the masses. A brain without form, she felt it gather its full strength, and when she thought it was behind her, she turned swiftly. As soon as she turned and faced that direction, she felt a presence approach from the other direction. Such a thing happened quite a few times; no matter which way she turned, the shadows advanced; she couldn't pick her target.

Her legs were trembling, and it was getting harder and harder for her to keep up; they felt like they were made from water. People were complaining that their legs were turning to jelly but that all was crap; it was more like her legs were more like water balloons, and she could barely carry her own weight. The fear was overwhelming, she couldn't swallow her mouth, and her throat was too dry. She was spinning on the spot franticly and firing energy, trying to hit something or anything.

All this time, it was getting closer and closer while existing all around her. It was like a predator stalking its prey, hiding in the long grass, slowly stalking from behind, looking for a moment to attack his target. She felt like someone was choking her, and she couldn't breathe; her chest wouldn't let her take full breaths, but just sharp, shallow and cold. Penny fell to the ground, defeated, covering her face, waiting for the hands, the hands that grabbed Mark Abbott when all this began.

Through her fingers, she saw the light. She was trying to see what it was, but the light was blinding her. The smell of Lillies was almost overwhelming. She could hear the creature's scream and what was left of its creations ran away to save its life. The light faded, but the smell stayed. Penny uncovered her face and finally opened her eyes and franticly looked around in confusion. That didn't come from her, she looked back up the hill, and there was a woman in white. She still had blurry vision.

"Penny couldn't see properly but, could it be Her mother?" She thought.

Penny started running, but by the time she got there, the woman was gone.

"MUM?" she yelled.

However, there wasn't any answer, but just the smell of Lillies.

#

Penny made her way back down the hill, feeling confused and walked into the camp. She saw what The Clan had done to their prisoners. The worst part of all this was that this was a government-sanctioned camp, but there was no doubt that fact would disappear or this camp would never be reported on.

Suddenly, an explosion erupted, and one of the prisoners neck popped. He fell to the ground and bleeds to death in seconds. The rest didn't react at all to it.

An evil cackling fills the air, "You've won this battle, but I'm going to make it feel like defeat. I never needed the control room to detonate the bombs in their necks; I always have a backup plan."

As the screeching stopped, each prisoner's neck exploded to the side one by one, and the whole scene was in a horrible slow motion as Penny tried helplessly to stop it. The ground was awash with blood, a river of it falling into the drain with a sickening sound. This was it for Penny. The laughter from The Operator was the last straw. Penny turned to him, and through a string of energy, he returned with his own, and they met in the middle. Arches of energy were bursting to the side, vaporising anything and anyone it touched. One of the blasts just missed Katy, but Penny was too caught up in her rage to care.

She was drawing power from her hate, rage, and her light energy. She was winning; she could see in his face that he was scared. His fear made her more powerful as she fed on it. The building behind him collapsed under the pressure of repeated strikes of energy. It landed on top of The Operator, and the battle was over. Penny was all drained and fell to her knees. She put her fists to the ground and screamed. The ground shook as if there was an earthquake; Penny wasn't Penny anymore. She was taken over by rage and hate. Katy walked over to her and put her hands on her shoulder. Penny stopped and looked up. The hate immediately dropped and was replaced by recognition and love.

"Let me be your anchor," Katy whispered.

Katy pulled Penny and helped her stand up. She helped her walk away but only got a few steps when The Operator emerged and screamed in rage, "I can't die, you stupid bitch!"

Penny, Katy and the company turned their face to him, and they were flabbergasted. They did not know what else to do. A voice behind him shouted, "Yes, you can."

It was Elliot, and he was holding the dark book. Then it disappeared again, but this time, it turned into a dark mist and went inside Elliot. Elliot's eyes were now black, and when he spoke, his voice echoed through the wind and vibrated through you're the ground0.

"It's time for you to end," He said and threw a bolt of lightning. The Operator put up a shield, but it went through as though it wasn't there and vaporised him.

He walked towards Penny and said, "I remember everything."

His voice was back to normal again, but his eyes were as black as coal.

"I've chosen, and the next time we meet, I'll kill you and take your power. This is the only time I'll respect our past and allow you to live." He said.

Penny was suddenly sick to her stomach.

"No, Elliot, you can come back with us." Penny was begging; she was desperate for her brother to return to her.

"Like hell, he'll come back," Anna yelled as she walked forward and opened fire.

The bullets disintegrated before they reached him; he didn't even look in her direction. Still, without looking at her, she burst into flames and died screaming.

Jacob came at him with a crystal plated sword and attacked, but the sword just bounced off his skin. Alex turned and shoved his hand into his chest, ripping his heart out. That was enough for Penny to know Elliot was dead.

"Retreat! Let's go home," Penny soon gave the order, and everyone had gotten out of there.

They headed back to New Pandora; the mission to retrieve the prisoners was a failure. The Operator was dead, but only to be replaced by someone worse and more powerful. They were at war – a war they couldn't win.

Chapter 35:
What Next?

The council chambers were solemn. They were mourning the loss of Jacob and his daughter along with the loss of every soul that died. They still didn't know who the traitor was; they only knew that it wasn't Jacob. He died an honourable death. Penny sat in the background for the debrief but intended to return below to her people. She felt more at home there.

"So Penny, that's a fair militia you've built. What do you plan on using it next?" Margaret asked.

The question was full of suspicion and accusation. Elder Claire stood and answered this question for Penny, "Margaret, this will not turn into another one of your witch hunts. If it wasn't for Penny, things would have been even worse."

The council murmured in agreement. Margaret left it; she knew when she wouldn't win an argument. She moved on to the next point, "Jacob had been succeeded by Marcus and would be replacing him on this council."

Claire whispered to Penny, "And also, one of Margaret's proteges."

Margaret continued, "We are at war! We cannot win this war by committee; we need strong leadership, a singular leadership."

Claire interrupted again, "Yes, you are right, and our laws dictate it should fall to Trevor, who we all trust."

Margaret ignored the interruption and continued, "I propose we install the council leader as a president, with all the executive power needed to win a war, providing the position complete control to make the right choices."

Trevor spoke up, "That would mean even more power than I would be granted; we risk a dictatorship!"

Claire chapped the table in agreement. Penny looked at the faces of the council, and it looked like Claire and Trevor were the only two against this.

John spoke up, "I second the motion."

Margaret put it to the vote. As expected, there were all white balls apart from two. The motion was passed, and Margaret was now the President of New Pandora.

Trevor felt very uneasy about these events. He believed Margaret was most likely to be the spy. Her behaviour toward Penny portrayed some suspicious concerns. He needed to know details about everything. However, He needed proof before he could accuse her, especially now she just became so powerful. This was a very bad turn of events.

There were birds chittering; Penny wondered why she hadn't heard the birds in the garden before. She was sitting there alone by herself and didn't want any company. She got up and made her way back to her room; she needed to consult with the Book of Light. She needed to know why her brother became so powerful and what happened to the black book. She walked into her small room, sat on the wooden framed bed, and sat the book on her lap. Uncertain of what she could find, she placed her hands on it.

"My child, you came back to me. I was worried that you had spent so much time with the dark one. I was a bit neglected," the book mocked, upset.

"Sorry, there were things going on that felt more appropriate for the dark book," Penny responded.

The book manifested in front of her as Claire, "Tell me, child, tell me more about that. Why were you called more to that book than me? Think carefully. It's important."

Penny explained that there were times for the dark book and times for the light.

"Yes, exactly. We all have our place in the great cycle, the grand balance of the universe. It's your understanding that there is a place for darkness, and the light, both must exist or neither can; it's that understanding that I find interesting in you." Book Claire explained.

Penny shook her head, "This isn't why I'm here. The black book disappeared and entered my brother. What happened there?"

Claire suddenly looked concerned. She said, "If the black book has chosen its vessel, then the final war is on its way, and the days of the prophecy are upon us."

"What prophecy?" Penny asked.

"'Both born of the blood of eve, one in darkness and one in light. The balanced one will destroy the gods.'" Claire revealed the prophecy.

The book version of Claire looked deep in thought

"What do you mean to destroy the gods?" Penny asked.

"Well, to be honest, that is not clear even to me. The Spark of Balance made that prophecy. I believe it to mean that it's your destiny to destroy the Shaitan. The Shaitan aren't the creators of darkness; they are just beings that live in it and abuse it, as do many other races." Claire explained to Penny.

Penny was back in her room with the book on her lap. It opened itself to the front page and said, 'Long ago, two sparks became books, one was this book The Book of Light and a second The Book of Darkness. These books and other artefacts have been used throughout time to wage war between light and dark. The Spark of Balance disappeared into the depths of Old Pandora. This Spark is what saved you on the battlefield. It's also choosing its own agent on Earth; it chose long ago but did not normally

interfere. There is something you need to know about the agent, the Harbinger of Balance. It's your mother."

Epilogue

This is not an ending, and it's not a beginning; it's a point in time where we are waiting for decisions. Decisions that will impact a world unprepared for what's coming, for the destruction and horrors that will come from my choice.

I stood up on the hill, watching the battle, as I always do. Unexpectedly, things weren't as one-sided as I thought they would be. I could see the human prisoners; I knew there was nothing left for them to save. They were now just hollow shells.

The light bearer was strong. She was destroying the mindless drones of the dark creature, but it could create more just as quickly. She was wasting her energy; she didn't understand her enemy. When she would fall, the battle would be over, the light would survive but would need a new host. Unknown territory, it had always favoured the same bloodline. Now, it will need to find another. Maybe that's why I did it.

Now the Light Bearer was failing; she was in a panic and getting overrun. The dark creature was surrounding her. She couldn't see it and couldn't get a hold of it; she was about to die.

#

I felt pain in my hands, realising there was blood. I had fidgeted so much I scraped a large oval-shaped wound in the palm of my hand. Something wasn't right. I had flashes of feelings and heard distant laughter in my head. No matter how I shook myself, I couldn't release myself from this. Have they detected me? Am I under some psychic attack? No, that's impossible. Balance has always been out of scope from dark and light.

#

When I looked down at the light bearer and realised I was here to watch her die, something took hold of my body. The primordial nature of the dark creature suddenly made sense to me. This was primordial, what I was feeling. I did it before I realised it wasn't something I was in control of; it was instinctual; I protected the light bearer. I crossed the line and wounded the dark creature and drove it away. This was something that would have repercussions that I couldn't predict.

#

I crossed a line; I am no longer balanced. I don't know what power this Light Bearer has over me. She has caused a chain reaction that she can't possibly understand. I am the Sparks Harbinger of Balance; imbalance always brings destruction and death.

I'm the harbinger, the bringer of balance, and now I bring death, the only question will be to who?

.

The End

Printed in Great Britain
by Amazon